# Three Boys in North Land

Egerton Ryerson Young

**Alpha Editions**

This edition published in 2023

ISBN : 9789357944144

Design and Setting By
**Alpha Editions**
www.alphaedis.com
Email - info@alphaedis.com

# Contents

# Chapter One.

"Welcome to this Wild North Land! welcome to our happy home in the Land of the North Wind! Welcome, thrice welcome, all and each one of you!"

Thus excitedly and rapidly did Mr Ross address a trio of sunburnt, happy boys, who, with all the assurance of a joyous welcome, had burst in upon him in his comfortable, well-built home, or "hunting lodge," as he preferred to call it, on the banks of the Nelson River. This cozy but isolated home was situated some hundreds of miles up in the interior of the country from York Factory, on the Hudson Bay.

Mr Ross had named his house "Sa-gas-ta-wee-kee," a beautiful Indian word which literally means a house full of sunshine. Mr Ross had spent many years as an official in the Hudson Bay Company's service, as had his father before him. A few years before this, being possessed of abundance of means, he had retired from active work in the great fur-trading company. He had tried to settle down in an older, civilised land, but had found it impossible to content himself away from those regions where he had spent the best years of his life. His wife and family were of the same mind, and so, after some years of travel in various lands, they returned to this northern country where they had spent so many happy years.

Every year or so Mr Ross with some members of his family was in the habit of visiting what he loved to call the mother country. So full was his life of varied and startling adventures that he was often asked to give addresses on some of the fascinating experiences through which he had passed.

Among the crowds who listened to him with intense interest, as he gave a series of addresses in one of the great historic schools in the home land, were the three boys who are to be the heroes of this book. Although they were from different families and nationalities, yet they were congenial spirits, and were equally filled with the love of sport and spirit of exciting adventure.

For such boys Mr Ross's addresses about the Indians, the wild animals, and the excitements of the hunt had the greatest fascination. With Mr Ross they had become personally acquainted, and had induced him to visit their different towns, where he lectured, and to be the guest at their homes, where his delightful stories had charmed every member of their households.

In some way or other they had persuaded their parents to consent to their spending a year or so in the wilds of the northern part of the great Dominion of Canada under the guidance of Mr Ross, who most importunately pleaded for this arrangement on behalf of the boys. As it was impossible for them to return with Mr Ross on account of their studies, several months passed away ere it was possible for them to begin their journey; so he had returned alone to his home, and had made all preparations for entertaining them as members of his household for an indefinite period.

Letters had been sent on in advance notifying Mr Ross of the probable time of the arrival of the boys. But, as often happened in that wild country, where there was no postal service, the letters never arrived, and so the first intimation Mr Ross had of the coming of the boys was their bursting in upon him. Abrupt as was their coming, of course they were welcome. In all new lands there is an open-hearted hospitality that is very delightful, and this was emphatically so in the vast lonely region of the Hudson Bay Territory, where the white men in those days were so few and so widely scattered apart from each other.

And now that they are snugly ensconced in the home of their good friend Mr Ross and his hospitable family, ere we begin to describe their many sports and adventures let us find out something about our heroes, and have them describe some of the exciting incidents of the long trip which they had already made on their journey to this Wild North Land.

Frank, the eldest of the three, was the son of a Liverpool banker. His friends had vainly tried to divert his mind from wild adventure and exciting sports, and persuade him to settle down to steady routine office work. Failing in this, they had listened to Mr Ross's pleadings on his behalf, and had commented to let him have the year in the Wild North Land, hoping that its trials and hardships would effectually cure him of his love of adventure and cause him to cheerfully settle down at his father's business.

Alec was from Scotland, a genuine son of "the mountain and the flood." While a good student when at school, yet, when at home on his holidays, his highest joy had ever been under the guidance of the faithful old gillie to follow on the trail of the mountain deer. For a wider field than that offered by his native Highlands he had been so longing that his friends yielded to his importunities, and so now here he is with his comrades, full of eager anticipations.

Sam was from what his mother used to call "dear, dirty Dublin." He was full of life and fun; a jolly Irish boy of the finest type. Storms and privations might at times depress the spirits of the others; but Sam, true to his nationality, never lost his spirits or his good nature. So rapid had been his progress in his studies that he had pushed himself beyond his years, and so even his tutors had joined in his request that he should have the year off, which, spent in the invigorating air and healthful adventures in the Wild North Land, would doubtless be a blessing to both mind and body.

In the good ship *Prince Arthur*, of the Hudson Bay Company, our three young adventurers set sail in the month of May from the London docks. They met with no adventures worth recording until after they had left the Orkney Islands, where they had called for their last consignment of supplies and the latest mails. Here they also shipped some hardy Orkney men and Highlanders, who were going out in the employment of the Hudson Bay Company.

The *Prince Arthur* was a stanch sailing vessel, built especially for the Hudson Bay Company's trade. She was employed in carrying out to that country the outfit of goods required in the great fur trade. Her return cargoes were the valuable furs obtained in barter from the Indians. Her port was York Factory, on the western side of the Hudson Bay. Here her cargo was discharged and carried by scores of inland boats and canoes to the various trading posts in the different parts of that great country, which is larger than the whole continent of Europe.

So remote were some of those posts from the seaboard, and so difficult and slow were the methods of transporting the goods, that several years passed ere the fur secured from them reached the London markets, to which they were all consigned and where they were carried each year in the company's ships.

Although the *Prince Arthur* was far from being a first-class passenger ship, yet she was a good, seaworthy vessel, with plenty of room for the few passengers who travelled by her each year. These were principally gentlemen of the Hudson Bay Company's service and their friends, or missionaries going out or returning home.

Letters from influential friends secured for our three boys the considerate attention of the captain and the ship's officers, and their own bright ways won the friendship of all the sailors on board. On the whole they had a glorious passage. Some fogs at times perplexed them, and a few enormous icebergs were so near that careful tacking was required, to prevent accidents. The boys were filled with admiration at these great mountains of ice; some of them seemed like great islands, while others more closely resembled glorious cathedrals built in marble and emerald. At times, as the western sun shone upon them, they seemed to take on in parts every colour of the rainbow. With intense interest were they watched as they slowly drifted beyond the southern horizon.

One of the most exciting incidents of the journey was a battle between a great whale and a couple of swordfish. The unwieldy monster seemed to be no match for his nimble antagonists. His sole weapon seemed to be his enormous tail; but vain were his efforts to strike his quicker enemies. As far as could be judged from the deck of the ship, the swordfish were masters of the situation, and the blood-stained waters seemed to indicate that the battle would soon be over.

In the southern part of Davis Strait they encountered great fields of floating ice on which were many herds of seals. The captain had the ship hove to and three boats lowered. In each one he permitted one of the boys to go with the sailors on this seal-hunting expedition. The seals, which are so very active in water, where they can swim with such grace and rapidity, are very helpless on land or ice, and so large numbers were killed by the sailors. While the boys were excited with the sport, they could not but feel sorry for the poor, helpless creatures as they looked at them out of their great eyes that seemed almost human. Some hundreds of skins were secured, much to the delight of the captain and crew, as the profit coming to them from their sale would be no inconsiderable item.

At the mouth of Hudson Strait the captain again had the ship hove to for a day or so to trade with a number of Esquimaux, who had come in their curious canoes, called kayaks, from along the coasts of Labrador. Their insatiable curiosity and peculiar fur clothing very much interested the boys. These Esquimaux were shrewd hands at a bargain, but their principal desire seemed to be to obtain implements of iron in exchange for their furs. They cared nothing for flour, rice, tea, coffee, or sugar. They knew no other food than meat and oil, and so craved no other things than those that could be utilised in improving their weapons. Guns were unknown among them, but they were very skillful in the use of the harpoon and the spear. When they are able to secure iron from the white man they make their harpoon heads, spears, and knives out of this metal, but when unable to secure it they manufacture their weapons out of the horns of the reindeer or the tusks of the walrus or narwhal.

They had among their other furs some splendid bear skins, and the boys were very much interested in hearing them tell through an interpreter how they, with their rude weapons, aided by their clever dogs, had been able to kill these fierce animals. All were very much delighted when told by these friendly Esquimaux how that with two well-trained dogs nipping at the hind legs of a great bear they could keep him turning round and round from one to the other and thus get him so wild and excited that in his efforts to catch hold of the nimble animals, which were able to keep out of his grasp, he did not notice the arrival of the hunters, who were able to approach so closely that they could easily kill him.

The ship crossed the great Hudson Bay, which is about six hundred miles in width, without any mishap, and safely dropped anchor in what the Hudson Bay officers call "the six fathom hole," some distance out from the rude primitive wharf. The signal gun was fired, and soon a brigade of boats came out, and the work of unloading the cargo began.

Our boys, eager as they were to land, were sorry after all to leave their snug berths in the good ship, where they had had some very delightful times during the thirty days that had elapsed since they had left the docks in old England.

A few gifts were bestowed among their particular sailor friends, and then, with the "God bless you" from all; they entered a small boat rowed by Indians, and were soon on the land that skirts this great inland sea. Great indeed was the change which they saw between the populous cities of the home land and this quiet, lonely region upon whose shores they had now landed.

Here the only inhabitants were the fur traders, with their employees, and the dignified, stoical Indians. The only signs of habitations were the few civilised dwellings, called in courtesy the fort, where dwelt and traded the officers and their families and servants of the great fur-trading company, and not very far off was the Indian village of the natives, where the most conspicuous buildings were the church and parsonage of the missionary, who had been marvellously successful in planting the cross in these northern regions, and in winning from a degrading superstition, to the blessings of Christianity, some hundreds of these red men, whose consistent lives showed the genuineness of the work wrought among them.

This great region, stretching from the Atlantic to the Pacific, far north of the fertile prairie region where millions will yet find happy and prosperous homes, has well been called "The Wild North Land." The Indians call it Keewatin, "The Land of the North Wind."

It has not many attractions for the farmer or merchantman, but it is the congenial home of the red man. On its innumerable lakes and broad rivers he glides along during the few bright summer months in his light canoe. Every waterfall or cataract has associated with it some legend or tradition. Its dense forests are the haunts of the bear and wolf, of the moose and reindeer, and many other valuable animals, in the excitement of hunting which he finds his chief delight.

To this land had come our three lads for sport and adventure, and we shall see how fully all their expectations were realised.

Frank's Upset from the Canoe.

# Chapter Two.

**Hudson Bay Company—Frank's canoe mishap—Duck shooting—
Clever Koona—Goose hunting—Queer battles.**

As our boys had come out to this great country for wild adventure and exciting sport, they were rather pleased than otherwise at the contrast it thus presented in comparison with the lands they had left behind. The fact was, they were simply delighted with the absence of the multitude to whom they had been so accustomed, and were at once filled with high expectations. Sam's explanation seemed to be the sentiment of them all when he exclaimed, "Sure if there are so few people in the country, there will be the more bears and wolves for us all to kill!"

The work of unloading the ship was necessarily slow, and so some days would elapse ere a brigade of boats could be prepared to take the first cargo to Fort Garry, on the Red River. The boys had been most cordially welcomed by Mr McTavish, the principal officer in charge at the fort, and by him they were all entertained most hospitably at his home.

Mr McTavish was an old sportsman himself, as nearly all the Hudson Bay Company's officials are; and so, as soon as the boys had made the acquaintance, as they call it, of their land legs; after the heaving and rolling of the vessel, he had an old clever Indian hunter clean up some guns and take the boys out in the birch canoe on their first wild hunting expedition. This first excursion was not to be a very formidable one; it was only a canoe trip several miles up the coast, to a place where the wild ducks and geese were numerous. Like all white people, on their first introduction to the birch canoe, they thought it a frail, cranky boat, and were quite disgusted with it, and some of the tricks it played upon them, on some of their first attempts to manage it. For example, Frank, who prided himself on his ability in pulling an oar, and in managing the ordinary small skiffs or punts on his native waters, seeing the light, buoyant canoe at the side of the little launch, boldly sprang into it, as he would into an ordinary boat of its size in the Mersey.

To his utter amazement, and the amusement of the others he suddenly found himself overbalanced and struggling in the waves on the other side. Fortunately, the water was not more than four feet deep, and he, being a good swimmer, was soon up and at once gave chase for the canoe, which had now floated out several yards from the shore. In this he was encouraged by the laughter and shouts of his comrades and others, who, seeing that no harm had come to him from his sudden spill out of the light boat, were eager to observe how he would ultimately succeed.

Quickly did he catch up to the boat; but, instead of listening to the Indian, who, in broken English, tried to tell him to get in over the end of the canoe, he seized it by the side, and there attempted to climb in. Vain were his efforts. Very skillful indeed is the Indian who can in this manner get into a birch-bark canoe, and of course it is out of the question to expect an inexperienced white person to accomplish the feat. So light is the canoe, that, when thus seized hold of, it yields to the slightest pull, and often causes the person who thus takes hold of it to tumble over ignominiously in the water.

Poor Frank was disgusted but not conquered, and so, amid the laughter of those on shore, he now listened to the advice and direction of the wise old Indian, who was the only one in the company who had not even smiled at the boy's mishap. At the Indian's advice he again caught hold of the canoe, but this time by the end, and carefully bearing his weight upon it he was at length enabled to work himself into it. Cautiously balancing himself, and seizing a paddle that happened to have been fastened in it, he paddled himself ashore amid the cheers of the onlookers.

"Well done, Frank!" said the old Indian.

He had done what some take months to accomplish. He had conquered the canoe in his first attempt, and never after in his many adventures was he afraid of that bonny craft, in which he spent many happy hours and in the paddling of which he became the equal of many a clever Indian.

Of course, there was some delay in the departure of the hunting party, as Frank had to return to his quarters at the Post and get on a dry suit of clothing. This is, however, an operation that does not take a boy full of eager excitement long to accomplish, and so it was not many minutes ere the party set off on their promised excursion.

The Indian decided that they should first go where the ducks were numerous, and to interest these young English lads they adopted a method of hunting them that was most novel and successful. Indeed, it is a very rare method which was here successfully tried, on account of the difficulty of getting a dog so trained as to correctly act his part. But this old native, whose name was Ooseemeemou, had by great patience and kindness so drilled his clever dog that he acted his part with extraordinary cleverness and tact. He called the little fellow Koona, which is the Cree for "snow," and was very appropriate, as the animal was of the purest white.

Taking the dog into the canoe with them, and giving all necessary directions, they soon were gliding along the coast of the great bay. Numerous flocks of ducks flew over their heads; and far away in the distance the water seemed almost alive with the numbers of them on the dancing, sparkling waves. This latter sight seemed to be what the old hunter was looking for, and so the canoe was quickly paddled ashore and carried up on the beach. There he carefully guided the party along. They had to cautiously creep behind some low, dense willow bushes that grew on the shore, with only a broad fringe of white sand between them and the waters.

Each boy, with his gun and ammunition, was now assigned his post behind a clump of bushes and given his final instructions. They were full of excitement and curiosity, and wondered how it was going to be possible for them to reach with ordinary guns the ducks, which were carelessly swimming in multitudes some hundreds of yards out from the shore. But they had not long to wait or conjecture. When the old Indian had seen that all were in their right places he gave a low whistle, which was more like the call of a sea bird than a human voice. So natural was it to a bird call that no bird around was startled by it; but the well-trained Koona, who had been left by the boat, fully knew its meaning, and now began his sagacious work. Like a little white arctic fox he was, and like one be began his antics on the shore. He frisked and danced around along the sand playing all sorts of antics. He walked on his hind feet, turned somersaults in quick succession, and acted as though possessed with perpetual motion, but not one yelp or bark or any sound did he utter.

A stranger would have imagined that his appearance and actions would have driven all the ducks that were near enough to the shore to observe him and his antics farther out to sea. But just the reverse happened. A spirit of curiosity seemed to possess those nearest the shore, and as they began to swim in closer and closer, their movements influenced those farther out, until hundreds of splendid ducks were soon swimming nearer and nearer the sandy beach on which the cunning dog kept up his unceasing and varied movements. At first he had kept at some distance from the sands, back of which grew the clumps of willows behind which the hunters were hidden; but when he saw that his manoeuvres had attracted the ducks near the shore, he gradually worked down the sandy beach until he had them fairly opposite the muzzles of the guns.

A low bird cry from his master was the signal for his change of tactics, and with loud, yelping, fox-like barking he sprang into the waves.

The ducks, thus suddenly alarmed, instantly rose up in hundreds, and the simultaneous reports of the guns rang out, and between thirty and forty ducks, dead and wounded, fell back into the waters. Our hunters, both the Indian and the three boys, sprang from their hiding places, and with Koona's aid secured their splendid bag of game. This was rare sport for the boys, and gave them so much delight that old Ooseemeemou decided to postpone the goose hunt until the next day, and give the boys another opportunity of seeing the sagacity of Koona, the clever little dog that had contributed so much to the success of the expedition.

They returned to their places, and were told to keep as much hidden as possible, as the ducks, now alarmed by the reports of the guns, and the death and wounding of so many of their numbers, would be shy and excited; and would keep flying around for some time ere they would again alight. Koona in the meantime had curled himself up like a ball of white wool, and was also quite hidden from the sight of the flying ducks.

In about half an hour the ducks began to alight again in the water. They were very alert and watchful, and seemed resolved not to be again so easily caught napping. But ducks are silly things and are easily deceived, or have very short memories. Anyway it was the case with these. When a goodly number of them were again seen swimming about, a peculiar sound like the cry of a sea gull was heard, and soon Koona was observed moving very cautiously out to a little point on the sandy beach, just in front of the clump of bushes behind which his master was hidden. Here he curled himself up into a little white bundle and remained perfectly still. Soon after the boys were startled by the sounds of the loud quacking of ducks over the very place where Koona lay so still and quiet. At first they were very much surprised at this, as not a duck was now seen flying in that direction. A little closer investigation showed them that the quacking sounds were all proceeding from the mouth of the old Indian, who, like many of his people, was able to imitate so perfectly the cries and calls of the birds and beasts of the lakes and forests that at times even the most experienced are completely deceived. In addition, this Indian was also a ventriloquist, and was able to so correctly throw his voice that the quacking of the ducks seems to be from the spot where the dog, now so motionless, was lying. The old Indian afterward explained that the calls were of ducks that had found something of interest, and were invitations for other ducks to come and see, and when he had induced some of the ducks to take up the call they would go on repeating it until so many others took it up, and all would then be anxious to see what the fuss was all about.

"Ducks," added the old man, "are like people, sometimes curious to see when there is not much after all to look at."

So, because of the calls to come and look, the flocks kept flying or swimming nearer and nearer, and all there was to see was only a ball of something very white and still. Not an hour before they were curious to see the antics of a lively little white dog; now they were curious to see him apparently motionless and dead.

By carefully peering through the dense bushes, the boys, with guns loaded, were able to see the dog quivering with suppressed excitement, as the many quackings of the ducks told him of the success of his ruse. However, he was so well-trained that he would not move until the welcome signal was given him, and then with a bound and a bark he was up, and again, as the startled ducks rose up, the reports of all the guns rang out, and nearly as many more fine ducks fell before the simultaneous discharge. This was capital sport for the boys. Koona's sagacity, and thorough training, in being thus able to bring the ducks within range of the guns, first by his comical antics, and then by his perfect quiet, very much delighted them. Their only annoyance was that when they wanted to pat and fondle him he resented their familiarity, and growled at them most decidedly. Indian dogs do not as a rule take to white people at first, but kindness soon wins them, and they often become fast friends.

The canoe was again launched, and the hunters proceeded a couple of miles farther and had some more capital shooting. Very proud and happy were they with this, their first day of duck shooting, and often did they in after days have much to say of the marvellous cleverness of the spotless Koona.

As the brigades were not yet ready to leave for the interior with the supplies for the trading posts, Mr McTavish readily consented to another excursion, quietly observing that the return of a few such well-loaded canoes would add materially to the fort's supply of food.

This second excursion was to be to a more distant place, where were some favourite feeding grounds of wild geese. They are very fond of a jointed quill-like grass, and when once they have found where their favourite food grows, there they resort in great numbers, and unless very persistently hunted will keep in the neighbourhood until they have about eaten it all.

As the distance was so great, it was decided to make an all day trip of it, and so two canoes were requisitioned with two experienced Indians in each, one of whom, of course, was Ooseemeemou. To him the boys had become very much attached, and, as he had some knowledge of English, they were able to get a good deal of reliable information from him. Some food and kettles were taken along with them, and old Ooseemeemou put in the bottom of each canoe a good-sized oilcloth and a couple of blankets, saying, as he did so, "Fine weather to-day, may not be so very long."

Frank and Alec were given good places in one of the canoes, and Sam was placed in charge of the other two Indians. Each boy was furnished with two guns and plenty of ammunition. Being eager to get to the hunting grounds, they each selected a paddle, and were found to be not unskillful in the use of them, even in birch canoes, after a few lessons from their Indian attendants.

With the best wishes of all who were not too busy to come down to the launch to see them off, they started on their excursion under the skillful, steady strokes of the Indians. Aided by the boys, they were able to make about seven miles an hour, and so in about three hours they reached their destination. The splendid exercise and the bracing air gave them all good appetites, and so they pulled up in a secluded little bay, where was to be found some dry wood. Here a fire was kindled, the kettles were filled with water and boiled, and soon a good, substantial meal of the delicacies of the country were spread before them. What the bill of fare was we know not, except that the principal part consisted of some of the ducks shot on the previous excursion. The dinner thus prepared and eaten on the rocks was much enjoyed by the boys; but they were kept in a perpetual state of excitement by the numerous cries of the wild geese that could be distinctly heard as well as seen, as they kept flying in great lines or triangles to and from their feeding grounds.

As this was a favourite resort for the Indian hunters, all preparations had been made for the goose hunting. Large nest-like piles of dry hay with reeds and rushes had been gathered in certain favourite places. In each of these a hollow had been formed in the centre like a bird's nest, large enough for two persons to cozily ensconce themselves, so low down as only to be observed by the geese when flying directly overhead. After dinner four of these big nest-like affairs were freshened up with some bundles of dry old grass, which was cut in an old disused beaver meadow.

A number of old decoys, made to look like geese when feeding, were arranged in the right position, which always varies according to the direction of the wind. Then Ooseemeemou, taking Frank with him, gave Alec and Sam each in charge of a clever Indian hunting companion. One Indian, whose name was Oostaseemou, had a nest to himself. Thus assorted, our party took possession of their four nests and awaited developments. The boys were greatly amused at the queer little white cotton caps which each one had to put on. Everything in the shape of colour had to be carefully hidden. Geese are not easily alarmed by anything white, and will come quite near to persons thus dressed.

While now waiting for the arrival of the game, the boys were each instructed how to act in case the geese should come within range. They generally fly down with the wind and arise facing it. Since the decoys are so arranged in the goose grass that the geese in coming down to join those already there must, in availing themselves of the wind to help them to alight, come within range of the nests in which are hidden the hunters.

Then, when the firing of the guns alarm them, and those unhurt rise to escape, they have to so use the wind to help them that they again come within range, and thus receive a second volley. When the second volley is fired the dead and wounded are quickly secured by the hunters, who jump out of the nests and make chase after them. There is lots of fun and some danger of ugly blows, for an old wounded goose sometimes makes a good fight.

Fortunately for our young hunters, a good stiff breeze was blowing when they took their places in these queer nests, and, with their two guns apiece in position, patiently waited the arrival of the geese. Several flocks had been seen in the distance, and their strange cries were heard on every side. While the men were on the move getting things ready, of course none of the wary birds came within range. However, now that all was quiet in the vicinity of the choicest feeding grounds, a few old out-guards which appeared cautiously flying over, seemed to have reported that nothing was to be seen but some patches of snow in the nests. The Indians say that the geese mistake them, when dressed in white, for lumps of snow. Soon after a great flock was seen coming with the wind from the south directly toward them.

Old Ooseemeemou began to imitate the call of the geese, and throwing his voice so that it seemed from the decoys, it appeared as if they in the goose grass were saying, "Honk: Honk: Honk:" which the Indians say is the goose language for "Food, food, food."

Ooseemeemou knew well how to imitate them, and so the great flock understood it as the call from some of their fortunate companions, and down they came with the wind passing in close range on the left-hand side of the hunters. Bang: bang: bang! rang out the guns of the three boys and of the four Indians, and five or six great geese tumbled to the ground, some of them dead and others badly wounded. The startled, frightened, surviving geese, that thought they were going to have such a feast among their fellows, had only time to turn round and strive to escape by rising up against the wind on the opposite sides of those dry nests. This was what the clever Indians knew they would do, and so, as they came within range, struggling against the wind, each hunter, white and Indian, now used his second gun, and nearly as many more plump geese dropped to the ground dead and wounded.

Now the fun began. There was a hasty springing out of the nests, and every man and boy dashed off for his goose. The Indians were wary and experienced, and so knew how to act; but our enthusiastic boys, in the excitement of securing their first wild goose, recklessly rushed in to the attack.

Alec was the first to come to grief. The old gander that he was pursuing had a broken wing, but as his legs were all right he led him a lively chase of several hundred yards. Then, seeing that he was being overtaken, he stopped suddenly and, turning the well wing toward the boy, awaited his coming. Alec, seeing him thus standing with one wing hanging broken to the ground, anticipated nothing but an easy capture, and so he thoughtlessly attempted to throw himself on the bird and quickly capture him in his arms.

Poor fellow, when picked up he could hardly tell what had

Knocked Out by a Goose.

happened, only that it seemed to him he had been pounded with sledge hammers and had seen some thousands of stars.

What had really happened was this: the instant Alec sprang forward and stooped to seize his game the goose with his unwounded wing had hit him such a blow on the head as to quite stun him, and this had been followed by several other blows in rapid succession. Fortunately old Ooseemeemou was not far off. He rushed to Alec's rescue and speedily dispatched the goose, and thus delivered the boy from the humiliating position of being badly whipped by a wounded goose. Poor fellow, he carried in the black and blue marks on his body the effects of the fierce blows which had been rained upon him.

Frank had conquered his without any mishap; but Sam, in reaching out to seize hold of the one he was chasing, had received such a blow from a wing on his elbow that he fairly howled with the pain, and was not able to fire another shot during the rest of the day's sport. It was news to the boys when the Indians told them that an old goose with one blow of his wing has been known to kill a large fox or to break the leg of a man. So the boys, while delighted with the success of their first goose hunt, ever after had a much greater respect for the poor despised goose than before.

With the veering of the wind the decoys were changed so as to bring the geese down in the right direction in range of the guns, and sport continued until evening. Then, after a hasty supper on the rocks in the glorious gloaming that exists for many hours in those high latitudes in the summer months, the canoes were loaded, and three very tired but happy boys who wanted to paddle went to sleep in the canoes long ere the hospitable home of their host was reached.

The Indians are the kindest men in the world with whom to travel. Hardly knowing how it happened, the boys were carefully helped to their quarters in the fort. Here their bruises were bathed, their suppers eaten, their prayers said, and then there was the long nine hours' dreamless sleep, "Tired nature's sweet restorer, balmy sleep."

When next morning the boys were discussing the, to them, glorious adventures of the two preceding days, it was agreed among them that the accidents and honours were about even—that while Alec and Sam had had their laugh at Frank for his misadventure with the canoe, the tables were completely turned on them in the incidents of the goose hunt.

Big Tom.

# Chapter Three.

### Writing Journals—Fur-Laden Brigades—Valuable Furs—Hunting Preparations—Big Tom, The Famous Guide—The Start—First Camp on the Rocks.

Soon after breakfast and a glorious plunge bath in the cold waters of Hudson Bay, the lads were informed by Mr McTavish that the ship's cargo was now about unloaded, and that just as soon as the brigades, with the last winter's catch of furs, which were looked for every hour, should arrive she would with the first favourable wind begin the return journey. He suggested that instead of hunting that day they should devote its hours to writing letters to their friends far away, as months would elapse ere another opportunity would be theirs. Of course this kind suggestion was most gratefully accepted, and in an unused office in one of the buildings Frank, Alec, and Sam were soon busily engaged in this very interesting work.

Before leaving home they had been furnished with regulation journals, and had been offered substantial rewards if they would write something in their books every day. Readily had they promised; but, alas! when the Atlantic storms had for some days assailed them their good resolutions, stimulated by the promised rewards, failed most signally. During the first few days after starting they had so much to write about, and had so filled up the pages, that they all regretted that their books were not larger, or that they had not three or four pages for each day. This, however, had all changed. The pages were now too large, and it was a burden to write even a few sentences.

We need not stop here to give any detailed accounts of these letters; suffice it to say they were just such as any of the bright, happy, boyish readers of these pages would have written under similar circumstances to their loved mothers and friends far away. It was noticed that while they were full of fun and laughter while writing to their school chums and other young friends, yet when they came to the writing of the letters to their mothers there was a quiet time among them, and some tears dropped on the pages, and some throats had lumps in them. All right, boys; we think not the less but much the more of you, because of the love and affection for your mothers, between whom and you now rolls the wide Atlantic. Months will elapse ere letters from home will reach you, or you will have the opportunity of writing again; and so now, while you have the chance, send loving letters to the precious mothers, whose love excels all other earthly love. Frank, Alec, and Sam all have, as you have, good mothers. They never gave bad advice, but always the best counsel. They never led the boys astray, but ever stimulated to a noble life. They always loved and were ever more anxious to forgive and forget than the boys were to be forgiven.

Great was the noise and excitement at the fort next morning, and very early were the boys astir to see what was the cause. The long-expected brigades of boats had arrived with the cargoes of furs. As they were all sorted in well-packed bales, weighing each about eighty or ninety pounds, the work of transferring them to the ship did not take very long. One boat in running some wild and dangerous rapids had been submerged and nearly lost, with all its crew, who escaped only because they could swim like otters. The cargo of furs had all gone under the waves ere rescued, and so it was necessary to open all the bales of fur with which the boat had been loaded and dry them in the bright sun as quickly as possible. This work very much interested the boys, and, as the assortment of furs was a varied one, they had their first opportunity of seeing what rich and valuable furs this wild country could produce.

There were no less than six varieties of foxes, the most valuable being the black and silver ones. Then there were cross foxes, blue foxes, as well as white and red ones. The rich otters and splendid black beavers very much interested them, and especially the prime bear and wolf skins. And as they looked at them and many other kinds their mouths fairly watered at the prospect of during the few months being engaged in the exciting sport of capturing the comrades of these in their native forests.

Yes, they would succeed in some instances, as our book will tell; but now as they looked at these splendid skins lying so quiet and still they little imagined the dangers and hardships which would be theirs ere the fierce bears and savage wolves they were to assail would render up their splendid robes.

Very much interested also were they in the hardy voyageurs, or trip men, who constituted these brigades. Dark and swarthy they were, with beardless faces, and long black hair that rested on their shoulders. From remote and different regions had they come. Here were brigades from the Assiniboine, Red River, Cumberland, and the Saskatchewan region. Many of the boatmen were of the Metis—half-French and Indian; and they spoke a language that was a mixture of both, with some English intermixed that was not always the most polite.

From the mighty Saskatchewan had come down that great river for a thousand miles, and then onward for several hundred more, brigades that had, in addition to the furs and robes of that land, large supplies of dried meat and tallow, and many bags of the famous food called pemmican, obtained from the great herds of buffalo that still, in those days, like the cattle on a thousand hills, thundered through the land and grazed on its rich pasturage and drank from its beautiful streams. The men of these Saskatchewan brigades were warriors who had often been in conflict with hostile tribes, and could tell exciting stories of scalping parties, and the fierce conflict for their lives when beleaguered by some relentless foes. Some of them bore on face or scalp the marks of the wounds received in close tomahawk encounter, and, for the gift of a pocketknife or gaudy handkerchief from our eager boys, rehearsed with all due enlargement the story of the fierce encounter with superior numbers of their bitterest enemies, how they had so gloriously triumphed, but had not come off unscathed, as these great scars did testify.

Thus excited and interested did the boys wander from one encampment of these brigades to another. The word had early gone out from the chief factor, Mr McTavish, that these boys were his special friends, and as such were to be treated with consideration by all. This was quite sufficient to insure them a welcome everywhere, and so they acquired a good deal of general information as they became acquainted with people from places of which they had heard but little, and from others of some regions until then to them unknown.

In addition to those already referred to, there were brigades from Lac-la-Puie, the Lake of the Woods, Cumberland House, Athabasca, and Swan River, and other places many hundreds of miles away.

As each brigade arrived it formed its own encampment separate from the others. Here the fires of dry logs were built on the ground, and the meals prepared and eaten. When the day's work was over, the men gathered around the fire's bright glow and smoked their pipes, laughed and chatted, and then, each wrapping himself in a single blanket, they lay down on the ground to sleep, with no roof above them but the stars.

As the goods brought from England in large bulk had to be made up into bundles, called in the language of the country "pieces," each weighing from eighty to one hundred pounds, that could be easily carried around the portages by the Indians, several days must elapse ere the return trip would be begun. Very interesting were these days to the boys, as from camp fire to camp fire they wandered, making friends everywhere with the Indians by their hearty, manly ways.

At first the wildest and fiercest looking fellows most attracted them; those wild warriors who could tell of scalping parties and horse-stealing adventures among the warlike tribes of the great plains. After a while, however, they found themselves most interested in the brigades that could travel fastest, that had the record of making the fastest trip in the shortest time. What at first was a surprise to them was that the brigades that held these best records were the Christian ones, who took time to say their prayers morning and evening and always rested on the Sabbath. This proved that these hard-working men, who rested one day in seven, could do and did better and faster work than those who knew no Sabbath, but pushed on from day to day without rest. Man as a working animal needs the day of rest, and with one off in seven will, as has been here and in other places proved, do better work in the remaining six than the one who takes no day of rest.

Soon after the arrival of the brigades with the furs, which were estimated as being worth in London over three hundred thousand pounds, they were all safely stowed away in the vessel, and a favourable wind springing up from the south-west, the anchor was lifted, the sails hoisted, and the good ship *Prince Arthur* started on her return voyage to the old land. The boys waved their handkerchiefs and shouted their farewells until the vessel was far out on the dancing waves like a thing of life and beauty.

To Big Tom, of the Norway House Brigade, had been intrusted the responsibility of safely taking the boys up from York Factory to the residence of Mr Ross. His Indian name was Mamanowatum, which means, "O be joyful," but he had long been called Big Tom on account of his gigantic size.

Ample resources had been sent with the boys to pay for all their requirements. Mr McTavish had an experienced clerk look after their outfit and select for them everything needed, not only for the journey, but for their requirements during the year of their stay in the country. So they were here furnished with what was called the yearly supplies, as York Factory is the best place, keeping as it does large reserve supplies for all the interior trading posts. The English boots were discarded for moccasins; fringed leggings manufactured out of well-tanned skins and various other articles of apparel more suitable to the wild country were obtained.

Two good Hudson Bay blankets were purchased for each boy, and, as they had come to rough it, it was thought best to give them no tent, but each one had in his outfit a large piece of oiled canvas in case of a fierce rainstorm assailing them. They were given the usual rations of food, with tea and sugar for so many days, and each lad was furnished with a copper kettle, a tin cup, a tin plate, a knife, fork, and spoon. As luxuries they furnished themselves with towels, soap, brush, and comb. In addition to these supplies for this first trip there were sent up all that would be needed during the long months that they were to spend in the country. The boys were specially anxious that the supply of ammunition should be most liberal.

For weapons they each had a good double-barrelled breech-loading gun—then just beginning to come into use—which had been carefully selected for them ere they left home. In addition they each had a first-class sheath knife with hilt, good for close hand-to-hand encounter with animals, and also useful in skinning the game when killed or in cutting kindling wood for a fire. A first-class knife is an indispensable requisite for a hunter in the North-west. Indeed, there is a saying in that country, "Give an Indian a knife and a string, and he will make his living and his way anywhere."

A brigade in the Hudson Bay service consisted of from four to twenty boats; each boat was supposed to carry from eighty to a hundred pieces of goods or bales of fur in addition to the supplies for the men. They were made out of spruce or balsam, and were like large skiffs, sharp at both ends.

They were manned by nine men. The man in charge was called the steersman; standing in the sharp angle of the stern, he steered the boat either by a rudder or a long oar, which he handled with great skill. The other eight men rowed the boat along with great oars, in the use of which they were very clever. Each boat was provided with a small mast and a large square sail. When there was no favourable wind the mast was unstepped and lashed on the outside of the boat under the rowlocks. Often for days together only the oars were used. This was specially the case in river routes. However, in the great lakes whenever there was any possibility of sailing the mast was stepped, the sail hoisted, and the weary toilers at the oars had a welcome rest; and often did they need it, for the work was most slavish and exhausting.

In each brigade there was a boss who had control of all the boats. He gave the word when to start in the morning and when to camp at night. His word was absolute in all matters of dispute. He had the privilege of selecting the best boat in the brigade, and was supposed to always be at the front when dangerous rapids had to be run, or death in any form had to be faced; in storm or hurricane his boat had to be the first to face the trying ordeal, and his hand to be on the helm. Only the well-tried old steersman of many years' experience could hope to reach to this position, and when once it was obtained unceasing vigilance was the price paid for the retention of the post. One mistake in running the rapids, or a single neglect to detect the coming of the storm in time to get to shore and the furs securely covered over with the heavy tarpaulins, with which each boat was supplied, was quite sufficient to cause him to lose the much coveted position. About the only liberty taken with him was, if possible, when the boats were crossing a great lake, with each big sail set, to try if possible by superior management of the boat to get to the distant shore ahead of him.

The start was made about three o'clock in the afternoon, as is the general custom of these brigades of boats; the idea being only to go a few miles for the first day and thus find out if everything is in thorough working order, and that nothing has been forgotten.

The camp was made on the bank of the river where dry wood was abundant, and where there was some sheltered cove or harbour in which the boats could safely be secured in case of violent storms coming up in the night, which was not an infrequent occurrence.

Big Tom appointed one of the Indian oarsmen to look after the boys. His duties were to cook their meals and select for their beds as smooth and soft a place as was possible to find on the granite rocks; or, if it happened to be in a soft and swampy place where the boats stopped for the night, he was expected to forage round and find some dry old grass in the used-up beaver meadows, or to cut down some balsam boughs on which the oilcloth would be spread, and then their blanket beds would be made. These boughs of the balsam or spruce, when broken up, make a capital bed. The boys, after a few nights' experiment with various kinds of beds, became so much attached to those made of the spruce or balsam that, unless very weary with some exciting sport during the day, they generally took upon themselves the work of securing them at each night's camping place.

Tables were considered unnecessary luxuries. The dishes were arranged on a smooth rock if one was to be found. The food was served up by the Indian attendant, and the three boys and Big Tom sat down and enjoyed the plain but hearty meal. It is generally the custom for the commodore of the brigade to take his meals with any travellers he may have in charge. When they have dined, the Indian servant or attendant then sits down and has his meal. After supper the Indians who have more quickly prepared and eaten their suppers, as they waste but little time in details, gather round the splendid camp fire, and for an hour or so engage in pleasant chat; and while having their evening smoke they show to each other their various purchases secured at York Factory. At this post they are allowed to take up in goods half of their wages for their services, and carry them along with them in their boats.

After a final visit was made by the different steersmen to their boats to see that everything was snug and tight, and a consultation with Big Tom as to the likelihood or not of a storm coming up, they all gathered round the camp fire for evening prayers. Big Tom took charge of the evening service. He first read from his Indian Testament, translated into his own language and printed in the clear, beautiful syllabic characters invented by one of the early missionaries. After the Scriptures were read Martin Papanekis, a sweet singer, led the company in singing in their own language a beautiful translation of the "Evening Hymn." When this was sung they all reverently bowed while Big Tom offered up an appropriate prayer.

Very sweetly sounded the voices of these Christian Indians as here amid nature's solitudes arose from their lips and hearts the voice of prayer and praise. The effect on the boys was not only startling but helpful. In their minds there had been associated very little of genuine Christianity with the Indians, but just the reverse. They expected to meet them with tomahawks and scalping knives, but not with Bibles and hymn books; they expected to hear war-whoops, but not the voice of Christian song and earnest prayer.

As the boys lay that night in their blanket beds on the rocks they could not but talk of the evening prayers, and perhaps that simple but impressive service did more to bring vividly and helpfully before them the memories of their happy Christian homes far away than anything else that had occurred since they left them.

Making a Portage.

# Chapter Four.

### The Early Call—The Picturesque Route—The Toilsome Portages— Rival Brigades—First Bear—Alec's Successful Shot.

So excited were the boys with their strange romantic surroundings that the first night they lay down in their beds, thus prepared not far from the camp fire on the rocks, they could hardly sleep. It was indeed a new experience to be able to look up and see the stars shining in the heavens above them. Then, when they looked around, on one side they saw the Indians reclining there in picturesque attitudes, smoking their pipes and engaged in quiet talk. When they turned and looked on the other side there was the dense dark forest peopled in their young imaginations with all sorts of creatures, from the fierce wolf and savage bear to the noisy "whisky jack," a pert, saucy bird, about the size and colour of a turtle dove, that haunts the camp fires and with any amount of assurance helps himself to pemmican and other articles of food, if a bag is left open or the provisions exposed to his keen eye. Still sounding in their ears were his strange, querulous notes, forming not half so sweet a lullaby as the music of the waves that beat and broke a few yards from where they lay.

But "tired nature's sweet restorer, balmy sleep," came after a time, and in dreamless slumber soon were they wrapped, nor did they stir until early next morning. They were aroused by the musical voice of Big Tom, from which rang out the boatman's well-known call:

"Lève, Lève, Lève!"

This is not Indian, but French, and has been taken by the Indians from the early French voyageurs, who long years before this used to traverse many parts of these wild regions to trade with the Indians. Quite a number of names still remain in the country as relics of these hardy early French explorers.

This ringing call met with a prompt response from all. No one dared to remain for another nap. At once all was hurry and activity. The fires were quickly rekindled, copper tea-kettles were speedily filled and boiled, a hasty breakfast eaten, prayers offered, and then "All aboard!" is the cry of Big Tom. The kettles, blankets, and all the other things used are hastily stowed away, and the journey is resumed.

If the wind is fair the sail is hoisted and merrily they travel on. If not, the heavy oars were brought out, and as they rose and fell in unison the boats were propelled on at the rate of about six miles an hour. Three or four times a day did they go ashore, boil the kettles, and have a meal, for the air of that land is bracing and the appetites are always good.

The route used for so many years by the Hudson Bay Company to transport their goods into the interior from York Factory is utterly unfit for navigation, as we understand that word, as the rivers are full of wild, dangerous rapids and falls. Some of these rapids can be run at all times during the summer, others only when the water is high. Many of them are utterly impassable at any time. The result is that numerous portages have to be made. As the making of a portage was exceedingly interesting to our boys, we will here describe one.

The boats were rowed up against the current as far as possible and then headed for the shore. Here at the landing place they were brought in close to the rocks and every piece of cargo was taken out. These pieces were put on the men's shoulders, one piece being fastened at both sides by a carrying strap, which in the middle is drawn across the forehead. Then, using the first piece thus fastened, one or two more pieces are piled upon it and the Indian starts with this heavy load along the rough and rocky trail to the end of the portage. This end is the place beyond the rapids where safe navigation again commences. In quick succession the men are thus loaded until all the cargoes are thus transported from one side to the other.

The boys were very eager to help. So they quickly loaded themselves with their guns and blankets, and, striking out into the trail along which they saw the Indians were hurrying, they bravely endeavoured to keep those in sight who had started just before them. To their great surprise they found this to be an utter impossibility. The swinging jog trot of an Indian does not seem to be a very rapid pace, but the white man unaccustomed to it finds out very quickly that it takes long practice for him to equal it. At first the boys thought that it was because they had loaded themselves too heavily, and so they quite willingly took a rest on the way; dropping their blankets and guns, and sitting down on a rock beside the trail, they watched with admiration the Indians in single file speeding along with their heavy loads. Many of these men can carry on each trip three pieces, that is a load of from two hundred and forty to three hundred pounds.

As Ayetum, the Indian who had charge of the white boys' cooking arrangements, was passing them as they sat there in the portage he said, in broken English:

"White boys leave guns and blankets, Ayetum come for them soon."

This was quite agreeable to the tired lads, and so they started up again, Frank saying as they did so:

"Now we will show them that we can keep up to them." Gallantly they struck out, but to a white boy running over an Indian trail where rocks and fallen trees and various other obstructions abound is a very different thing from a smooth road in a civilised land. For a time they did well, but when hurrying along on a narrow ledge of rock an unnoticed creeping root tripped up and sent Sam flying over the side of a steep place, where he went floundering down twenty or thirty feet among the bracken and underbrush. Fortunately he was not much hurt, but he needed the assistance of two Indians to get him up again.

Thus rapidly passed the days as the brigade hurried on. Not an hour was wasted. It was necessary to move on as quickly as possible, as not twenty-four hours would elapse ere the next brigade would be dispatched from York Factory, and not only would it be a great disgrace to be overtaken, but the rivalry and strife of the boats' crews in the portages, in their efforts to see which could get their cargoes over first, would be most intense; and sometimes there is bad blood and quarrelling, especially if the brigades happen to be of rival tribes.

Hence it was ever the plan of the great company that employed them all to keep them at least a day or two apart on these adventurous and exciting journeys. To Big Tom and his men had been given the post of honour, and it was well-known that such was his skill as a leader, and so well was he backed up by his well-trained, stalwart men, that unless some great accident happened, no brigade following would have any chance of catching up to him ere his journey was finished.

One day when passing through a lakelike expanse of the river they saw a large black bear swimming as fast as he could directly ahead of them. At length a cry was raised, "A bear! a bear!" The men bent to their oars and there was an exciting chase.

Fortunately for the pursuers, it was a wide open space and the bear was far out from land. Even in these heavy boats the men can row faster than a bear can swim. Knowing well the habits of the bear, the men's first efforts were to cut him off from the mainland, and thus oblige him to swim for one of the many islands which could be seen on ahead. If they could succeed in this, of course he would have a poor chance, as the boats would speedily surround him there. Bears know that they are not safe on islands when hunted, and so cunningly endeavour to keep from them; or, if so unfortunate as to be obliged to take refuge on one when closely pursued, they do not seem able to keep quiet and try to lie hidden and unseen, but just as soon as possible they make the attempt to reach the mainland, and there hide themselves away from their pursuers in the dense forest or underbrush. This peculiarity of the bear is well-known to the Indian hunters; so in this case the first object of the men, as they would hardly be able to get near enough to this big fellow to shoot him in the water, was to head him off from the mainland and thus force him on an island. In this they succeeded, as they anticipated.

Frank, Alec, and Sam were, of course, intensely excited as the chase advanced. In their Zoological Gardens they had often seen and watched various species of bears. There, however, they were in captivity and could do no harm. Here, however, away ahead of them like a great Newfoundland dog, was this big, fierce fellow, wild and free, making the race of his life, to escape from his relentless pursuers.

At first he struck out for the mainland, and made the most desperate efforts to reach the shore; but when at length he saw one of the boats surely crawling along so that it would soon be between him and the point of land toward which he was swimming, he accepted the situation and struck off for a large island that seemed to be densely covered with trees and underbrush.

Nearer and nearer came the boats, propelled so vigorously by the muscular, excited men, whose great oars rose and fell with all the precision of clockwork, as they saw they were sure of gaining on their prey.

As Big Tom's boat was at the front, he said to the excited boys, who could hardly restrain themselves:

"You boys want to shoot him?"

Of course they did. What boy under similar circumstances would not have given almost anything for a shot at a bear in a position like this?

So the guns were quickly loaded, and under Tom's direction the boys were given a position one after another in the stern of the boat. Grandly did the men row so as to bring the bear within range ere the island should be reached. When the bear was about two hundred feet from shore Tom, who had had some difficulty in restraining the boys from firing, now ordered the men to cease rowing, and, as had been arranged with the boys, he gave the word to Sam to fire. Quickly rang out the report of his gun.

"Did you hit him?" said Big Tom.

"I think I did," was Sam's odd reply; "for see, he is swimming faster than he did before I fired."

This quaint answer was met by shouts of laughter from all who understood its comical meaning.

"Now, Frank, it is your turn," said Big Tom.

Carefully aiming for his head—and really there was not much of it to be seen, for a bear swims low in the water—Frank fired, and a howl and a vigorous shaking of the head told that he had been hit somewhere, but not enough to stop his progress. The boat, under the momentum it had received from the oars, was still moving on about as fast as the bear was able to swim.

"Now, Alec," said Big Tom, as the lad took his position in the stern of the boat, "when he tries to run through the shallow water near those rocks, your turn comes. Hit him behind the shoulder, good young Scotchman."

At the kindly mention of his nationality the blood of Alec suddenly rose, and he felt his hand grip that gun and his eye strangely brighten, and he resolved if possible he would make the shot of his life. Steadying himself, he waited until the bear was exactly in the place and position mentioned by the experienced old hunter, who stood just behind him. Then he fired. As the report rang out there was also heard a dull thud, that told that somewhere the

Alec Shoots the Bear.

fierce brute had been struck, but to Alec's mortification he gave some desperate bounds and finally reached the shore. There among the rocks he suddenly dropped as in a heap. A few seconds after, some of the Indians jumped overboard and cautiously waded toward him through the shallow water. Their caution, however, was altogether unnecessary. Alec's bullet had done its work, and the bear was stone dead. The Indians found, when cutting up the body, that the ball had gone completely through him. The wonder was that the great brute had been able to move at all after being so struck. The bears have an immense amount of vitality, as hunters who shoot them often find out to their own cost. So here was the first bear killed; Alec was the hero of the hour. While modestly he received the congratulations, he naturally felt very proud over the accuracy of the shot that had brought down a great black bear.

Speedily did some of the Indian hunters get out their knives and begin skinning the great animal. While doing this they made a discovery that very much pleased Frank, and that was that his bullet had gone clean through the ear of the bear, and had thus caused his howls and the angry shakings of his head which had been observed by all after Frank had fired. As a bear's ear is very small, Frank's shot was an exceedingly good one, when we take into consideration that he fired from a moving boat at such a small object as the bear's head.

"First blood, anyway, for Frank," said Alec.

So it had turned out to be, although Alec's had been the shot that had brought down the game.

The beautiful black robe and the meat were soon carried by the stalwart men to the boats, and the journey was resumed. That evening at the camp fire all had abundance of bear's meat for their supper. It was very much enjoyed by all, as the meat of these animals is good, tasting something like young pork, with a gamey flavour.

Spearing Sturgeon.

# Chapter Five.

**Robinson's Portage—Gunpowder Transportation—Hole in the Keg—The Frightful Explosion—Ensconced at Headquarters—Delightful Home in the Wilderness—Sturgeon Fishing—Involuntary Plunges.**

At Robinson's Portage there occurred a startling accident of a most unique character. It caused much consternation both among the boys and the Indians.

In one of the boats, which was most carefully guarded, were quite a number of barrels of gunpowder for the different trading posts. Large quantities of this dangerous material are required for the Indians all over the country. The company is very particular in its transportation, and only the most experienced men are allowed to have charge of the powder boat.

When the brigade reached Robinson's Portage, which is a long one, some men who had charge of the powder carefully rolled or dragged the barrels across the portage, which has over its whole length a fairly good forest road. The rest of the men, with their carrying straps, conveyed, as usual, the many "pieces," and piled them close to the landing stage. Three boatloads of supplies, as well as the cargo of gunpowder, had been taken across and piled up ready for reshipment. Before bringing over the other cargoes and dragging the great boats, which were as usual to be dragged overland by the united strength of all the men, it was resolved to have dinner at the end of the portage where they had landed, and then go on with their work. Wood was gathered and a fire was kindled and dinner was prepared.

While the men were dining it was noticed that the fire had increased, and had at length reached in the dry grass the place where the powder kegs had been placed when they had been taken out of the boats, and from which spot they had been carried to the other end of the portage. Soon the Indians and boys were interested in seeing a fuselike running of fire spluttering and flashing on the trail. On and on along the road it sped, until at length it disappeared over the hill leading to the other end of the portage, where the barrels of powder and bales of goods were now piled. For a moment or two the men continued their dinners; then suddenly there was a report so loud and so deafening that those who were standing were nearly thrown to the ground, and all were so shaken that it seemed as though a small earthquake had occurred.

In an instant the cause was well surmised, and away they hurried as rapidly as possible to the other end of the portage. A strange sight, indeed, met their gaze. Some of the trees were badly shattered, and the parts of those left standing, instead of being covered with green foliage, were well decorated with coloured calicoes and ribbons, tattered blankets, men's clothing, and many other things. The well piled up bundles and pieces had disappeared, and the contents seemed to be anywhere within the radius of half a mile. A large quantity had been blown out into the river, and had gone floating down the stream.

Where stood the piles of powder kegs was an excavation in the ground, but, alas! no powder was left. All had gone to cause that great explosion that had borne such a near approach to an earthquake. Of course, Big Tom and his men were a humiliated lot, as there is a great deal of ambition among these hardy boatmen to deliver their cargoes in as good condition to the Hudson Bay Company's officials as possible. But here was a disaster. Three boatloads of supplies, as well as a cargo of gunpowder, were simply annihilated, or nearly so.

Quickly did they set to work to secure what was in the water, but it was of little value. Some of the most adventurous climbed the high trees and managed to pull off a few of the garments there securely lodged, but much was beyond their reach, and for several years the articles fluttered in the winds of winter and of summer, and vividly reminded all who passed over that portage of that singular disaster.

And how had it come about?

This was easily found out. One of the powder barrels had a little unnoticed hole in it, and from this had silted out a tiny little stream of powder all along the whole length of the portage. When the fire was kindled at the other end, where the dinner was cooked, it touched the beginning of this strangely laid fuse, which in running along had so interested those who had seen it at the beginning, but who had had no idea of there being any danger in it or of the damage it would inflict upon the supplies.

"Well," said Big Tom, in his quiet way, "I am sorry for John Company to lose so much property; but he is rich, and it will not hurt him. I am glad we did not do as is our general way—come over here and have our dinner near our loads. If we had done so perhaps some of our arms or legs might be now hanging up there in the branches where those red calicoes and other things are."

So, while all regretted the great misfortune, they were very thankful that there had been no loss of life or anybody even wounded. With a will they set to work, and soon the other cargoes were carried over, and then the boats were dragged across by the united crews. Soon were they launched and loaded, some with only half cargoes on account of the disaster, and then the journey was resumed.

How Big Tom explained the story of the explosion to the Hudson Bay officials and what were their answers we know not; suffice to say, Big Tom was very glum for some time after, and was not anxious to have many questions put to him in reference to the interview.

To the residence of Mr Ross the boys were escorted by a party of Hudson Bay clerks, after they had dined at Norway House. All their outfits, which fortunately, like their owners, had escaped the explosion, were brought over a few hours later by some of the servants of the company.

Of the hearty welcome which the boys received from Mr Ross and his family at Sagasta-weekee we have already made mention.

During the evening the chief factor and some of the other officials of the fort, who had had advices of the coming of our three young gentlemen, Frank, Alec, and Sam, came over to meet them. They most cordially welcomed them to the country, stating at the same time that they had received, by way of Montreal and Fort Garry, advance letters in reference to them, and would gladly carry out the instructions received, and do all they could to make the year's sojourn in the country as pleasant and interesting as possible.

This was good news to the boys, and was especially welcome to Mr Ross, who, now that he was no longer actively in the employ of the company, was a little nervous about the reception which would be accorded to these young hunters, who in this way had come into the country.

Strange as it may now appear, yet it is a well-known fact that persons coming into these territories were not welcome unless they came on the invitation and kept themselves completely under the company's direction and guidance. However, the old despotic rules were being relaxed, and especially was it so in the case of our boys, as thoughtful friends at home, who had influence with the London directors, had so arranged matters that everything was most favourable for their having a delightful time. That they had it these pages will surely testify.

As we have stated, very cordially were they received and welcomed by Mr Ross, whose home was on the mighty Nelson River, a few miles away from Norway House Fort. This great establishment of the Hudson Bay Company was for a great many years the great distributing centre for the supplies sent out from England to the many smaller posts throughout the country. The houses were very substantially built of hewn logs, boarded over and painted white. They occupied the four sides of a hollow square, room only being left for two or three massive gateways. The interior was kept during the summer months beautifully green, and was the favourite resort of officials, employees, and servants, and white and Indian visitors.

The relations between Mr Ross and the officials from this large establishment were most cordial, and visits were frequently interchanged.

The house which Mr Ross had built was as good as the material of the country afforded. The walls were of squared logs, the interstices between them being made as nearly frost-tight as possible. The outsides were well boarded, and so was the interior. As there is no limestone in that part of the country, the partitions dividing the rooms were all made of timber.

In the fall of the year, ere the ground freezes up, the house was banked up to the lower edges of the windows. Double sashes were placed in every window. As there is no coal in that part of the country, wood is used altogether in its place. Great iron stoves are used, in which roaring fires are kept burning incessantly from October until May. In this genuine native house the three boys were cordially welcomed, and soon felt themselves to be as members of the delightful family.

Shortly after their arrival, of course, there were many conversations as to the various excursions that could be made, and the different hunting expeditions that would be possible. While they expected to have some good times hunting the bears, beavers, wolves, reindeer, and other animals that were within easy reaching distance of their present headquarters, they were also ambitious enough to hope that they would have time to reach the haunts of the buffalo on the great western prairies, the musk ox in the far north, and even the grizzly bear in the mountain ravines.

In the meantime they had much to interest and amuse themselves with in studying the habits and customs of the Indians, who were constantly coming to see Mr Ross, whom they found to be a universal favourite, and the wise counsellor and adviser of all when in trouble or perplexity. With the twelve or fifteen splendid dogs which were owned by their host they soon became fast friends, and with them they had many a run, either in the forests or along the shores of the great water stretches that were near. Each boy soon had his favourite dog, and naturally did all he could to develop his intelligence and bring out all of his latent sagacity. While in a measure they succeeded in this, they also found, in some instances, that in some dogs downright mischief and trickery could be about as easily developed as the more noble qualities.

The canoes, of course, were tackled, and after a few laughable upsets they all soon became experts in the use of them, and had many a glorious trip and many an exciting adventure. Often did they go in the company of Mr Ross and with some experienced Indians to the place still retaining the name of the Old Fort, although the buildings were destroyed long ago. There the accumulated waters of some scores of rivers that pour into Lake Winnipeg rush out in one great volume to form the mighty Nelson River.

Here in this picturesque region, rich in Indian legends, and the resort of various kinds of game, and a favourite spot for the fishermen, many happy days were spent by our young friends in fishing and hunting. Then, when wearied with the varied sport, delightful hours were passed away, as, gathered round the bright, blazing camp fires, they listened to various reminiscences of the past as given by white or Indian.

These excursions often lasted for a number of days at a time. The party, which often consisted of from eight to a dozen persons, carried with them in their canoes not only their guns and ammunition, but their kettles and supplies and blankets. When the day's hunting was ended the supper was cooked at a fire made on the rocks, the principal item of which was supposed to be some of the game shot or fish caught.

As the boys' dexterity in the use of the canoes increased, they became more adventurous in their excursions, and one day they struck out, of course in company with experienced Indians, from the Old Fort and went as far as to the mouth of the great Saskatchewan River. The long trip across the north-west end of Lake Winnipeg was most exhilarating. The boys up to that time had no idea that birch canoes could ride in safety such enormous waves, or be propelled along continuously with such rapidity.

They camped on the shores of the great river, near the foot of the rapids, which are the only ones to be found in it for a thousand miles. Here they pitched their camp and lay down to sleep. The music of the rapids was a pleasant lullaby that soothed them into refreshing slumber.

Early the next morning they were visited by a number of friendly Indians, who informed them that the sturgeon were very numerous in the river at the foot of the rapids, and that excellent sport could be had in killing some of them.

While the usual method of capturing the sturgeon is with large gill nets, a more exciting way is by spearing them at the foot of the rapids, where at times they gather in large numbers, or by shooting them as they spring into the air. To spear a large sturgeon from a birch canoe, and not get an upset, is a difficult matter. For a time the Indians alone did the spearing; but after the boys had watched them at it they imagined that it was not such a very difficult matter after all, and so asked to be allowed to try for themselves. The Indians at first hesitated, as they well knew how really difficult it was, and thought that the boys had better keep at the safer sport of trying to shoot those that sprang, porpoise-like, out of the water. This itself afforded great amusement, and, while exciting, was not very successful, as it is extremely difficult to strike a sturgeon in this way, so rapid are its movements.

The boys had been fairly successful, and as the great fish, which were from five to eight feet long, when shot floated down the rapid current some old Indian men and women, on the lookout in their canoes, were made the richer and happier by being allowed to take possession of the valuable fish as they came along. This was the thought ever in the minds of the boys, that, whenever possible, no matter what they caught in the waters or shot in the forests, or elsewhere, if they could not use it all themselves, to have it reach some old or feeble Indians, who would be thankful for the gifts thus bestowed. This conduct on the part of the boys was most commendable, and everywhere secured them the good will of the Indians, who are never jealous of those who, visiting their lands for, sport and adventure, do not merely kill the animals for the love of killing, but are also desirous that somebody may be benefited by having for their use the fish or animals thus slaughtered.

As the boys were still anxious for an opportunity of trying their skill in spearing, they at length induced the Indians to let them make the attempt, even if they should not be very successful.

To be ready for any emergency, the cautious Indians arranged their canoes so that if any accident should occur to these adventurous boys they could prevent anything more serious than a good ducking taking place. In this method of capturing the sturgeon, the one using the spear takes his position in the front of the canoe, while the other men noiselessly paddle the boat against the current to the spot where sturgeon are seen to be quietly resting or rooting in the gravelly bottom of the shallow places in the current.

Alec was the first to make the attempt at this new and rather uncertain sport. In a good canoe manned by a couple of skilled Indians, he took his position in the bow of the canoe, and with a good strong fishing spear in his hands he steadied himself carefully in the cranky boat, while the men silently paddled him to a spot where the occasional appearance of part of a sturgeon above the water betrayed its presence. The sun shining gloriously made the day delightful, but its very brightness was the cause of Alec's discomfiture.

Nothing more quickly disturbs sturgeon than a sudden shadow thrown on the water. Alec, not knowing this, was being quietly paddled against the current, thus facing toward the west. As it was now about noon, the bright sun was on his left. In this position he ought only to have attempted to spear the fish on the left side of his canoe, where he would have thrown no shadow. Ignorant of this, as soon as he observed a large sturgeon not far ahead of him he quietly indicated by signs to the canoemen which way he wished them to paddle, so as to bring him close enough to spear the fish. The men from their positions not being able to see the sturgeon paddled as directed, and soon Alec was brought close enough to make the attempt. The sturgeon seemed to be an enormous one, and so Alec, knowing that only a most desperate lunge would enable him to drive the spear through the thick hide of the fish, which was just now a little before him on the right, made the attempt with all the strength that he could possibly muster.

But, alas, how different from what was expected! As Alec threw himself forward to plunge the sharp spear into the body of the fish, he found that it met with no firmer substance than the water, and so, instead of the spear being buried in the body of the fish, the momentum of his great effort threw him out of the boat, and down he went head first into the river. Fortunately the water was not deep, and as the other canoes were not far behind he was soon pulled into one of them, a bit frightened, but none the worse for his involuntary plunge.

Nothing daunted, Sam was the next to volunteer to try his skill, and on being informed that Alec's trouble was that he had raised his arm with the spear so as to cast a shadow which had frightened the fish, he resolved not to make a similar mistake. Taking his position as directed in the front of the canoe, his men paddled him where he would be able to strike his fish without casting his shadow. Soon the appearance of the fins of a great sturgeon were seen, and noiselessly the Indians paddled Sam's canoe close up to it. He was resolved if possible to succeed where Alec had signally failed. When close enough to the large fish, which seemed to be utterly unconscious of the canoe's presence, Sam, taking the spear in both hands, plunged it well and true into the body of the great sturgeon, that up to that instant seemed to have been sound asleep. However, there was a great awakening when it felt that spear thrust. Giving a great spring, so strong and sudden that it seemed to fairly lift Sam, spear and all, out of the canoe, it started for the great lake. Sam let go of the spear when he found himself being dragged over the side of the boat, but the Indians afterward declared that he hung on for some time, and had a ride on the back of the great fish.

Like Alec had been before him, he was quickly picked up and dragged into another canoe.

The Indians imagined that now that two of the boys had come to grief the third would not wish to attempt this risky sport. Those lads of ours were not easily daunted, and so without any hesitancy Frank asked to be allowed to see what he could do. Frank had this advantage, that he had observed what had caused Alec and Sam to fail in their attempts. Arming himself with a sharp spear, he took the position assigned to him, and was paddled up to a place where the fish were numerous. The spear that he had selected, instead of being one of the three-pronged variety, was more of a chisel shape, and exceedingly sharp. With this in his hands, he firmly braced himself in the narrow front of the canoe, while the now intensely interested company watched his efforts. Even Sam and Alec refused to leave until Frank had made his attempt. Some sturgeon were observed very near, but Frank, even in the excitement of the moment, was not to be diverted from his resolve, and so had the Indians paddle him on and on until they brought him close to an enormous fellow, lying quiet and still on the gravelly bottom.

With all his strength Frank struck him a blow, so quick and strong that the first intimation of danger to the fish was the sharp spear crashing through the strong bony scales, through flesh and vertebrae, into the spinal cord, just behind the head. So instantaneous was the death of the great sturgeon under this fatal stroke that there was not even the usual spasmodic spring. Like as a log might have lain there on the water, so did the great fish. The only movement was, as is the case with most large fish thus killed, he rolled over, and at once began to float away on the current.

"Well done, Frank!" shouted the dripping boys, who had pluckily refused to be taken ashore until Frank had made his attempt, in which he had so well succeeded. The Indians were delighted and, in their way, quite demonstrative, and for long after at many a camp fire the story of that strong, true, successful spear thrust had to be described and acted out.

Thoroughly satisfied with these first adventures at sturgeon fishing, the party went ashore, and at a large camp fire Alec and Sam dried their garments as well as possible. Changes, of course, they had not on such an excursion. However, they suffered but little inconvenience, and no bad results followed from their submersions.

They spent another day or two at the mouth of the great Saskatchewan River, and in the canoes of some of the experienced Indians, who there reside, they several times ran the rapids. This was wild and exhilarating sport, and was vastly enjoyed by the boys. During the return trip nothing of very great importance occurred. They shot a number of wild ducks from the canoes as they paddled along, and in due time reached Sagasta-weekee tired and bronzed, and full of the adventures of their first outing from the home of their kind host.

# Chapter Six.

### Indian Implements—Canoeing Excursion—Gunpowder Versus Jack Fish—Loon Shooting—Sam's Successful Shot.

The Indians were originally very skillful in the manufacture of the few essential articles that were absolutely necessary for their use. The style and curves of their graceful canoes, although only made of the bark of the birch tree and strengthened by supple bands of cedar or balsam, and made watertight by the gum of the pine or other resinous trees, have never been improved in any boat builder's yard in civilisation. True, fancy canoes are being turned out for the pleasure and enjoyment of canoeists in safe waters, but whenever the experiment has been tried of using these canoes in the dangerous rivers of the Indian country they are not found to be at all equal to those manufactured by the natives. In the manufacture of their paddles, and in the spring and lightness of their oars, they have never been surpassed; and, while often imitated, many a skillful white artisan has had to admit that after all his efforts there was a something of completeness and exact fitness for the work required about the Indians' production that he felt was in some way lacking in his own handiwork.

To the Indian women and clever old men were left the duties of making the canoes. Our boys were very much interested in watching them at the work of canoe building, but naturally annoyed at the spasmodic way in which they carried on their operations, as while perhaps for some days they would work incessantly from early dawn to dark, they would then lay off for days and do nothing but lounge around and smoke.

As the weeks rolled on, and the boys became more and more acquainted with the natives, and acclimated and accustomed to the methods of travel, a more ambitious trip for their pleasure was arranged by Mr Ross.

It was decided to go to the Old Fort, and after shooting and fishing there in the vicinity of the place previously visited, then to push on to Spider Islands, and after a short stay in order to enjoy the beauties of that romantic place, then to push on across the north-eastern part of the great Lake Winnipeg to Montreal Point, and there to hunt along the coast as far south as Poplar Point, if the sport were good and the necessary supplies of ammunition and other essentials held out. The boys were wild with delight at the prospect, and were anxious to do all in their power to expedite the undertaking.

The Indians of all these regions in which our boys were hunting do not now give much prominence to the old picturesque style of dress with which we have all been so familiar. Feathers and paints are with them now quite out of date; still their coats, pants, leggings, and moccasins are principally made of the beautifully tanned skins of the moose and reindeer, and handsomely ornamented with bead work, at which the Cree women are most skillful. Of course Frank, Alec, and Sam were speedily fitted out in the dress of the country, and were quite proud of their appearance. They were also very anxious to have the natives give them Indian names, as is quite customary. The Indians, however, after some councilling, in which a large quantity of tobacco was smoked, decided that as the boys were to remain some time in the country they had better wait for the development of some strong peculiarities in them, or until some great event occurred that would suggest some expressive name. While disappointed with this decision of the council, the boys had to rest content.

At first they found the use of the soft, pliable moccasin very strange, after the heavy boots of civilisation, and for a little while complained of a soreness in the soles of their feet. These, however, soon hardened, and then they much preferred the soft Indian shoes to all others.

On the contemplated trip Mr Ross decided that, in addition to some younger Indians, he would take with him two old, experienced men, who were perhaps the most famous hunters of their tribe. One of these was our old friend, Big Tom; the other was called Mustagan. He was almost as large as Big Tom, and had a wonderful record. We shall hear much about him as these pages advance, and will be delighted to have him with us in many an exciting hour.

Three canoes were employed on this excursion. Mr Ross had Mustagan, another Indian, and one of the boys with him; while the other two canoes, which were not quite so large as Mr Ross's, had in each two Indians to paddle them, and one of the boys. So when the party started it consisted of ten persons. Everyone was well supplied with guns and ammunition. The guns used were the muzzle-loaders of the country, as after some experiments with the breech-loaders there was found to be a good deal of difficulty in reference to the supplies of cartridges. The usual camping outfit and supplies for a month's outing were taken along with them.

While passing through Play Green Lake, they amused themselves one day by catching some very large jack fish, or pike, in the usual way. It seems very surprising that the mere concussion of the air caused by the firing of blank charges of gunpowder could so stun or paralyse such enormous fish.

As they journeyed on, a quiet "Hush!" from Mustagan caused them to look toward the shore, and there, not far up from the sandy beach, were to be seen four beautiful young deer. As Mr Ross was anxious to get on, and nothing specially was to be gained by hunting these beautiful young creatures, they were not even disturbed or frightened. The boys watched them for some time, and were delighted with their graceful movements as like young lambs they gambolled on the shore. Genuine sport is not butchery of inoffensive creatures that cannot be utilised for the benefit of parties shooting them.

They had some rare sport in trying to shoot the great northern diver, called in this country the loon. It is a bird as large and heavy as the wild goose. Its feathers are so thick and close that they easily turn aside ordinary shot. Its bill is long and sharp, and with it in battle can inflict a most ugly wound. The feathers on its breast are of snowy whiteness, while on the rest of the body they are of a dark brown colour approaching to black flecked with white. Its peculiar legs are wide and thin; its webbed feet are so large that it can swim with amazing rapidity. On land it is a very awkward and ungainly bird, and can hardly move along; but in the water it is a thing of beauty, and as a diving bird it has, perhaps, no equal. It has a strange mournful cry, and seems to utter its melancholy notes more frequently before an approaching storm than at any other time. The Indians, who are most excellent judges of the weather and quick to notice any change, have great confidence in the varied cries of the loon. It is a marvellous diver, and is able to swim great distances under the water with amazing rapidity, only coming up, when pursued, for an instant, at long intervals to breathe.

The loon is very hard to kill. A chance long-distance bullet or a shot in the eye does occasionally knock one over, but as a general thing the Indians, none too well supplied with ammunition, let them alone, as when shot they are of but little worth. Their flesh is tough and tasteless, and the only thing at all prized is the beautiful skin, out of which the Indian women manufacture some very picturesque fire-bags.

As several of these loons were seen swimming in Play Green Lake as our party paddled along, Mr Ross decided to give the boys a chance to show their skill and quickness in firing at them, although he hardly imagined any of them would be struck. The sportsman who would strike them must have an alert eye and quick aim to fire the instant they are up, as they are down again so suddenly, only to reappear again some hundreds of yards off in the most unexpected place.

The three canoes were paddled to positions about a third of a mile apart, like as at the points of an equilateral triangle. In this large space thus inclosed several loons were surrounded, and the work of trying to shoot them began. Before beginning to fire, the boys had been warned never under any circumstance to pull a trigger if one of the other boats should be in line, no matter how distant. Bullets even from an ordinary shotgun will sometimes so bound over the waves as to go an immense distance, and very serious injuries have resulted. As has been stated, it is almost impossible to kill a loon even when struck with ordinary shot, so it was decided here to use either buckshot or bullets as the hunters preferred.

Part of the fun of loon hunting is in the absolute uncertainty as to the spot where the bird, after diving, will next show itself. It may appear a quarter of a mile away, or it may suddenly push up its bright head and look at you out of its brilliant eyes not five yards from the side of your canoe. It has, when hunted, a certain dogged stubbornness against leaving the vicinity it was in when first assailed, and will remain in a small area, even of a large lake, although repeatedly fired at.

Hardly had the canoe in which were Mr Ross and Frank with their two canoemen taken its position, when a beautiful loon rose up about a hundred yards away, and not having been frightened, as no gun had as yet been fired, he sat there in all his beauty on the water watching them.

"Fire at him," said Mr Ross to Frank.

No sooner said than done, and away sped the bullet well and true on its errand, and fairly and squarely hit the water exactly where the bird had been, but no bird was there. Quicker than could that bullet speed across those hundred yards the bird had dived, and ere Frank could recover from his chagrin its brilliant eyes were looking at him from a spot not twenty yards away. The loon had been facing the canoe when fired at, and in diving had come on in a straight line toward them, and now here he was, so close to them and looking so intently that he seemed to say by his appearance, "I've come to see what all that noise was about."

So sudden was his appearance that no one in the canoe was ready for him, and ere a gun could be pointed he was down again and, swimming directly under the boat, rose again on the other side, more than a hundred yards away. While this had been Frank's experience, the others had not been idle. As was quite natural, there was a good deal of good-natured rivalry among them as to which canoe would come the honour of killing the first loon. Mustagan, who had charge of one of these canoes, was an old hand at this work, and, as he was a keen hunter, had caught this spirit of rivalry that had arisen. He determined to put his long experience with these birds against their cleverness, and it was interesting to watch the contest between him and them. For a time his efforts met with complete failure, and the birds fairly outwitted him.

Mustagan, however, was not discouraged, and he resolved on one more effort to succeed. He had learned from observation that the loon with its marvellously brilliant eye seemed to be able to see the flash of the gun, and so quick were its movements that it could dive ere the bullets or other missiles reached it. Acting on this knowledge, he rigged up in the canoe a kind of a barrier behind which Sam was seated, concealed from the sharp-sighted bird. For a time they were not able to get a successful shot, although a great deal of ammunition was expended.

Alec, with Big Tom and his other Indian canoeman, was equally unsuccessful. The loons themselves seemed to have entered into the spirit of the thing, and kept bobbing up here and there, at most unexpected places, taking good care, however, that each time the bullets struck the spot where they were, they were somewhere else when it arrived. It was at first strange to the boys that the bullets did not follow them in the water, but went bounding off and skipping over the surface often for great distances.

At length, when Mr Ross began to fear that the ammunition had suffered enough, and the boys had had sufficient of this kind of shooting, which, after all, was a most capital drill at quick firing, and was about to stop the sport, Mustagan pleaded for time to try one more experiment. He had been watching the movements of a splendid loon, that had saucily and successfully challenged the guns from each boat in succession for quite a time. Mustagan's quick eye noticed that the bird was not quite so vigilant as he had been, and resolved that he could be shot, and that Sam should have that honour. Strange as it may seem to those who have not had the fun of trying to shoot loons, these birds get to know that the hunters they are to watch are those who handle the guns. Knowing this, Mustagan had Sam well load his gun with buckshot and slugs. Swinging the canoe so that Sam would be completely hid by the barrier prepared, he with his gun rose up in a conspicuous manner flourishing his weapon, and thus kept the eyes of the bird on himself every time he arose. This went on for some minutes, until at length, as Mustagan did not fire, although brandishing his gun about, the loon seemed to lose his caution, and remained up longer each time he came to the surface.

This was what the wily old Indian was expecting, and so, speaking to Sam, he told him to be on the watch and soon he would have a successful shot. Sam, however, had to wait for quite a time, so erratic were the loon's movements, and in such unexpected places did he suddenly come up. However, success generally comes to those who have patience long enough to wait, and so it was in this case. The fortunate opportunity came at last, for there right in front of the canoe not fifty yards away rose up that beautiful bird, and the same instant from the unseen gun and lad, behind that little barrier, rang out the report which followed the fatal missiles that had done their work, for one of them had cut clean through the neck of the loon, severing the vertebrae, and there he lay in the water with the snowy-white breast uppermost.

A rousing cheer told of the successful shot, and at once when the bird was secured the canoes were headed for the shore. There a dinner was quickly prepared, and in glorious picnic style it was enjoyed by all. The loon was skinned by one of the Indian men, and subsequently was tanned in native fashion, and a beautiful fire-bag was made from it of which in after years Sam was very proud.

Sam's Race with a Bear.

# Chapter Seven.

## The Old Fort Camp—Sam's Race with the Bear—Indian Comments.

As the day was now advancing, and they had already had so much sport, they decided not to try and reach the Old Fort on Lake Winnipeg, where the Nelson River begins, that evening. So they paddled their canoes to the ashore and there formed a camp. While the older members of the party remained at the fire, some of the younger and more eager ones took their guns and went off to see what they could shoot.

Frank succeeded in bringing down a great pelican that, with some others, had been gorging itself with gold-eyes, a beautiful kind of fish, similar in appearance to large herring, but with eyes so bright and golden that the appropriateness of the name is at once evident to all the first time they see it. Frank carried to the camp his great bird, but was disappointed when told that as an article of food it was about worthless. One of the Indians, however, pleased him when he said that a very beautiful ornamental bag could be made of the great sac that hung down from its enormous bill.

Alec was more successful, and returned soon after Frank with a number of fine ducks, which he carried hanging around him with their heads crowded under his belt in real Indian fashion.

The different Indians, who had also gone off hunting, returned one after another, and so when supper was ready at the camp fire about sunset all were returned but Sam.

Where was he? Who had seen him last?

These were the questions put, but no one seemed able to give any satisfactory answer.

As it was supposed he would return any minute, the supper, which consisted principally of the fish they had caught and game shot, was eaten and much enjoyed.

Still no signs of Sam. Mr Ross began to feel uneasy, and now, as the shadows of the coming night were beginning to fall around them, he called Mustagan and some of the older Indians to him, and asked what had better be done. Promptly they responded that he must be found ere the last glimmering light faded away and the auroras began to dance and play in the northern sky.

"Let us at once get on his trail," said an old Indian, "and we will soon find him."

So the question was again anxiously asked who had last seen him.

But there was little need for an answer, as Sam, pale, excited, and panting for breath, suddenly dashed into their midst.

"What is the matter?" said Mr Ross, while all the rest, with intense interest, waited for his answer.

All poor Sam could say was, "The bear! the bear!" as he lay panting on the ground.

Mustagan, quick to read signs, was the first to see what had happened, and so, hastily catching up his gun and crowding down the barrel a bullet on the top of the buckshot with which it was already loaded, he slipped out from the circle of light around the camp fire in the direction from which Sam had come.

Not five minutes was he gone ere the report of his gun rang out. With all the imperturbable nature of an Indian he returned, and when within easy calling distance of the camp fire he asked for a couple of Indians to join him. Quickly they glided away in the darkness. It was not for a long time, however, that they were required. Soon their voices were heard asking that additional wood might be thrown upon the fire in order that they might have a better light. Why they needed it was soon evident, as they shortly afterward appeared dragging into the camp a splendid bear, the sight of which at first made Sam jump again, as though he would continue the journey he had so abruptly ended when he had dashed into their midst.

When Sam had quieted down he told the story of his exciting adventure.

Like the others, he had taken his gun and gone off to see what he could shoot. As at first he did not meet with much success he pushed on and on until he reached a long stretch of sandy beach, on which he detected the fresh footprints of a bear. Putting a bullet into his gun, he bravely started off to get that bear. On and on he hurried, reckless and excited, until at length he saw the fine fellow, not two hundred yards away, sitting on a flat rock a little way out from the shore, busily engaged in capturing fish.

Without any fear Sam pushed on until he was, as he thought, near enough to kill the bear that was sitting on his haunches with his back toward him, utterly unconscious of his presence.

Raising his gun he fired. That he hit him he was sure, as he said he saw the fur fly from a spot on his back. The instant the bear felt the wound he gave a roar of pain, and, turning around, without a moment's hesitation dashed into the water and came for Sam.

"All at once," said Sam in a most comical manner, "as I saw what a big fellow he was and his resolve to try and cultivate a closer acquaintanceship, I thought I had had hunting enough, and would like to go home and see my mother. But, as this was impossible, I decided that the next best thing was to get back to the camp as soon as I could. So I dropped my gun and started at a great rate. However it did not take the bear long to get across that bit of water, and then on he came.

"My! but he did run, and quickly did he gain upon me. Then I dropped my brightly coloured beaded Indian cap, hoping that that would delay him.

"But he only seemed to give it a sniff and a tear, and then on he came. Finding he was still gaining on me, I pulled off my leather coat and dropped it on the trail and hurried on. Glancing behind me, I noticed that that seemed to make him suspicious for a time, as he carefully examined it. This delay was fortunate for me, but soon, to my alarm, I found he was once more coming on after me.

"It was now getting dark, but fortunately I knew the way, and so dashed in upon you in the manner I did, just about used up."

The recital of Sam's adventure and narrow escape very much excited Frank and Alec, and Mr Ross looked grave and anxious, and seemed to be thinking of what would have been felt and said in the home land if, during the first few weeks after the boys had arrived in the Wild North Land, one of them had been killed by a bear.

The Indians smoked their pipes and listened in silence to Sam's story, which was translated for those who did not understand English. It was evident by their clouded faces that they were not pleased. Their actions said, even before they uttered a word:

"The young white brave should not have run away from a bear. Suppose that the bear had not been killed, and after chasing the white hunter into the protection of the camp fire had escaped and gone and told the other bears of his success, what a rejoicing there would have been among the other bears! And how bold and saucy all the bears would have been ever after!"

Thus the Indians thought, for they have queer ideas about bears. Because of the handlike appearance of the paws of the bear they say there is a good deal of the human in them. So they talk about them as holding councils and taking advice one from another. And when they attack them, especially the Indians of these great Algonquin tribes, they always address them as Mr Bear, and apologise to them for being under the necessity of killing them.

Thus these Indians at this camp fire were simply disgusted with Sam for running away from that black bear.

So after a good smoke and much cogitation one of them, who was a paddler in Sam's canoe, turned to him and said:

"You have a good knife?"

"Yes," said Sam, and he drew the keen, sharp, double-edged weapon from its sheath in his leather belt, and handed it to him to examine.

The Indian took it, and, after carefully examining it, passed it on to the other Indians, who all admired it. But it was noticed that in their low utterances among themselves there was much of sarcasm, and even contempt, in some of their expressions.

After some more smoking another Indian turned to Sam, and said:

"No tree along the trail where the bear chase you?"

"O yes," said Sam, "plenty of them. But I was afraid to take time enough to try and climb up into one of them."

This answer, which Sam gave in all honesty, was too much for the Indians, and the look of disgust that passed over their faces was a study. However, the one who had asked the question about the tree spoke up and said:

"No good climbing a tree. Bear better climber than any hunter. Tree only good for you to fight bear at the bottom. Put back against tree. Black bear rise up and come to hug you to death. He then never bite or tear. Only hug. He try to squeeze the life out of you. So with good knife, and your back against a tree, keep cool. Let bear come, and when he stand up on his hind legs and try to hug, you just give him your good knife straight in the heart. Bear fall over dead. You not hurt at all. All needed, keep cool all the time. No brave white boy with good knife and plenty trees must ever run away from black bear any more."

Thus he went on in his broken English to Sam's mortification, and he found that in using his good legs, that had often carried him in first in many a race at school, he had gone down very much in the estimation of the Indians, who think it is simply foolishness, as well as cowardice, if armed with anything like a decent knife, to refuse to give battle to a bear from the trunk of the nearest tree. Thus the boys were getting points and learning lessons by experience in reference to hunting.

Mr Ross did not chide the lad, but thought that it would have been better if, when he discovered the fresh track of the bear, he had immediately returned to the camp for assistance. The fact is, Mr Ross was very thankful that nothing worse had happened.

Frank and Alec listened with intense interest to Sam's account of his race back to the camp with the bear at his heels, and both declared that they would have done likewise. Later on we will find that they were able to successfully adopt the Indian methods, much to their delight.

Alec Shooting the Wolverine.

# Chapter Eight.

### Preserving Meat—Cunning Partridges—Celestial Phenomenon—The Fearful Hurricane—Caught in the Storm—Disaster—The Mischievous Wolverine—Alec's Shot.

The sun was shining brightly next morning ere the musical "Koos-koos-kah" rang out, calling them from their slumbers. When the boys arose they found the big bear already skinned, and some portions of his hams, cut as steaks, were being broiled, while his spareribs were skidded on a couple of sticks, and were being roasted a nice brown colour in front of the fire which burned so brightly on the rocks. The savoury odour of the cooking breakfast was welcome to the boys.

A hasty plunge in the fresh water of the lake was a refreshing bath, and soon they were ready for their morning meal. Indians, if they have the chance, are not bad cooks, especially when working for those whom they respect; and so here, under the eye of Mr Ross, whom they so loved, they did their best. With some of the supplies from home, added to the fish, duck, bear steaks, and spareribs, they had a breakfast of which any hunters might be proud. The delicious bracing air, the wild romantic surroundings, the congenial friendship, the picturesque, attentive red men, gave to this meal on the rocks under the blue sky such an exhilaration of spirits to the boys that they were fairly wild with delight.

Even Sam had forgotten in some degree his exciting race and fright in the rare enjoyment of the hour. Soon after, preparations were begun for continuing the journey. The question was, what was to be done with all the bear's meat, as there was too much to carry in their canoes, with the other supplies considered more necessary. So the Indian plan of preserving meat fresh and sweet was adopted. A hole was dug in the fresh earth to a depth of three or four feet, and here the meat, well wrapped up in the bear's skin, was deposited. Meat will keep fresh and good in this way for many days. The hole was then carefully covered up and packed down by the Indians. Then on the top a large fire was kindled, and then allowed to burn itself out. This was done to destroy the scent and thus save the "cache" from being discovered by prowling wolves and wolverines that would in all probability visit the camp not long after the hunters had left.

Nothing of much importance occurred during the trip to the Old Fort. Their favourite camping ground was reached in due time, and the boys had a couple of hours' duck and partridge shooting ere they sat down on the rocks to dinner. Each had something to say, but Frank most amused the party by a description of an old partridge that kept tumbling down ahead of him and acting in the queerest manner possible. In fact, so amused was he in the queer antics of the bird that he could not find it in his heart to shoot her. When Mr Ross heard Frank's story he said he was delighted to hear that he had not tried to shoot that partridge, as it was undoubtedly a mother bird with a brood of little ones not far off. Then he went on to tell not only of the cleverness he had often witnessed in the old mother birds themselves, but also how cunningly the little ones acted when suddenly disturbed. They would apparently make themselves invisible. Some would quickly disappear in little openings or under leaves, others would cleverly catch up old brown leaves in their mouths and suddenly turn over on their backs, and then lie still and quiet thus hidden under the leaves. Mr Ross said he had seen them do this so quickly that he could hardly believe his eyes until he went and picked up the brown leaf and the little partridge that had so cleverly hid itself out of sight, and not until the little bird was in his hands did it show any sign of life. Then, indeed, it was wild enough.

During the afternoon the sky became hazy and slightly overcast. The boys were treated to one of the peculiar phenomena not unfrequently seen in those high latitudes. First, a great circle surrounded the sun, and at the east, west, and top and bottom in it were seen very vivid mock suns. Shortly after another ring appeared inside this first one, and then another one on the outside of all, and in each circle there appeared four mock suns, clear, distinct, and startling. In all there was the sun himself, in a beautiful halo in the centre, and around him were visible no less than twelve mock suns.

While this sight very much interested the boys, the older Indians were somewhat troubled, and at once proposed to Mr Ross the removal of their camp to a sheltered spot where some dense forests of balsam and spruce would be a barrier against the coming storm, which they said was not more than an hour off. Marvellously clever are these Indians in reading these signs in the heavens, and very rarely do they make mistakes.

To the boys there was not in these beautiful visions in the heavens anything that portended a storm, and they were somewhat disappointed when told that in all probability there would be but little hunting for perhaps some days. While this was not pleasant news, they willingly fell to work and did their share in removing to the place appointed. They were very much interested to see how skillfully the Indians cut poles, and, taking the oilcloths from the canoes, improvised a watertight roof over a "lean-to," as they called it, against the storm that they said would soon be on them from a certain point indicated. Large dry logs were cut and rolled into position to make a fire in the front of this improvised tent, under which they would have to find shelter. Kettles, food, and blankets were brought up to this camp, and then the canoes were carried to a sheltered spot and turned over and fastened down with heavy logs and stones.

Very busily were the men employed, and yet more rapid were the changes that were taking place in the heavens above and around them. One by one the circles with the mock suns disappeared. Dark clouds began to arise up in the north-west horizon, and rapidly they came up in the heavens. Vivid flashes of lightning were seen and the rumbling thunder was heard from the rapidly darkening clouds all around. The birds that had been singing now seemed to fly off to dense coverts, and uttered only frightened cries. A dense, stuffy sensation seemed to be in the air, and there for a few moments every sound was hushed, and a calm, the most profound and ominous, seemed to fall upon the whole face of nature. Not a blade of grass or a tall reed in the marshy places near the shore made the slightest movement. Nature was absolutely still. It was the dead, weird quiet before the awful hurricane; the quietude of death before the elemental war.

Only for a short time did it last, and to judge by the feverish haste with which the Indians, under Mr Ross's stern orders, worked, it was evident they knew the danger of this ominous calm, and what would speedily follow. Large logs were piled up as a barrier behind the improvised tent, while every rope available was used to tie down the poles which held up the roof of canvas and oilcloth. Poles were lashed across the top, and tied down with the fishing nets, which had to do as substitutes for something better. Guns were well wrapped up in the oilcloth covers, and, with the axes, were placed at a distance from the camp.

"Get under cover, and hold on to something fixed and strong!" shouted Mustagan, who had been on the lookout, and saw that the storm was close at hand.

And it *was* a storm! A strange greenish appearance came into the north-west sky, and then suddenly there was heard and seen the oncoming tornado. The clouds that during the calm had apparently become motionless in the heavens for a time suddenly became strangely broken and twisted, and then, as though impelled by some irresistible impulse, started with a speed that seemed incredible on their wild career. There seemed to roll up before them the strange green colour in the sky, which now appeared like a great monster on the crest of the coming clouds. Blacker, denser, and darker, on they came. Far away the sound of the storm could be heard, while now the forked lightnings and peals of thunder were almost incessant.

Crouching under the shelter was our party. Mr Ross and the three boys were in the centre, while the stalwart Indians took the outside positions, each man with a grip of iron upon the poles and canvas.

Very strange and very different were the sensations of the boys. "This is glorious!" said Alec, who had often, with his Highland friends, been caught in storms amid the hills of his beloved Scotland.

"Wait until it is over," said the other boys, "and then we will tell you whether it is 'glorious' or not."

"Hold on!" shouted Mr Ross. For, in almost an instant, a dark as like as midnight was on them, broken only by a vivid flash of lightning, while the very ground seemed to shake under the awful thunder. Then the storm in all its fury was upon them. How they escaped seemed a miracle. Great trees all around them were bent and twisted and broken, and went down in scores, until the air seemed full of the falling trunks and branches. Large branches fell upon the frail roof under which they were sheltered, but fortunately, while some holes were made, none of them were large enough to break through or injure them, and those that did fall on them were really a benefit, as they helped to hold down the canvas over them.

Fortunately these tornadoes are not of long duration. With a speed of perhaps over a hundred miles an hour they sweep along with irresistible power in their wild career.

Their fury is soon spent, and years may pass ere they occur again. As a very heavy fall of rain immediately followed this hurricane or tornado, our party were obliged to remain under their frail tent, which, in spite of the fury of the winds, thanks to the strong arms of the Indians, skillfully directed by Mustagan, had been kept from being blown away. However, some of the larger branches that had fallen upon it had pierced the roof in some places, and now, like out of a huge funnel, about a gallon of water suddenly struck Alec on the back of the neck, and caused him to change his position, while he fairly howled from the suddenness of the dousing.

"Is that sousing 'glorious,' Alec?" asked Frank, who was doing his best to dodge the little streams that through some other rents were trying to reach him.

"Well, no, not exactly," was Alec's answer;—"this beats anything I ever saw or heard of in the Highlands; and now that the worst is over I would not have missed such a thing for a good deal."

"What do you think of it, Sam?" said Frank.

Sam had cuddled down between Mr Ross and Mustagan, and, at the advice of the latter, had taken the precaution to double up a blanket like a shawl and throw it over his head and shoulders. Very little wet had reached him, yet he had to confess that he had been terrified by this storm, which had excelled any dozen ever witnessed before in his life.

"Think of it!" said, he; "faith, I have just been thinking which is the worst, being chased by a fierce old bear or frightened out of a year's growth by a tornado. Next time, if I am to choose between the two, I'll tackle the bear."

This answer caused a hearty laugh, and even the Indians, who had remained so quiet, yet alert to watch for any change in the storm, smiled at it and exchanged significant glances, and said that the boy would yet redeem himself.

After a time the rain ceased, the blue sky appeared, and the sun shone out again. But what a change met their gaze as they came out from under their quickly improvised tent and wandered about! The beautiful forests seemed about ruined. In one direction, like as though a great reaper had gone through a splendid meadow and cut clean to the ground a great swath of grass, so had this cyclone gone through the forest. In the centre of its path not a tree had been left standing. Every one had gone down before this irresistible force. Fortunately it had swerved a little to the right as it passed by our friends, or they would not have escaped so well. As it was great trees had fallen all around, and it was a providential escape that had been theirs, and for this they were more than grateful as they saw by investigation more and more of the fury displayed by the effects of the tempest as it passed. The spot where the canoes had been hid away was, of course, one of the first to which their steps were directed. A great tree had fallen across one of them that had not been placed low enough in the hollow between the rocks, and it was so crushed and broken as to be absolutely worthless. The others, however, had escaped, and were none the worse of the storm, although fallen trees were all around them.

Blankets, supplies, and other things were overhauled, and everything that had caught the rain was soon drying in the warm sun, which was now smiling serenely upon them. The mock suns, or "sun dogs," as they were commonly called, all disappeared with the storm of which they seemed to have been the harbinger. Beautiful as had been their appearance, the boys all agreed that if their coming was to be so speedily followed by such a storm they would gladly dispense with them in the future; nor did they see them again until when, in the depth of winter, they showed up in their weird splendour and heralded forth a blizzard storm which played its wild pranks upon the boys most thoroughly. But we must not anticipate.

Mr Ross and the Indians quickly shifted the camp to a pleasant place. A fire was kindled and a hot meal was cooked and eaten, and then there was a consultation as to the future. One canoe was destroyed; could the whole party go in the other two, or had they better return to Sagasta-weekee? Mr Ross was anxious to hear whether the cyclone had done any damage at home, although he had not much fear, for it had apparently come from another direction. However, it was eventually decided that three of the Indians should return home, and bring along with them another canoe as well as news from the home. They were also to call at the camp to take home the bear's robe and meat, which had been cached in the ground as we have described. Very soon were they ready to start, and, to the surprise of Mr Ross, Alec asked to be permitted to go with them. This request was readily granted, and soon in one canoe, with their four paddles at work, they were speeding along at a great rate.

They pushed on without stopping until they began to round the point of a narrow tongue of land which would bring them into full view of their camp, although it was still some hundreds of yards away. The instant the point was turned and the distant camping place came into view the Indian in the front of the canoe suddenly ducked down his head and whispered a sharp, quick "Hist!" and at once arrested the forward movement of the boat. Noiselessly and quickly was the canoe paddled back out of sight.

"What is the matter?" said Alec, who was surprised by the suddenness of this quick retrograde movement and of the quiet, suppressed excitement of the Indians.

"Wolverine!" was the only word he heard, which was whispered from one Indian to the other. The utterance of this one word made Alec no wiser until one of the men, who understood a little English, said, "Wolverine find the camp; smell the meat; dig him up; carry him away; we kill him."

This was no easy matter, as the wolverine is, without exception, the most cunning animal in the woods. He far outstrips in this respect the fox or wolf or bear. What these Indians were going to do must be done quickly. The first thing was to see that their guns were well-loaded with bullets. The next was to find out if his quick eyes had seen them when for the few seconds they must have been visible when they rounded the point. The wind was in their favour, as it was blowing from him to them. The oldest of the crew was appointed the leader, the rest were to follow his directions. First of all he quietly went ashore, and, noiselessly crawling through the underbrush across the point, he was able to see that the wolverine was still at work. It was evident that he had not the slightest suspicion that his enemies, the hunters, were near him. Returning to the canoe from this inspection, the leader gave orders that they were to paddle back into the deep bay so that there would be a possibility of their landing and getting in behind him, as their old camp which he was robbing was close to the shore.

Very noiselessly and yet rapidly did they hurry back, and then as quietly as possible they landed at a suitable spot. It was here decided that three of them, with their guns, should try and get into the rear of the camp, while

Alec, who had not yet the ability to travel with the speed and quietness here essential to success, was to take his place just across the neck of land where, with his gun, he could command the shore if the wolverine, disturbed by those in the rear, should attempt to escape over the rocks in that direction. Before leaving the leader said to Alec:

"Do not fire until you see the whites of his eyes, and then hit him, if possible, between them; or, if it is a side shot, strike him behind the foreshoulders."

Alec was excited, but he soon conquered his nervousness, and prepared to play his part as well as possible. His instructions were to wait for a few minutes ere he began to crawl to his assigned position. He thus had an opportunity of witnessing the cleverness and alertness of the three Indians starting on their critical work. Making a deep détour, they were soon out of sight in the forest, without making as much noise as the breaking of a single twig beneath their moccasined feet. More like phantoms they seemed, as so quietly they flitted away. When he thought it was time for him to move he began, Indian-like, to advance to his assigned position, imitating as far as possible the movements he had witnessed in the Indians. To his great satisfaction, he reached the designated spot without any trouble.

Carefully looking over the rocks and through some underbrush, he was able to see, through a pocket telescope which he fortunately had with him, the busy wolverine still at work. Very interesting it was to watch him, even if it meant the destruction of all the meat. The wolverine is about as large as a first-class retriever dog. His legs, though short, are exceedingly muscular, and he has quite a bushy tail. These animals are very powerful, and in breaking into an Indian's "cache" can remove logs and stones much larger and heavier than one man can lift. They are very destructive when they find a "cache" of this description. They not only have an enormous capacity for devouring the meat cached by the Indians, but they will carry away and cunningly hide large quantities. Over the whole they emit an odour so pungent and so disagreeable that neither hungry Indians nor starving dogs will touch it. The Indians simply detest the wolverine on account of its thievish propensities and its great cunning. There is always great rejoicing when one is killed. As Alec, through his telescope, watched the mischievous, busy animal he became very much interested in his movements. He was amazed at the strength which enabled him to dig out from the ground a hindquarter of the bear and easily carry it away to another place, where he cunningly hid it. His next effort, which much amused Alec, was to take the bear's skin in his mouth and attempt to climb up into a tree that he might hide it among the branches. It was laughable to see the skin slipping under his feet, and thus causing him to lose his grip, so that, with it, he fell heavily to the ground. Failure, however, was not in his vocabulary. Again and again he seized the robe in his mouth, and endeavoured to carry the awkward thing up that tree. But, alas for him, his very determination proved his destruction. So absorbed had he become in his efforts to succeed that he was, for once in his life, caught off his guard. The three Indians had succeeded in getting behind him, and had thus cut off his retreat into the forest. The first consciousness he had of his enemies was when three simultaneous shouts, from different parts of the forest behind him, told him of his danger. Cunning as he was, the Indians had clearly outwitted him. They knew that the loud shouts from different parts at the same time was about the only way by which he could be puzzled, and this plan they had successfully adopted.

For an instant only he waited, and then, as rapidly as possible, he started along the only route that seemed open to him, which was the one from which no sound had come. This was the way that led him exactly in the direction where Alec was waiting for him. This was what the Indians were anticipating. Their hope was that Alec would make the successful shot; then, even if he failed, so narrow was the tongue of land on which the wolverine was running that they felt that by spreading out they had him so securely hedged in that it would be impossible for him to escape.

In the meantime Alec had been watching him through his glass, until there fell upon his ears the shouts of the Indians. When he saw the effect upon the wolverine he was amused at the sudden change. While busy robbing the "cache" he seemed the monarch of all he surveyed, by his saucy appearance. Now he looked and acted as a craven coward, whose one thought was in reference to his escape. Alec, watching him, saw him spring upon a fallen log, and for an instant look in different directions toward the deep forest. The prospect did not seem to satisfy him, for, springing down, he at once began his journey directly toward where Alec was in hiding. When Alec saw this movement, he quickly put up his telescope, and, seizing his gun, prepared for his opportunity. It was fortunate that the distance over which the wolverine had to travel was considerable, as it enabled Alec to get his nerves steady and his hands firm. When the wolverine had come about half the distance his cunning suspiciousness seemed to return, and, fearing some danger ahead, he stopped and acted as though he would like to retrace his steps and try some other plan. Fortunately for Alec, the wind was still blowing toward him, and so the wolverine had not caught his scent. While thus halting and undecided about his movements he was startled by another shout, which told him that his retreat was cut off, and so he quickly resumed his journey. Knowing the cleverness of these animals, Alec had taken his position behind a rock, and there, with trigger drawn back, he awaited his oncoming.

"Wait until you can see the white of his eyes," had been his instructions, and faithfully did he obey.

With his strange, slouching gait, along came the treacherous, cunning brute until he reached a point where he stood fairly exposed on the lower one of some steplike rocks. With eye keen and nerve firm, Alec stepped out from behind his cover, and ere the animal could get over the start of his sudden appearance the report of the gun rang out and the wolverine fell dead, struck by the bullet fairly and squarely between the eyes.

Alec's shout of triumph brought the Indians to him on the run, and they, in their quiet way, congratulated him on doing what but few white hunters have ever done—he had had the honour of shooting one of the largest wolverines that had been killed in the country for a long time.

While one of the Indians hurried across the tongue of land for the canoe and paddles it around to the camp, the rest of the party dragged the dead wolverine back to the scene of his depredations. Here they had an opportunity of seeing the destructiveness of this animal. Every pound of meat had been removed from the "cache," and so cunningly hid away that not one piece could be found except the one which Alec had seen him hide as he watched him through his telescope, and this piece was so permeated by the offensive odour that it was worthless. Fortunately, the bearskin was none the worse for its overhauling. While waiting for the coming of the canoe the men set to work and speedily skinned the wolverine. The fur is not very valuable, but, to encourage the Indians to do all they can to destroy them, as they are so destructive on hunters' traps as well as supplies, the Hudson Bay Company always gives a good price for their pelts.

A few hours' paddling brought them to Sagasta-weekee. Here they found all well. Fortunately, the cyclone had passed some miles to the west of them, and so they had escaped its fury. Hunters, however, had come in who had been exposed to its power, and had some exciting tales to tell of narrow escapes and strange adventures.

Mrs Ross had become alarmed when, from some Indians, she had learned that the march of the cyclone was in the direction in which Mr Ross and his party had gone. She was pleased and delighted to welcome Alec, and to hear from him and the Indians the story of their deliverance and escape from accidents during the great storm.

The skins of the bear and wolverine were opened out and much admired, and then handed over to some clever Indian women to carefully dress for their home-going. The story of Sam's race from the bear very much amused them all. Nothing, however, so much delighted the Indian hunters who gathered in as the destruction of that old wolverine. It seems that same fellow had haunted that region of country for some years, destroying traps, robbing fish scaffolds and meat "caches," and playing with all the steel traps that the cleverest hunters could set for him. Now, however, his reign was over, and here was his hide—and a big one it was. Alec was the hero, and, although he modestly disclaimed all the honour except the first-class shot, the Indians were very proud of him, and showed it in various expressive ways.

The Fight with the Wolves.

# Chapter Nine.

**Montreal Point—The Governor and the Iroquois—The Herd of Deer—Ominous Sounds—Packs of Wolves—The Fierce Battle—Welcome Reinforcements—The Victory—Playing "Possum".**

As Mr Ross was anxious to get news from Sagasta-weekee and hear how his family and home had fared during the cyclone, Alec and the Indians started on their return trip early the next morning, taking with them a new canoe to replace the one that had been destroyed by a falling tree. They tarried not on the way, except to shoot a few ducks that were directly in their route. The result was they arrived early in the forenoon at the Old Fort, and were glad to bring the good news that all were well at Sagasta-weekee, and that the storm had passed by several miles away from them.

Of course the story of the destruction of the cache by the wolverine, and then his being killed, had to be told, much to the delight of Frank and Sam, as well as to the satisfaction of the older members of the party, who all rejoiced that at length that cunning fellow, that had so long been a terror and a nuisance, had been destroyed.

As the storm had completely died away, and the weather seemed fine and settled, it was decided to have an early dinner, then push on to Spider Islands, and there camp for the night. The rearrangement of their outfit was soon completed and the journey commenced.

Lake Winnipeg is nearly three hundred miles long, and about eighty wide in its northern part. It is thus like a great inland sea. Great storms sweep over it at times with tremendous fury. It has many shallows and sunken rocks.

The result is, it requires careful navigation for vessels that need any considerable depth of water.

There are some laughable stories afloat about the nervous, excitable captain of the first schooner, who carefully came up to the northern end of the lake from Manitoba and pushed on as far as Norway House. He had secured as a guide an old Hudson Bay voyageur, who had piloted many a brigade of boats from Fort Garry to York Factory, on the Hudson Bay. Of course the small boats to which he was accustomed did not draw nearly as many feet of water as this three-masted schooner. Still he imagined he knew where all the rocks and shoals were, and quickly accepted the offered position as guide or pilot for the first schooner.

In spite of his skill and care several times the vessel bumped against a rock, much to the terror and alarm of the captain, but all the satisfaction he could get out of the imperturbable old native was, as they repeatedly struck them:

"Ah, captain, I told you there were many rocks, and there is another of them."

Fortunately these rocks are very smooth, and as the vessel was moving along very slowly she was not at all injured by the merely touching them. When, however, she had in passing over some sunken ones nearly stranded on one or two, the peppery old captain could stand it no longer, and so he shouted to the guide:

"Look here, old fellow, I'll not have my ship's bottom scratched any more like this."

All the answer he could get from the stolid man was:

"Um, bottom all right, only a few more rocks."

And these few more rocks they managed to get over, much to the delight and amazement of the Indians, who had never seen such a large vessel before.

With birch canoes, our friends had no such troubles among the rocks. As the wind was fair the clever Indians fastened two paddles and improvised a sail out of a blanket for each canoe, and they were able to sail along at a great rate. But it requires careful steering, as the canoe is a cranky vessel at the best, and only those thoroughly accustomed to them ought to try to sail them.

The trip across to the Spider Islands was safely accomplished. The boys were pleased with their run, which was most exhilarating. Those who travel on the water only in great ships miss much of the healthful excitement and delight that is the portion of those who are brave and adventurous enough to take some of these trips in the light canoes of the Indians.

The boys were charmed with the few picturesque islands, and had a joyous time of it, for the weather was most glorious. Yet, as there was no game, except some passing ducks that lit at times in the little indentations that served as harbours, it was decided to push on to Montreal Point, which is the first landing stage on the mainland on the east side of Lake Winnipeg. The point derived its name from the fact that in the old days of long trips made by Sir George Simpson, in the birch canoes manned by the famous Iroquois Indians, this was the first stopping place from Norway House on their return voyage to Montreal, some two thousand miles away. Marvellous are the stories told of the skill and endurance of those matchless crews of Indians. Sir George Simpson was a hard master, and pushed them to their very utmost. No dallying along the road was allowed when he was on board. He would put his hand over the side of the canoe into the water, and if with a swish the water did not fly up perpendicularly before him he would reprove in language that could not be misunderstood.

Very strange does it now appear when we read of those days, or talk to old men who were participants in those events when the officials of the fur-trading company, from the despotic governor himself down to the lowest clerk, travelled over half the continent in birch canoes, manned by Indians or half-breeds, looking after the interest of the greatest fur-trading company the world has ever seen. It is after all no wonder that they worked in a hurry when the weather was favourable, as there were times when storms swept over the lakes with such fury that, in spite of all their skill and anxiety to push on, they were detained for days and days together. The wonder ever was that more lives were not lost in the daring recklessness that was often displayed. A characteristic story of Sir George Simpson, so long the energetic governor of the company, is still repeated at many a camp fire.

It seems that on one of his return voyages to Montreal from Norway House he was, if possible, more arbitrary and domineering than ever, and especially seemed to single out for his spleen a big burly fellow, a half-French and half-Iroquois voyageur. This half-breed, who was making his first trip, stood all this abuse for time good-naturedly, and tried to do his best; but one day at one of the camping places, where Sir George had been unusually abusive and sarcastic, the big fellow turned on him and gave him one of the handsomest thrashings a man ever received. The rest of the canoemen pretended to be so horror-stricken that they could not, or would not, interfere until the thrashing had been well administered to the governor, and then they made a noisy show of delivering the tyrant out of the clutches of their enraged comrade.

When the governor recovered his voice, and was able to get the better of his anger and indignation at the fact that he, the great Sir George Simpson, had been treated with such indignity by a miserable voyageur, he vented in not very polished French his threats upon his assailant. He said:

"Just wait until we reach Montreal, and I will soon clap this villain into prison, and have him kept there until the flesh rots off his bones."

With this and other threats of what he would do, the governor worked off his passion. The imperturbable canoeman, having obtained his satisfaction in the thrashing administered, returned to his duties, and paid no more attention to the threats of Sir George. What cared he? It would be many days ere Montreal was reached, and there were many rapids to run and portages to cross, and so there was no need of worrying about what was distant. But the governor, although he had ceased to scold, became very glum and distant, and the voyageur began to think that perhaps it would go badly with him and he would have to suffer for his doings. His fears were not allayed or lessened any by his chums, who conjured up all sorts of dire calamities that would befall him, and invented any amount of stories of pains and penalties that had been inflicted on others who had dared to resent his tyrannies.

Thus the days passed, and at length they reached Lachine, at the end of the Ottawa River, not very far from Montreal. Here the company had in those days a large trading establishment. Shortly after they landed, and Sir George, who had been met by the officials of the company there stationed, went with them into the principal building and was in close consultation, while the feelings of the voyageur were not enviable. As was feared, the big men were not long in consultation ere his name was called in a loud, stern voice. There was nothing for him to do but obey, and so he marched up into the building and met the officials and Sir George.

To his surprise and astonishment Sir George reached out his hand and there made a full apology for his hasty words and petulant temper, and stated that the thrashing he had received he had richly deserved, and that it had done him good, as it had opened his eyes to see that he had grown tyrannical and overbearing and was expecting more than possibilities of the men. Then, to show the genuineness of his apology, he ordered the clerk to give to this man the best outfit of clothing and other handsome presents, and to charge the whole to his, Sir George's, private personal account.

A couple of hours were quite sufficient to take the boys and Indians across the wide open expanse of lake that lay between Spider Island and Montreal Point on Lake Winnipeg. When drawing near the coast they were pleased to see some deer sporting on the shore. It is a peculiarity of some animals when on the edge of a lake, that while they are exceedingly alert and watchful against surprises from the land, they seem to have no idea of danger from the water side. The result is, the experienced Indians can, by cautious stalking, get quite near to them.

This is true of some of the deer tribe, and here the boys had an illustration of it. These deer are called in that country by the Indians "wa-was-ka-sew." They are very graceful in their movements and full of play. The canoes were halted two or three hundred yards from the shore, and the movements of the small herd were watched with great interest by the boys. Then Mr Ross quietly passed the word that an effort would be made to get a successful shot or two. As the guns then used were not to be depended upon to accurately carry a bullet more than a hundred yards, it was decided to back up and make a long detour and land some hunters ahead of the deer in a clump of timber toward which they seemed to be moving.

Noiselessly the paddles were plied, and when they were several hundreds of yards out they rapidly paddled on to the designated place, which was perhaps half a mile ahead of the deer. As Alec had had such a successful time with the wolverine, it was decided that this was Frank and Sam's opportunity, so they, with one of the younger Indians from each boat, under the leadership of Mustagan, were cautiously landed, each one with his gun, knife, and hunting hatchet. Then the boats put out again from the shore to watch the progress of events.

Not long were they kept waiting, for hardly had they reached a position where they imagined their presence would not be observed before they saw that the deer had become very much excited, and at first had all huddled close together on the shore. Mr Ross and the rest at first thought that they must have observed the canoes or had caught the scent of those who had landed. A moment's observation revealed that this was not the case. The very position of the deer showed that the fears were caused by enemies behind them, and they had not long to wait ere they were at first heard and then seen. Faintly coming on the wind were heard the blood-curdling howls of a pack of wolves.

To judge by the movements of the herd of deer it looked as though the beautiful creatures seemed to think of defence. The bucks formed a compact line with their antlered heads down toward the point from which the rapidly increasing howls were coming, while the does and young deer crowded in behind. Not long did they there remain. A louder chorus of horrid sounds reached them, which seemed to tell of their triumph at having struck the warm scent of their victims. These dreadful howlings were too much for the timid deer, and so with a rush they were off with the speed of the wind, running directly toward the point where Mustagan had placed the two boys and the Indians. It was very fortunate for them that in this hour of peril they had the cool-headed and courageous Mustagan in command.

He had been watching the deer from his hiding place and had observed their sudden fear and precipitate retreat. His long experience at once came to his help, and so, before his acute ear had caught the sound of the distant howlings of the wolves, he was certain of their coming. With a celerity most marvellous he gathered in the boys and Indians and quickly explained how matters stood, and told them that their bullets would probably be required for other game than deer.

Taking a hasty survey of the ground along which he was sure the deer would fly, pursued by the wolves, he arranged his men, keeping the boys with himself.

His instructions were to let the deer go by unharmed by them; then, as the wolves followed, for each to pick out one and fire. Then, if attacked by the rest of the pack, they were to close in together and fight them with their axes and their knives. If, however, they were not attacked after they had fired, they were to again load their guns as quickly as possible.

"Down to your places!" sternly spoke Mustagan.

And hardly a moment passed ere the herd of deer flew by, some of them so close to the hidden hunters that they could almost have touched them with their guns.

"Steady, boys!" were Mustagan's whispered words to the white lads, who, crouching down near him with their fingers on the triggers of their guns, had caught his cool, brave spirit; and although the blood-curdling howls of the wolves were now distinctly heard they flinched not in the strain of those trying moments.

As Frank and Sam's guns were on this excursion only single-barrelled, while the rest were double-barrelled, Mustagan said:

"When first wolf reach that stone, Frank, kill him. Then Sam hit the next one. Then I kill some. Then other Indians fire. Perhaps other wolves run away. Perhaps not, so have axes handy."

This advice was not neglected, for each axe, keen-edged and serviceable, was at the side of its owner.

"Now here they come!" shouted Mustagan.

Nothing can be more trying to brave hunters than was such a position as this. The travellers in Russia and elsewhere who have been assailed by packs of these fierce wolves, sending out their merciless, blood-curdling howlings, can appreciate the position of Frank and Sam. Yet they were true as steel, and when the word was given by the old Indian, in whom they had such implicit confidence, the guns were raised, and with nerves firm and strong they fired with unerring accuracy, and two great grey wolves fell dead, pierced through by the death-dealing bullets.

Then Mustagan fired. He was too wise a hunter to waste a bullet on a single wolf, if with it there was a possibility of killing two; and so, as the two leaders who had been a little in advance of the pack had fallen, he fired at two who were running side by side. His bullet first went through the body of the one nearer to him and then broke the back of the second.

In a second or two there rang out the reports of the other guns, and as many more of the wolves lay dead or dying on the ground. Now was the uncertainty of the battle. Wolves are the most treacherous and erratic animals to hunt. Sometimes they are the most arrant cowards, and will turn and run away at the slightest appearance of resistance or attack. At other times they will continue to advance against all odds. Their courage and ferocity seem to increase with their numbers, and are of course greatest when they are half-famished for food. Gaunt and half-starved those fierce ones seemed to be. And so, when the guns suddenly rang out and numbers of them fell, the others were at first somewhat disconcerted; but the hot scent of the deer was close, and the fact that their enemies were invisible made them determined not to yield at this first alarm.

With a rush the survivors, perhaps about twenty in number, dashed into the thicket into which the deer had disappeared, and from which their enemies had fired upon them. Sudden as was this rush it was not quicker than the movements of the hunters, who had closed in together, and with axes in hand were ready for their wild, mad attack. Mustagan and his three Indians were in front, while the two boys were placed a little in the rear.

As the pack came on some of them seemed disconcerted by the appearance of the hunters, and especially by the loud shouts which, at Mustagan's orders, they now made. All wild animals seem to have a dread of the human voice. And thus it was on this occasion. Some of the wolves were startled and fell back, but numbers of them resolutely dashed on to the attack. Then it was axe against teeth, and one wolf after another fell dead or badly wounded under the heavy, skillful blows. Frank and Sam each had the satisfaction of finishing off some of the wounded ones.

But the conflict was a fierce one; and how it would have gone with them eventually is hard to say, but it was victoriously ended by a welcome arrival of additional forces. Mr Ross and the others in the canoe had also been watching the deer, and had seen their startled movements and sudden flight. This had caused them to use their paddles as vigourously as possible and make for the shore. Ere they reached it the howling of the wolves fell on their ears. Then they had seen the rapid flight of the herd, and soon after the wild rush of the wolves not far behind them. So, as speedily as possible, Mr Ross and the party had landed in the rear and had hurried on.

The firing of the guns of Mustagan and his party plainly told them of danger, and also indicated the position of their friends. So they cautiously hurried along, and were in good time to pour, from the side, a volley into the wolves, that were now making a fierce attack on the men and boys.

This second attack was too much for the wolves, and so with howls of baffled rage they turned to the east, and soon disappeared in the forest, to be seen no more.

Many and sincere were the congratulations of all at their success and deliverance.

This was the largest pack of wolves that had been seen or heard of in this part of the country for years. The great northern wolves do not, as a general thing, hunt in very large numbers, as do the smaller wolves of the prairies or of the steppes of Russia, or as the brown wolf used to do in the new settlements of Canada and in some parts of the United States. A pack of eight or ten of these big, fierce northern wolves was considered by the Indians as many as generally hunted together; although sometimes, when a few got on the trail of a large moose or reindeer, that led them for a long time, they were apt to be joined by others until they mustered quite a number. So Mustagan's idea was that a number of small, separate packs had been on the trail—it may have been for days—of the different deer, which had at length gathered in this herd. All they could do, of course, was thus to conjecture; but here was the startling fact—they had encountered the largest pack of great northern wolves seen in that land for years at least.

There was still something to be done. While a number of dead wolves lay where they were shot, others badly wounded were making desperate efforts to escape. These had to be killed, and while some were being dispatched with axes by the Indians, to the boys was given the pleasure of sending the deadly bullets into others, and thus quickly putting them out of misery.

"Be careful," said Mustagan, "as you move around among the apparently dead ones. Wolves are most treacherous brutes, and sometimes badly wounded ones will feign to be dead when very far from it. By doing this they hope to escape the extra bullet or fatal blow of the axe that would quickly finish them. Then when the hunters are off their guard, or night comes on, they hope to be able to skulk away."

This cunning feigning of death when wounded or captured is not confined to wolves. There are several other animals that often try to play "possum" in this manner.

This warning advice of the old Indian did not come too soon, and fortunate indeed it was for one of the party.

The skins of some fur-bearing animals are not considered *prime* when they are killed in the summer months; the bitter cold of winter very much thickens and improves the fur. However, sometimes the bears and wolves are almost as good then as in the colder months, and bring nearly as high a price in some foreign markets. As soon as the work of killing the wounded ones was apparently over, Mr Ross began feeling the fur of them as they lay around, ere the Indians commenced the work of skinning them. To the boys, who were closely following him, he explained the difference between what they called in the fur trade a *prime* skin and one of inferior value. After several had been tested in this way, and all signs of movements on the part of any of the wolves had ceased, they happened to come to one very large fellow, settled out flat on his belly, apparently stone dead.

"Here is the finest one we have seen thus far," said Mr Ross, as he stooped down and began pulling at his dark grey fur, while the boys stood around with their guns held by the barrels in their hands with the butt resting on the ground.

While listening to Mr Ross's explanations in reference to the different grades of skins, Sam's sharp eyes fancied they detected a slight quiver in the eyelids of the fierce brute, that was apparently unconscious of the thorough way in which Mr Ross was pulling his fur and testing it in various places. Not wishing to be laughed at, Sam said nothing about his suspicions that life was still there, but he nevertheless, without attracting attention, so changed the position of his loaded gun that it would not take him long to fire if necessity arose. And very soon the occasion came. As Mr Ross moved around to the front of the animal he stooped down to feel the thickness of the fur that grows between the short ears. No sooner had he done this than with the fury of a demon the wolf sprang up at him, and made a desperate attempt to seize him by the throat.

Mr Ross was completely thrown off his guard, but fortunately as the brute sprang at him he threw up his arm, and thus saved his throat. But the arm was pierced by the sharp teeth, that seemed to penetrate through the clothing and flesh to the very bone. However, that was his last spring and his last bite, for before even Mustagan or anyone else could seize a weapon the report of Sam's gun rang out, and the wolf fell, dead enough this time. Sam had put the muzzle within a yard of his side, and the charge had fairly torn its way through him.

So savage had been the attack, and so viciously had the wolf fastened onto the arm of Mr Ross, that, when the brute fell over dead, the jaws remained set with the teeth in the flesh, and so Mr Ross fell or was dragged to the ground by the weight of the animal. Mustagan and the others had to use the handle of an axe to force open the jaws before the wounded arm could be released.

"Well done, Sam," was the chorus that rang out from all. After Mr Ross's arm had been stripped, and some decoction of Indian herbs, which were quickly gathered, had been applied, Sam told of his suspicions when the eyelids quivered, and of his precaution in getting his gun ready. Of course it would have been better if he had mentioned it at the time, but he feared to be laughed at, and he said that he thought at the time that perhaps the wolf's eyelids had the same habit as a snake's tail, of moving for some time after the animal is dead.

The dead wolf was examined for other wounds, and found to be shot through the body, behind the ribs, where no vital organ had been touched. This shot had given it a momentary paralysis, which had caused it to drop so flat upon the ground. The Indians' idea was that it recovered itself while they were all around it, and so it cunningly lay still, hoping to get away when they left, but Mr Ross's handling was too much of an insult to be ignored, and so it suddenly sprang at him as described.

Of course this wounded arm must be promptly attended to more thoroughly than it could be on this wild spot, and so every Indian was set to work to skin the wolves, and then the home trip began.

A Woman's Successful Shot.

# Chapter Ten.

### Romantic Courtship—The Happy Family—A Canoe Picnic—Mustagan—A Prowling Bear—A Woman's Shot.

When the full details of the battle with the wolves came out, and the fact of the prominent part that Sam had played in the rescue of Mr Ross, his family were at first very much excited at his narrow escape, and then full of congratulations for Sam for his shrewdness and the promptitude with which he acted.

We have as yet said but little about this interesting family, and so we will use some of the time while Mr Ross is recovering from his wounds in giving a few details which we are sure will be most interesting, as some of them partake most decidedly of the romantic.

Mr Ross, like many a Hudson Bay official, was rather late in life in choosing his wife. His busy life in the service, where on each promotion he was removed from one post to another, made it almost impossible to set up a home. When he decided to do so his plan was very romantic. In those remote, lonely regions there are not many white families from which the young gentlemen in the service can select wives. The result is, many of them marry native women, or the daughters of mixed marriages contracted by the older officials. These women make excellent wives and mothers, and, being ambitious to learn, they often become as clever and bright as their white sisters, to many of whom they are superior in personal appearance. Into many a cozy home can the adventurous tourist go, and never would he dream that the stately, refined, cultured woman at the head of the home, honoured by her husband and beloved by her children, if not of pure Indian blood, was at least the daughter or granddaughter of a pure Indian.

Very romantic is the story of Mr Ross's love adventure, and here it is given for the first time. Long years before this, when Mr Ross was comparatively a young man, he saw in one of the Indian villages a little dark-eyed native girl, who looked to him as beautiful as a poet's dream. Although she was only ten or twelve years old, and he approaching thirty, he fell desperately in love with her, and said she must yet be his wife. He knew her language, and soon found that the bright and beautiful child was willing some time in the future to be his bride.

So it was arranged that she should be sent to the old land to be educated. Fortunately good Bishop Anderson was returning to England in connection with his work in the Red River Settlement, going by the Hudson Bay Company's ship. Wenonah was placed in charge of his family on the voyage, and at the journey's end was sent to a first-class school, called "The Nest." Here at Mr Ross's expense she was kept for several years, until she was not only highly educated as a student, but loving, interested ladies taught her, in their kindness, the things essential for a good housekeeper to know.

When she was about twenty years of age she returned to the Hudson Bay territories, and was married by the missionary to Mr Ross, who had so well-earned the skillful, loving wife she ever proved to be. Over twenty years of wedded life had been theirs before Mr Ross retired from the service, and several more had passed ere our story opened. Two sons were away from home as clerks in the company's service at some remote stations similar to those in which most of the officials had begun their apprenticeship.

At home were two bright girls about ten and eight years of age, and a younger brother hardly six, whose name was Roderick. The names of the girls were Minnehaha and Wenonah. A delightful home was theirs, even if in a place so remote from civilisation. Mrs Ross had devoted much of her time to the education of her children. The house was furnished with a splendid library, which Mr Ross himself had gathered with a great deal of care. For music, the piano and harp were their favourite instruments, and several members of the family were able to play exceedingly well. So well cultured were they that they would be considered a well-educated and intellectual family in any land.

There was for a time some anxiety about the wounds which Mr Ross had received when the wolf so savagely sprang at him. However, he was under the careful treatment of Memotas, the Christian Indian doctor, whose fame was in all the land, not only for his marvellous skill, but for his noble, upright character.

During the days of Mr Ross's recovery, when it was thought best for him to keep quiet, so that there might be the more rapid recovery, there were no long excursions made by the boys. The fact was, they had been so surfeited with excitement that they were quite contented to remain at Sagasta-weekee and revel in its library, where they found many an interesting volume.

Of course this did not mean that they were not much out in the canoes and among the wigwams of the Indians, who were camped about on the various points within easy reaching distances. The natives were always delighted to see the boys, and utilised what little English they possessed in order to impart to them as much information as possible. The visits to Big Tom and Mustagan were always a great pleasure. As Mustagan talked English they were not obliged to have an interpreter, and so enjoyed his company very much, and were always delighted when they could get him talking on his arctic adventures and narrow escapes in polar regions. He was a man with a marvellous history, as he had been employed in no less than five arctic expeditions. He was with Sir John Richardson and Dr Ray on their desperate expeditions, when they so courageously and persistently endeavoured to make the sullen North reveal the story of the destruction of Sir John Franklin and his gallant comrades. Some of his wonderful adventures we must have from his own lips after a while.

Although Mrs Ross was, as has been stated, such a refined and cultured woman, still she had all her nation's love for the canoe and outdoor life. The result was, many short excursions were undertaken by her and her children to various beautiful and picturesque spots within a few miles from home.

On these excursions one or two faithful well-armed old Indians were always taken, as it might happen that a fierce old bear or prowling wolf would unexpectedly make his appearance. That this precaution was necessary was clearly proved by an adventure that had occurred some time before the arrival of the boys. Mrs Ross, accompanied by her three youngest children, had taken a large canoe, manned by a couple of Indians, and had gone to spend the day at Playground Point, which was ever, as its name would imply, a favourite spot for old and young, Indians and whites. They had with them a large basket of supplies, and anticipated a very pleasant outing. They reached their destination in good time, and in various ways were intensely enjoying their holiday. They had all wandered some distance from the spot where they had landed, and where the canoe had been drawn up on the beach by the Indians. These men, after seeing that everything was made right, and that there were no signs of prowling wild beasts around, had, as Mrs Ross suggested, taken their axes and penetrated some distance into the interior of the forest, to see if they could find some large birch trees, the bark of which would be suitable for a new canoe.

After the young folks had amused themselves for time with their sports they began to think it was time for a raid upon the lunch basket, and so Mrs Ross, who had been sitting on a rock reading, shut her book and accompanied them back to the canoe, where they had left their supplies. An abrupt turn in the path brought them in plain sight of the canoe, which was about a hundred yards directly in front of them. There was a sight at which they had to laugh, although there was a spice of danger mixed with it. Seated up in the canoe, with a large hamper in his lap, was a good-sized black bear deliberately helping himself to the contents. Gravely would he lift up in his handlike paws to his mouth the sandwiches and cakes, and then he cleared out with great satisfaction a large bowl of jelly, spilling, however, a good deal of it on his face.

Mrs Ross would have endeavoured to have noiselessly retreated back with the children, but the sight of their dinner disappearing down the bear's throat was too much for them, and so ere the mother could check them, a simultaneous shout from them alarmed the bear and quickly brought his meal to a close. The sudden shouting and the apparition of these people were too much for him, and so, jamming what food he had at that instant in his paws in his mouth, he sprang out of the canoe into the water, and began swimming at a great rate toward a small island that was directly out from the mainland. Seeing him thus retreating, and wishing to keep him at it, Mrs Ross and the children, with all the display and noise they could make, rushed forward, and thus, if possible, caused him to redouble his efforts to get away. This was the wisest thing they could have done. A bear is quick to notice whether his presence causes alarm or not. A bold front will generally cause him to retreat, while on the other hand, if he sees any signs of cowardice, or thinks he can terrify his enemies and cause them to fly from him, he is not slow in being the aggressor and making the attempt.

Mrs Ross, well knowing some of the characteristics of bears and their habits, was not to be taken off her guard, and so she was resolved to be prepared for every emergency. Her first precaution was to take out one of the guns and load it well with ball. Then she explored the lunch basket to find out the extent of the bear's raid upon it. To the children's sorrow they found that the best part of the contents, from their standpoint, of the hamper was gone. The cakes and most of the jam, which in that country is such a luxury, being imported all the way from England, were all gone. However, there were some packages of bread and butter and cold meats, and so they did not starve.

But what about the bear? The island which he had now reached was not more than a quarter of a mile away from them. No other one was near, and a frightened bear dislikes to be on an island. He seems to be conscious of the fact that he is at a disadvantage, and so he will endeavour to leave it for the mainland as quickly as possible. Mrs Ross knew this, and so she felt after she had thought it over that, in all probability, very soon after the bear had reached the island and observed its limited area and lack of dense forests in which he could hide himself, he would take it into his head for his own personal safety to quickly return to the mainland. With this knowledge of the bear's habits, she resolved to be ready for him in case he made the attempt. The first thing she did, however, was to endeavour to recall the men who were at work in the forest. This was done by taking the other gun from the boat and heavily loading it with powder. This when fired made a very loud report. Three times in quick succession did Mrs

Ross thus heavily load the gun and fire. She well knew that if the men were within hearing the sounds of these three reports, when there were only two guns, would indicate that something was wrong and that it was necessary for them at once to return.

But while the reports were heard by the men and caused them to start on their return at once, as was desired, they also startled the bear, and so alarmed and frightened him that he immediately sprang into the water and began swimming for the mainland.

The situation was exciting and decidedly interesting. Here on the mainland was a lady and three young children.

Their Indian protectors were a couple of miles or so away in the rear, and directly in front, swimming toward them, was a great black bear. When halfway across from the island he veered a little in order to reach a point of rock that projected out a little from the mainland not two hundred yards away from where were Mrs Ross and the children. The majority of people would gladly have let the animal escape. Mrs Ross and her children, however, were not of this opinion. His skin would make a beautiful robe, his flesh was good for food, and his fat was the substitute for lard in that land, and was therefore valuable. Then, worst of all, had he not eaten the cakes, and especially the jam? So, of course, mother must shoot him when he comes near the shore, if the Indians do not arrive in time. Thus thought the children, anyway.

Mrs Ross first took the precaution to load both guns with bullets. Then launching the canoe, she had her children get into it, and giving the older two their paddles, which, young as they were, they could handle like the Indian children, she gave them their orders. She would go to that point toward which the bear was swimming, keeping herself well hid from his sight. When he was near to the shore she would fire; if she did not kill him with the two shots, or only badly wounded him, she would after firing hurry to a spot where they were to wait for her in the canoe, and then embarking with them they would all be safe on the water, as they could paddle much faster than the bear could swim, even if he should try to catch them.

These were wise precautions in case things did not go as were anticipated. Everything was soon arranged, and then Mrs Ross, taking the guns, dropped back a little in the rear, and quietly and quickly reached a good position behind a rock not far from where it was now evident the bear intended to land. Carefully arranging her weapons, she waited until the animal was about fifty or sixty yards away, when resting one of the guns on the rock, she took deliberate aim at the spot between the eyes and fired.

No second ball was necessary, for suddenly the head went down and a lifeless body rose and fell on the shining waves. The bear was stone dead, and all danger was at once over.

A shout from the children caused her to look, and there she saw it was caused by the arrival of the two Indians, who, almost breathless, had at that moment come into view.

As though it were a matter of everyday occurrence, Mrs Ross said to her men as they reached her:

"Please carry the guns back to the landing place; tell the children to come ashore; and then you two take the canoe and go and bring in that dead bear."

The anxiety that had been in the minds of these two Indians during the last twenty minutes, while they had been running two or three miles, quickly left them, and there was a gleam of pride in their dark eyes to think that this cool, brave woman, whose unerring shot had thus killed the bear, was of their own race and tribe.

Mrs Ross, although cultured and refined and the wife of a great white man, was always the loving friend of her own people, and did very much for their comfort and happiness. Here was something done by her that would, if possible, still more exalt her in their estimation; and so this story, with various additions and startling situations added on, long was a favourite one in many a wigwam and at many a camp fire.

The bear was soon dragged ashore and skinned. It was then cut up and the meat packed away in the canoe. And the children rejoiced that that bear would never, never steal any more jam.

# Chapter Eleven.

### The Wonderful Story of Apetak, the Grateful Indian, and the Description of the Trip to and View of the Silver Cave, as told by Mr Ross at Sagasta-weekee.

"Tell us a true story to-night," said little Roderick, the youngest in the family and the pet of all, as he climbed up on his father's knee.

"Yes, please, Mr Ross," said Sam, "tell us that wonderful story your father told you about the old Indian and the silver cave."

It was a capital night for a good story. The rain was pattering against the window panes, while the winds, fierce and wild, were howling around the buildings, making it vastly more pleasant to be inside than out, even on a first-class hunting excursion.

As Sam's request was re-echoed by all, Mr Ross cheerfully consented, and so, when they had gathered around him and taken their favourite places, he began:

"My father was in the service of the Hudson Bay Company for many years. He began as a junior clerk and worked his way up until he became a chief factor, which is the highest position next to that of the governor. During his long career in the service he was moved about a good deal from one post to another. The result was, he became acquainted with various parts of the country and with different tribes of Indians.

"Many years ago, when he had been promoted to the charge of a fairly good port, the incident I am about to tell you took place. As master in charge my father was, of course, as all Hudson Bay Company's officers are, very anxious to make large returns of fur each year. The dividends were greatest when the sales were largest.

"Father had perhaps a hundred hunters at his port, who all were more or less skillful and successful in this fur hunting.

"There was one old Indian whom we will call Apetak, who was, by all odds, the most skillful hunter father had. Not only was he successful in bringing the greatest quantity of furs to the port, but he was most fortunate in being able to capture more of the valuable black and silver foxes and other of the richest fur-bearing animals. His great success as a hunter thus made him very much of a favourite with my father. But, in addition, he had many very excellent qualities which made him respected and trusted by all, both whites and Indians.

"One winter, however, he nearly lost his life. Shortly after the ice had formed on one of the great lakes in his hunting grounds he shot at and wounded a great moose. The animal, mad with the pain of the wound, dashed out of the forest and made for the lake, on which was but a covering of thin ice. He was only able to run on it a few yards ere it broke under him and let him through into the water. Apetak did not like to lose the animal, as there was good meat enough on him to keep his pot boiling for weeks; so he made a noose in a lasso and tried to get near enough to throw it over the moose's head, and thus to burden him until he could get help to get the body out.

"But unfortunately for him he ventured too far out on the poor ice and broke in. He managed to get out, but the day was bitterly cold and he suffered very much. A bad cold settled upon his lungs, and it seemed as though he must die. When my father heard of this he sent his own dog-sled and plenty of blankets to Apetak's wigwam and brought him to the trading post, and had him put into a warm, comfortable bed and well cared for. He kept him there all winter, and it was not until spring that he was strong and well. He had thus lost that winter's hunt, as he had not been able to set a trap or fire a gun. However, my father gave him the necessary supplies in view of his past services, and for this he was very grateful.

"With the bright spring weather he regained his usual health and once more entered upon his work. But he could never forget my father's kindness, and was anxious in some way to show his gratitude. Money there was none then in the country, as everything in the way of trade was done by barter. He could not give a present of the rich and valuable furs, as he well knew father would not be allowed to accept of them, as the company had made a very strict law against anything of the kind. They demanded that all the furs should go into their sale shops, and not one of their officials, from the governor to the lowest clerk, dare accept as much as a beaver skin as a present from an Indian.

"Thus was Apetak troubled because he had no way of showing his gratitude. The spring passed away and the summer was about half gone when one evening Apetak, who had not been seen around the trading post for some weeks, suddenly returned.

"During the evening he asked for the privilege of having a few minutes' talk with my father. This, of course, was readily granted. To my father's great surprise he had a strange request to make, and it was this: He wanted my father to allow him to blindfold his eyes, and in that condition take him on a journey of several days' duration into the more remote wilderness. There would be travelling both by the canoe and walking on land. Then at the right time he would uncover his eyes and show him a sight that would please him very much indeed.

"This was a very strange proposition, and for a time my father hesitated; but knowing so well the reliable character of Apetak, and having in his constitution a good deal of the spirit of adventure, he at length consented. Apetak imposed some conditions upon him that were very stringent. One was that he was under no circumstances to divulge to anyone the fact that he was going away blindfolded. Another was that when the journey was completed, and he was safely back at home, he was not to try and get there again. And the last was that for so many years he was never even to mention or refer to the matter to anyone, white or Indian. These seemed rather hard conditions, but as father's curiosity had now been aroused he at length consented, and in a day or two he said to his head clerk:—

"'I think I will go off on a bit of an excursion for a few days.'

"As these were of frequent occurrence, there was no stir or curiosity excited. So, leaving orders as to the business for a few days, he and Apetak started off with their guns, blankets, and the usual outfit in a birch canoe. When away from the post Apetak got out the mask with which he blindfolded my father. It was a most thorough one, not a ray of light penetrating it. When it was fastened on Apetak said:—

"'It will be all right, and you will not be sorry for this trip.'

"Taking up his paddle again, Apetak really began the journey. At first he paddled the canoe round and round, until my father was completely bewildered and knew not the north from the south. Then on and on the strong Indian paddled for hours. Of course he and my father talked to each other, and they laughed and chatted away at a great rate. They landed at some portages, and Apetak helped father across, then he went back for the canoe and supplies. Thus on they went for several days. At the camp fire long after the sun was down Apetak would remove the mask that so blindfolded father, and leave it off until nearly daylight. But he never took it off until he had so confused him that, when his eyes were uncovered he could not tell which way they had come. Early in the afternoon of about the fourth day Apetak said:—

"'We are nearly at our journey's end. Soon I will show you what I have brought you so far to see.'

"This was good news to my father, who had begun to feel this travelling so long with the close covering on his face very irksome.

"Shortly after, Apetak stopped paddling, and, after helping my father to land, he lifted his canoe out of the water, and hid it carefully among the bushes. Then, placing a large bundle on his back, including his axe and gun, he started on a land journey of some miles. As my father was led along, although he could see nothing, he knew by the rush of air, and the way they went up and down hill, that they were in a very broken country.

"'Here is the place,' said Apetak. 'Now very soon I will uncover your eyes, but before I do it you must follow me into the earth.'

"Then he led my father into what seemed to be an opening on the side of a great hill or mountain, and, entering first in, he told my father to walk close behind him and keep his hand on him so that he would not be lost. Sometimes the opening was so low that they had to stoop down, and in other places they had to squeeze through between the rocks. After a time they stopped.

"'Now,' said Apetak, 'I will take off the covering from your face, but you will see nothing till I make a light.'

"So it was just as Apetak said. When the covering was removed from the eyes so dense was the darkness that my father saw no better than he did with it on.

"However, that great bundle on Apetak's back was composed of torches for this place. And so when the Indian struck a light with his flint and steel, and lit up some of these torches, they both could see very well. At first sight what my father saw was a great cave, like a large church or cathedral, here in the hill or mountain. Strangely broken was it in places, and great columns, like stalactites, were very numerous. There were others that looked like filigree work.

"Said Apetak: 'Look at these great things that look like old lead bullets.'

"Said my father: 'Sure enough, as my eyes became accustomed to the place, lit up by these flaming torches, I discovered that a great deal that I thought was native rock was really metal. At first I thought it was lead, as so long exposed there it looked like old lead pipes. But when I tried to scrape it with my knife I found it was too hard. Then Apetak used his axe, and managed to cut down a little for me, and to scrape or hack it in some other places, and, lo, it was pure silver.

"'At this discovery,' said my father, 'I was amazed, for here, visible to the eye, were thousands of pounds of silver.'

"We both continued to look around and examine it until we had burnt all but the last torch. It seemed in some places as though the softer rocks had gradually dissolved and left the silver here just as we found it. In other parts it looked as though in some remote period intense fires had melted it, and it had run down and then hardened in these strange formations. Anyway there it was in vast quantities and in various forms.

"'How did you find it?' asked my father of Apetak.

"His answer was: 'I was hunting in this part of the country, and I caught a fine silver fox by one hind leg in a trap. Just as I came up he succeeded in cutting off his leg with his teeth and thus got away. I, of course, ran after him, when he suddenly disappeared in the mouth of this cave. As his skin was so valuable I hurried and got some birch-bark and balsam gum, and made a large torch, and tracked him by the blood from his leg into this place. My torch went out before I caught him, and I was very much frightened for fear I would here die; but I managed to find the opening, and got out. Then I made plenty of torches and came in again. I had to search quite a while before I found my fox and succeeded in killing him. Then I looked around to see what kind of a place it was into which the fox had led me. For the first time I now saw all this metal. I first thought it was lead and would supply me with bullets. I tried to cut it with my knife and could not succeed. Then I saw that it was good metal which you call silver, and I knew you would be pleased to see it. So that is the reason that I have brought you here.'

"Soon after my father was again blindfolded and brought safely back to his home. He was very much pleased with his wonderful adventure, and honourably carried out his part of the agreement. He never in after years attempted to find the cave, nor did he even speak about it for many years. But it is there, nevertheless, and some day the world will be startled by the story of its discovery, and of the richness of its hidden stores."

With intense interest the boys, as well as the others present, listened to this wonderful story. When it was concluded very many were their questions and comments.

Then Sam, springing up on a chair, said:

"I move a hearty vote of thanks to Mr Ross for this splendid story about the cave, and when it is discovered may I be on hand!"

Alec seconded the motion and added:

"With great pleasure I second this motion, and may I be a good second, close at hand when Sam rediscovers the cave!"

Frank put the motion, and it was carried unanimously.

Mr Ross gracefully responded, and as the fierce storms were still raging without, and they listened to the howling of the winds, their thoughts went out to those who were upon the stormy seas, and so they heartily sang the beautiful hymn wherein is the expressive prayer:

"O hear us when we cry to Thee
For those in peril on the sea."

Sam Towed by a Jack Fish.

# Chapter Twelve.

### Novel Fishing—Guns and Gaff Hooks—Frank's Plunge—Light-hearted Sam and his Story—Strange Battle—Pugnacious Jack Fish.

The boys were quite fascinated by the wonderful story, which is undoubtedly true, of the silver cave. Their imaginations were fired, and they longed to start off to find those treasures of silver that in that hidden cave somewhere in the foothills of the northern Rockies are still hidden away from man's curious, greedy gaze. Uncertain as are the whereabouts of Captain Kidd's long-sought-for treasures is the locality of the cave of silver.

Long years ago Apetak, the old Indian, died and carried with him to the grave the knowledge of its whereabouts, and old Mr Ross, honourable man that he was, made no attempt to find it; neither did he state his impressions as to its locality beyond what is mentioned in his recital of the story. But it shows how a good Providence has his treasures of wealth for the generations to come. By and by, when it is needed, it will be found and utilised, as will the vast resources of other mineral wealth which this great new country has in reserve when the supplies in older lands begin to be exhausted.

However, in a few short days the story of the silver cave was less and less talked about, and the lads with Indian attendants were more or less busily employed in various undertakings.

Sam, who was an enthusiastic fly fisherman, was quite amazed and disappointed on finding that there was so little of his favourite kind of fishing in this part of the country. However, although there was a lack of success in that kind of fishing, there were many other methods that were very successful. One plan that very much interested them was fishing with a net attached to the small end of a pole. This they used in the water in the same method in which they had been accustomed to catch moths and butterflies with their lighter and frailer nets. They felt quite elated when a large whitefish or lively trout was brought up in the almost invisible net.

One day Mr Ross organised a fishing excursion for them, and equipped three canoes, with a couple of Indians in each to paddle them. He placed one boy in charge of each of the canoes, and sent them off in high spirits to see which canoe would return with the largest load of fish. To the boys alone was to be left the work of securing the fish. The Indians were only to attend to the paddling, and as the men in the canoe that succeeded in securing the greatest load were to receive, in addition to their wages, a flannel shirt apiece they all keenly entered into the spirit of the expedition.

All was needed in each boat for this kind of fishing was a good gun and a gaff hook with a long handle. The boys decided to go to Jack River, which takes its name from the number of jack fish that used to swarm in its waters. Not many hours' paddling brought them to their destination, and then the fun began.

To start even they drew up side by side, and then at the given word away they all paddled toward a distant spot, where the Indians knew the fish were likely to be found in large numbers. So evenly matched were the canoemen that they were not far apart when they arrived at the designated locality. So they widened the space between their canoes and noiselessly paddled up to where the disturbed waters and many back and tail fins told of the presence of the gamey fish.

For the first firing it was decided that it should be simultaneous, and then after that it was each canoe for itself, and they were not to meet till they reached Mr Ross's launch.

This method of fishing is very novel. The guns, heavily loaded with powder, are fired as nearly over the fish as it is possible to be done from the canoe. The concussion of the air seems to so stun them that they stiffen out on their backs, and there lie apparently dead for a minute or so. The men hunting them, aware of this, the instant they have fired immediately set to work with their long-handled gaff hooks, and gather in as many as they can ere the fish return to consciousness, and those not captured instantly swim off.

When all have been secured at that place as the result of that one heavy discharge of the gun, the canoe is paddled away to another spot where it is observed that the fish are plentiful near the surface and the process is repeated. So for this kind of fishing all that is necessary is the gun, with a plentiful supply of powder, and the gaff hook. A good deal of skill is required for the efficient management of the hook in seizing the fish so that it can be successfully landed over the side of the canoe.

For a time the success of the boys was about equal, but they did not capture after each shot anything like the number of fish that their able-bodied, experienced Indians would have done. It is no easy matter to lift a twenty or thirty pound fish by a hook over the side of a canoe. The boat itself is so cranky, and the fish themselves are generally so full of life and fight, that there is a good deal of risk and excitement, after all, about this kind of sport. It is no uncommon thing for an upset to occur in the risk and glorious uncertainty of capturing a large, gamy fellow who makes a stubborn fight.

The three canoes gradually separated, and to judge by the frequent reports of the guns they were having a good deal of sport. About eight p.m. they were all back at Sagasta-weekee, and each had a different story to tell.

Frank had over a score of very fine fish, and had had only one fall into the water. He had hooked in his gaff a large, vigorous fish, and was making the most careful efforts to hang on to him and to lift him over the side of the canoe. Just as he had him nicely out of the water, the fish, by a sudden furious struggle, wrenched himself off the hook and fell back in the water.

Frank had been so firmly holding on that when the weight of the fish was so suddenly gone he could not master his balance, and before an Indian could seize hold of him he tumbled head first into the water on the other side of the canoe, and the last the Indians saw of him for some seconds were the bottoms of his moccasins. Quickly did he reappear and was soon helped into the canoe; but while he pluckily stuck to the sport for some time, the prudent Indians persuaded him to allow them to early paddle him home. So he had been the first to arrive.

Sam's canoe arrived somewhat later; he also had a goodly supply of fish. As he was saturated with water, the question was at once asked, what had been his mishap.

At first he was a little glum about it, but the cry of "Tell us all about it," had to be responded to.

It had been decided some time before that on their returning from these different excursions each one was to fairly and squarely give the story of his misadventures, blunders, and failures, as well as of his triumphs and successes. So Sam had to own up, and he began by the odd question:

"Have you any whales in these lakes or rivers?"

This odd question was met by a hearty laugh all round.

"Well, then, I'm after thinking you must have plenty porpoises, or the likes of such things; for I am certain that it was one of such gentry I struck to-day."

Happy, light-hearted Sam, bright and cheery he ever was, it was a joy to hear him when, with a twinkle in his bright eye, he came out with his quaint remarks. His odd question only the more excited the curiosity of his listeners, and so amid the laughter and call for the story of his mishaps, he had to let them have it:

"Well, the fact is, we were having a good time, and at every discharge of my gun I would stun quite a number and succeeded in getting some of them into our canoe with the gaff hook all right. Getting a little careless with my success, I asked the Indian sitting before me to let me get in the very front of the canoe. At one place where I saw a big beauty I stood up and reached out as far as I could, and getting the gaff hook under him I gave him a great jerk to be sure and have it well hooked into him, when, lo and behold, before I could say 'Jack Robinson,' I was out head first into the water hanging on to my end of the pole, while the monster of a fish was at the other on his way to York Factory, it seemed to me."

"Why didn't you let go?" said Alec.

"Let go!" he replied, with a comical look, "sure the creature didn't give me time to let go; and then, when I came to my senses, didn't I remember that the gaff hook, pole, and all belonged to Mr Ross, and how could I face him and his gaff hook on its way to York Factory."

No one laughed more heartily than Mr Ross at the quaint answer. He had most thoroughly entered into the enjoyment of this odd adventure.

"Well, where is the gaff now?" he asked.

"Sure, it's in the boat, sir, and the fish, too," said Sam. "Do you think I'd have had the face to come home so early without it?"

This answer amused and more deeply interested all, and so Sam had to give the full account of his doings after his sudden jerk over the front of the canoe.

Some of these jack fish grow to be six feet in length, and are very strong. It seems it was one of the very largest that Sam had the good or ill fortune to hook.

With a tremendous jerk he was fairly lifted out of the boat, and seemed to skim along on the water with the fish like a small tug in front towing him along. Fortunately it was in a large, shallow place, where the water was not more than four feet deep, and so the fish was unable to dive and had to keep near the surface. As rapidly as possible the Indians used their paddles, and so were soon able to seize hold of Sam. They found him holding on to the one end of the gaff hook, while on the other the now about exhausted fish was still securely fastened. This was the Indian statement of the adventure.

Sam's account was that when he went out of that canoe so suddenly he resolved to hang on to his end of that gaff hook as long as the fish did at the other. It was a new sensation, and he enjoyed it amazingly to be thus ploughing along through the water towed by a fish. Then he felt sure that the fish could not keep it up very long and the canoe would not be far off; so he resolved to hang on to his fish until the men picked them both up. After the first sensation of the ducking, he said he much enjoyed the fun.

The water was warm, and he knew that if he had to let go he could easily swim until the canoe came to his assistance.

Alec had had no accidents or adventures. He had often gone out with older people fishing in the streams of his native country, where he had helped to land the spent salmon after they had been well played by the fishermen, and this training had come to his help here; so he had the greatest number of the finest fish and the largest, excepting, of course, this one monster of Sam's that had played him such a trick.

Only for a short time in each summer can these jack fish be successfully captured in this way. So during the next few days the boys went out several times and had some rare sport without any very startling adventures.

One day, however, when resting on a high rock that overhung the deep waters of the lake they were visiting, they were the spectators of a battle between two fierce jack fish that fought and grappled and tore each other with all the ferocity of bulldogs.

As such sights are extremely rare, we will give a description of this marine battle. A number of the female fish were first observed slowly passing through the clear waters and depositing their roe on the gravelly bottom. Following in the rear were several of the male fish. They were, as usual, extremely jealous of each other, but for a time made no attempt at hostilities.

It is a well-known fact that a person situated some height directly over water can see much farther down into it than those who are close to its edge. So in this case the boys could see the fish distinctly, and also the gravelly bottom of the lake. While interested in watching the movements of the fish, suddenly there was a commotion among them, and the boys were excited and amazed to see two of the largest of the jack fish suddenly seize each other in their enormous jaws and make the most determined efforts to conquer. So securely locked together were their jaws that in their struggles they several times rolled over and over in the water.

After a minute or two of this desperate struggling they separated and seemed to be in distress. But their fury was not spent, and so after circling around in the water a little they rushed at each other with the greatest speed, almost like two fierce rams. Then with open mouths again they bit and tore each other, until once more locking their jaws they each exerted all their strength to vanquish their opponent. Thus it went on until they had had several rounds in this fierce way. How it would have ended we know not. As they fought they moved along the coast, and in order to see them to advantage the boys had to shift their position. One of them unfortunately rose up so high that, the sun being behind him in the heavens, his shadow was cast on the waters over the two fierce combatants. As quick as a flash they let go their grip on each other and dashed off in opposite directions.

Very much disappointed were the boys that the battle came to such an abrupt termination. They would have liked to see such a strange conflict fought out to the end.

The Wrestling Match.

# Chapter Thirteen.

### Mission Village—Self-Denying Toilers—Pleasant Visits—
### Flourishing School—Syllabic Characters—Competitive Sports—
### Archery—Foot Races—Wrestling—Swimming—Canoe Races.

Not many miles from Sagasta-weekee was an Indian mission village. There a devoted missionary, Mr Evans, with his brave wife and a lady teacher, Miss Adams, were nobly toiling and were not unsuccessful in their efforts to Christianise and then to civilise the Indians. They were pursuing the right methods in trying to Christianise first, as it has ever seemed an impossibility to get much of an abiding civilisation out of a pagan Indian. However, this devoted man with his helpers was not toiling in vain. It is true that there were not many encouragements in their efforts to civilise in a land where hunting and fishing were nearly the only way by which a livelihood could be obtained.

One day there came from the mission an invitation to all at Sagasta-weekee who could come, to attend the annual examination of the village school, and to observe the progress made by the Indian children in the studies both in the Indian and English languages.

Mr Ross had taken, since the beginning of the mission, a great interest in the school, and not only attended at these examinations, but donated prizes for competition among the children.

Frank, Alec, and Sam were delighted to be included among the invited ones, as their curiosity was aroused to see the Indian youngsters in the school. They had seen them at their sports, and had admired their cleverness with their bows and arrows, and had almost envied the skill and daring with which they could, in rapids or on stormy waters, manage their light canoes.

When the morning arrived for the visit, Mr Ross sent on a canoe well-loaded with supplies for a substantial lunch for the children when the examinations were over, and he gave a hint to the boys that if they had anything extra lying around that they did not specially need they would doubtless have an opportunity to make some little dark-eyed, swarthy-faced Indian children rejoice. So the hint was taken, and in due time they all embarked in their canoes, and, adding their own strokes to those of the strong Indians who had been secured by Mr Ross, they were at the mission village before nine o'clock. They met with a very cordial greeting from Mr and Mrs Evans, and also from Miss Adams.

It was a great pleasure to the boys to see the Indian children in the school. Very frequently when the weather was fine had Mr Ross brought his family and guests to church on Sabbath mornings, but, as up to the present time the young white gentlemen had not yet visited the mission on a week day, all they saw now was novel and interesting. It was arranged that the school examinations should take place in the forenoon; then, after they had partaken of the handsome lunch which Mr Ross had prepared for them, they were to have the usual games and sports in the afternoon.

A number of prizes were to be contended for by the young Indians. It is true that from a civilised standpoint these prizes would not be considered of much value, but by these young Indians they were much valued. And then the honour of being the winner is just as much prized by them as it has ever been in more highly favoured lands.

The missionary had the worthy idea in his mind that, as these native races have so little literature in their own language, the sooner they learned English the better for them. The result was that all the lessons were in the two languages, with a decided preference for the English as their studies advanced.

This was the first opportunity the boys had had of seeing the methods by which Mr Evans's syllabic characters were taught to the Indians. With a home-made blackboard, and a very white kind of clay as a substitute for chalk, these syllabic characters were put down upon the board like the alphabet, and there to be studied like the A, B, C's. It was committed to memory. The peculiarity about it, as the name "syllabic" implies, is that each character is a syllable, and so there is really no spelling in the language.

These are phonetic in character, and so, when the thirty-six characters are impressed upon the memory, all that remains to be done is to open the book, be it Bible, Testament, hymn book, prayer book, or catechism, and begin to read; no long, tedious efforts at learning to spell first words of one syllable, then words of two syllables, and so on. Each character is a syllable, and thus the method of learning to read is so simple that the intelligent boys and girls learn to read in their own language in a few weeks. Even many of the old people, when they renounce their pagan life and become Christians, readily get to understand these characters and learn to read.

With the mastery of English, and learning to read in the ordinary way, the work is very much slower. Still even here there is some progress, and the visitors were all pleased with the intelligence and aptitude of the scholars, both boys and girls. Mr Ross, who understood their language perfectly, at Mr Evans's request conducted the examinations, and Mrs Ross presented the prizes.

After the hearty lunch, which was very much enjoyed by the youngsters—
for Indians have glorious appetites—the sports and competitions for
various prizes began.

The highest prize, a good gun, presented by Mr Ross for archery, was won
by a son of Mamanowatum, "Big Tom," and richly did he deserve it. At a
hundred yards he sent every arrow of his well-filled quiver whizzing
through a paper hoop not three feet in diameter. For this prize there were
several competitors, and some of the lads did well; but only the winner
sent every arrow through, so this one was easily decided.

The "many arrow" prize was not so easily decided, as there were many
competitors and they were evenly matched. This was a competition among
them to see who could get the greatest number of arrows into the air at
the same time. The method is this. Only one competes at a time. He fills
his quiver with arrows and places it on his back as he would to carry it in
hunting. Then he steps out a few feet in front of the crowd, who to escape
accident from falling arrows are all behind him. He is allowed to feather
the first arrow in the bow string, and then at a given signal he instantly
shoots. The object is to see how many arrows he can shoot into the air
before the first one fired reaches the ground. It is a very interesting sight
to watch a contest of this kind. The eye can hardly follow, not only the
arrows, but the rapid movements of the archer, as he draws the arrows
and shoots them with all his might up into the blue sky above. Eight, ten,
yes, sometimes even a dozen arrows are thus sent with wondrous rapidity,
sometimes following so closely that it seems at times to the eye as though
some succeeding would catch up to the ones just on ahead. The greater
rapidity of the arrow just leaving the bow than that of those some
hundreds of feet up adds to this delusion.

This was ever with the Indians, ere the introduction of guns, a very
favourite sport, not only in these forest regions, but among the wild,
warlike tribes of the prairies. Exciting contests were numerous, and
sometimes rivals from different tribes contended for the honours in this
and other kinds of archery practice and feats of skill with the bow and
arrow. Catlin's brush has given us one of these exciting scenes.

After the various kinds of archery competitions the foot races began. The
first was the long race over a course that had been marked out for two
miles of a shore and back. It was not all an unbroken sandy beach. Out in
some places there were rock obstructions, and in others dense underbrush.
It was a race over a course that could well be styled good, bad, and
indifferent. It was one not only to test the endurance of the lads, but to
develop their judgment in the quickness of decision when in a part full of

difficulties. About a dozen competitors entered for this race, and there were three prizes that were well-earned.

Then there were races for shorter distances, which were well run.

When the half-mile race was about to be run, which was open to all comers, Alec rather mischievously suggested to Sam that he ought to enter for this, as his practice in that famous escapade with the bear, where he ran with such marvellous rapidity, might have turned out a good training for this occasion. To the surprise of all, when Frank added his banter to the others, Sam sprang up and asked permission from Mr Ross, who was somewhat amused at this request, as he felt sure Sam would be hopelessly beaten; but he readily granted Sam's desire. Surprises often come from unexpected quarters. Sam quickly stripped off his outer garments and, much to the Indians' delight, took his place among them. Over twenty competitors started. The race was a spurt from the beginning. To the surprise and delight of the whites, Sam came in second, being only beaten by Emphasis, a noted runner, and whose name means "the young deer."

Old Kapastick, the chief, was so delighted with Sam's success that he presented to him a second prize, which was a pair of beautiful Indian moccasins.

After these running races were the wrestling matches, and as Sam's success had fired the ardour of both Alec and Frank, and had raised him so much in the eyes of the Indians; they asked permission to try their sturdy English and Scottish strength against the supple agility of these lithe Indians. For good reasons Mr Ross only permitted one of them to enter into this competition, and as Frank had a school reputation among his chums at home he was settled on to uphold the honour of the paleface against the dark-skinned Indians. Eight competitors entered the lists, so there were four pairs of wrestlers, and the conquerors in each bout would have to wrestle with each other, until eventually the prize winner would have to throw three competitors.

At this time there was great interest in wrestling contests, but being objected to by so many they have about disappeared in these later years from the Indian mission schools.

The competitors were all placed in pairs upon the green, soft grass, and warned not to get angry, but each to do the best he could to down his opponent. It was "catch as you can," and get your opponent down until both of his shoulders at the same time touch the ground.

Face to face, and with their hands extended so that they just touched their opponent's, they waited the "How" of the chief to begin the exciting struggle.

Frank was matched against a splendid young fellow, lithe and supple as an eel. So quick was he that, as Frank afterward said, "Before he had more than heard the word 'go,' the fellow seemed to wind himself around me and twist all over me." But Frank had what boys know as the "power to hold his feet," and so, in spite of the cyclonic attack, he stood firm and solid merely on the defensive, until he got a home grip that suited him, and then with one quick, skillful twist he laid out his opponent so neatly on the grass that the crowd gave him quite a cheer, a difficult thing for an Indian crowd to do.

The other three pairs of contestants being Indians, and up to all Indian wiles, struggled much longer ere the victors were announced. Now the four conquerors in these struggles were again matched, two against two.

When Frank tried his favourite trick, which had won him his first victory, he found that his second competitor had, although busy at the time with his first opponent, observed it, and was not to be so easily caught. Then Frank, after they had each tried various schemes well-known to good wrestlers, very suddenly seized him fair and square around the waist as they stood face to face, and, by what the boys know as the "back-hold," threw him neatly and cleverly on his back. So Frank by throwing the two had thus won the right to contend in the final struggle for the prize with the victor who, like himself, had also thrown two opponents.

Very excited yet very good-humoured were the people, whites and Indians. There was no betting or anything else to make anyone mad or angry. It was a friendly tussle of strength between young lads under the eye of the missionary, who was ever at the front in their sports, and hence his marvellous influence over them for good.

The final struggle was a very close and continued one. Each had his clever tricks and plans, but they were well met by the other side. After a time Frank thought he had a splendid back-hold, and suddenly tried to finish the contest like he had the second one. But he had a different lad this time. His supple *vis-à-vis* so quickly turned around in his grasp that, when Frank landed him on the ground, the laughing Indian lad was fair on his face instead of on his shoulders. Mr and Mrs Ross and the mission party led the crowd in the applause as they witnessed the clever trick. Up again and at it with varying success. There was one other method sometimes tried elsewhere that Frank had in his mind when he had failed in his other plans. He had sometimes tried it, but had not often been successful in doing so, as his white competitors were generally on their guard against it. He hesitated to try it here from the fact that his supple opponent was so slightly clothed there was but little upon which to get much of a grip. All these Indian lads had stripped to their moccasins, leggings, and loin cloths, while Frank had only taken off his coat and vest. However, as Frank was not able to succeed in other ways he determined to try it, but to insure success he must not let his opponent have any suspicion of it. So as they struggled in various ways Frank several times so gripped him that he lifted him off his feet in a way that, after the first few times, the Indian seemed to be amused at it. This was just what Frank wanted, and so he let him have his laugh, while, alert against any surprise, he watched for the right instant, and then suddenly, when it came, he gripped him by the loin cloth and so completely threw him over his head that he had him on his back with both shoulders on the ground ere the crowd, quick and watchful as they were, could realise how it had been done. A cheer greeted this well-earned victory, and Frank said he had had enough for one day.

Frank was the idol of the Indian lads from that hour, and to many a one had he to show how that clever feat had been performed, until they were able to do it themselves, to the astonishment of Indian boys from other villages with whom they competed.

As the spirit of emulation was up in every heart, Frank and his comrades went in for the swimming contest, which took place in the beautiful bay not far from the spot where stands the schoolhouse.

The white lads held their own for a time, but as the course marked out was new to them and they were out of practice, while the Indian lads had been in almost daily drill for the event, until they were as much at home in the water as otters, they gradually forged ahead, and not being so fleshy as their white competitors they nearly all of them came in as victors.

However, our boys were glad to have had the glorious swim, and only regretted that, amid the many other sports in which they had had such pleasure since their arrival, they had not given more attention to swimming. Alec was not slow in saying that he believed, if they had been in practice for a few days, they would not have all been at the tail end of the string at the close of the race.

The closing contests were the canoe races. For them the prizes were given by the Hudson Bay Company's officials. These gentlemen were present at the previous contests, and had been very much interested. First there were races where only one lad was in each canoe. In addition to paddling out to and around a certain island they were to twice, out in deep water, upset their canoe and, unaided, get into it again. This was rare sport, and while to persons unacquainted with these youngsters, who are as much at home in the water as beavers, it would seem dangerous, such a thing as any of them coming to harm is unknown. The cleverness with which they would turn over and upset the canoe and then get into it, never over the side but at the end, was marvellous.

These various races, some with two, and others with four, Indian lads in them, were well contested, and gave great pleasure to all the spectators.

At the close the Indian boys, who perhaps were none too well satisfied with the white lads for having carried off both a first and second prize, went to Mr Ross, and through him challenged the white boys to a canoe race. This our lads promptly accepted, but, of course, demurred against the canoe upsetting process and climbing in again. This was agreed to by the Indian boys, and it was decided the race was to be to a large rocky island about a mile out and return. They were, however, both to paddle twice around the island ere they returned on the home stretch.

Two canoes were selected; and the Hudson Bay chief Factor was appointed the judge. Ever since the arrival of the boys in the country they had been learning how to manage the frail but beautiful birch canoe, and so were no unworthy competitors to these young Indians, whose summer lives were almost all spent in paddling their light canoes. A good start was made, and while the alert Indians secured the advantage the good, steady paddling of the heavier white boys enabled them, ere the island was reached, to have their canoe a good half-length ahead of their dusky opponents. But here at the island the long practice of the Indians in the management of the canoe gave them a decided advantage. While Alec, who plied the stern paddle, and thus was responsible for the turning round and round the island, was cautiously and safely doing his work, the Indians with a flash and a laugh went round and round, cutting off corners where he never dreamed there was sufficient depth of water, and were away on the home stretch with so many lengths to their advantage that, in spite of their magnificent finish, our boys were utterly unable to catch up.

The Indians winning this race put everybody in the best of humour, and when, after a hearty lunch at the Mission House, our party paddled home in the long summer gloaming it was voted to have been one of the most delightful of days.

Good resulted from this visit in various ways. From that day forward Frank and his comrades were very much more interested in mission work. Although their families were members of different churches in the home land, and all were interested in missionary operations for the genuine benefit and uplifting of earth's millions who were in the darkness of paganism, here for the first time the boys had the opportunity of seeing for themselves something that was being done for these once degraded red men, around whom such a halo of romantic interest has ever gathered.

Then it was instructive to these sturdy, active white boys to come in contact with young Indians in their sports and hunting, and to observe the points in which each excelled and to study the reasons why.

In the management of the canoe the white boys never learn to equal the Indian lads, neither could it be expected that they could attain to the accuracy with which they use their bows and arrows; but in all trials of physical strength the Anglo-Saxon ever excels, and, surprising as it may appear to some, in shooting contests with gun or rifle the pale faces are ever able to hold their own.

Defeat of the Medicine Man.

# Chapter Fourteen.

### Conjurers—Old Tapastanum—Boasting—Challenge Accepted—Medicine Man's Tent—Bogus Bullet—Detected—Conjurer's Defeat and Fall.

Not long after the visit to the mission and the School Mr Ross was visited by a number of old pagan medicine men and conjurers, the most noted of them being old Tapastanum, who, having heard of the visit of the young gentlemen from across the sea to the family of Sagasta-weekee, was anxious to make them a visit of ceremony. Tapastanum's principal reason for a ceremonious visit was that he should not be eclipsed by "the Black-coat Man with the Book."

Mr Ross, while receiving these old men as he received all Indians, in a civil manner, was not at all kindly disposed toward them, as he knew their influence was harmful and that they were a curse and a malediction to the people. Their very presence in an Indian village is a source of terror and fear. They never hunt or fish themselves as long as they can frighten other people into being blackmailed by them.

The coming of these men very much excited Sam and Alec, who had heard such extraordinary things about them. Some firmly believe that they are in league with the devil, and by his direct assistance are able to perform all the wonderful things of which they boast. Others, however, believe that they are rank impostors. The boys, who had heard so many conflicting things about these conjurers, tried to coax Mr Ross to get them to show off some of their pretended power.

For a time Mr Ross, who considered them only as clever scoundrels or unmitigated humbugs, objected, as he did not wish to seem in any way to encourage them. However, one day as they, from Mr Ross's reluctance to put them to the test, became exceedingly boastful of their powers to do such wonderful things it was decided to give them an opportunity.

"What do you say you can do?" asked Frank of old Tapastanum.

"Do," he replied, "I can so conjure that you cannot hit me with a bullet, or tie me so that I cannot spring up loose; and fire will not burn me, or water drown me."

"All right," said Frank, "one thing at a time. We will try the first, and see if we cannot hit you with a bullet."

"What you give?" was the request of the old fellow.

"O, indeed, that is what you are after; well, what do you want?"

At first his demands were very unreasonable, but after some dickering it was decided that if he stood the ordeal he was to get an agreed amount of flour, tea, sugar, and tobacco. It was also settled that the ordeal should come off the next day. The conjurer said that he would spend the night with his medicine drum and sacred medicine bag, to call back his familiar spirit, who might be away hunting. The boys discussed very much the coming contest, and, of course, were profoundly interested. They had learned much since their coming into the country about these strange, wild, fearsome people, and this with what they had read in other days filled them with great curiosity to see what would be the outcome.

With Mr Ross and the family the matter was well talked over, and it was determined—as Mr Ross considered the conjurer who was to go through the ordeal an unmitigated fraud—that he should be taught a lesson that he and his cronies would never forget.

When the morning arrived the old fellows were there in good time, and the ordeal, which was to-day to be by bullet, was decided upon.

The conjurer selected for the ordeal had not proceeded far in his talk before he asked to see laid down at his wife's feet his pay. This was brought out and measured to his satisfaction, with the understanding that it was not to be his unless he succeeded.

His preparations were soon completed. Aided by his comrades, a small conjuring tent was made by sticking some long green limber poles in the ground, and bending them over like bows until the other ends were also made fast in the earth. Then over these poles a skin tent, made by sewing a number of dressed deerskins together, was thrown. Taking his medicine bag and magic drum into this tent, the conjurer disappeared. Soon the monotonous drumming began. In addition there were heard the barks and howls and cries of nearly all the animals of the forest and prairies. The sounds were like that proceeding from a wild beast show when all the animals are let louse and are uttering their discordant notes. The tent quivered as though in a cyclone. Thus, for a time it went on—the drum beating, the beasts howling, the tent quivering—until it seemed utterly inexplicable how one man, could create such a din.

Among the boys, Sam was most excited at these strange proceedings. Much to the amusement of those around, he said:

"I'm thinking the safest place would be on the top of the house, if all those reptiles should break loose."

The conjurer now began crying out in his own language: "To help me he is coming, my own familiar spirit. Soon the bullet cannot pierce me; soon waters cannot drown me; soon fires cannot burn me. To help me he is coming! coming! coming!"

Thus on he went, while the drumming and howlings were almost incessant.

Mr Ross, who had resolved that there should be no nonsense, had asked one of his servants, who was an unerring shot, to do the firing. In the meantime one of the conjurer's associates had asked to see the gun that was to be used, and kindly offered to load it. The suspicions of Mr Ross were at once aroused by this request, but wishing to see through the man's trick he did not oppose his request. Soon after a good gun was sent for, and also some powder and bullets. Full measure of powder was poured into the gun, and the usual wadding was well driven down upon it. When Mr Ross selected a bullet the friend of the conjurer, with a great pretence of awe, asked to see it, and holding it in his hand said, "This is the bullet that the familiar spirit will turn aside."

Mr Ross let him look at it, and saw him handling it with much apparent reverence, but he also saw him quickly and deftly change it for another bullet.

"That's your game, is it?" said Mr Ross but not out loud. After a little more humbuggery the bullet was handed back to be dropped into the muzzle of the gun.

If Mr Ross's thoughts could have been heard they would have been something like this:

"I have seen through that little trick, and will show you that two can play at that game."

And so without exciting the suspicion of the Indian, whose trick he had detected, he changed the bullet for another, and dropped it into the gun. When the wadding was driven in and placed upon it, the confederate of the conjurer asked for the privilege of being allowed also to help ram it down. Mr Ross saw his meaning and cheerfully granted it. The weapon was now loaded and ready for use. All this time the drumming and the conjuring had continued with all their accompaniments of howls and shrieks.

In a short time a shrill, low whistle, like the call of some bird, was heard, and Mr Ross observed that it was from the lips of the old Indian who had pretended to examine the bullet with such awe, but who had in reality exchanged it for a perfectly harmless one. He and the conjurer were associates in their trickery. The bullet had been made in this way: A pair of bullet moulds had been heated quite hot, and then some bear's fat, which is like lard, had been put inside of them. Holding the moulds shut, and placing them in very cold water, they kept turning them around until the melted fat had hardened into a thin shell exactly the size of a bullet. Then a small puncture was made through this thin casing of fat, and the interior carefully filled up with fine sand. It was not difficult then to stop up the orifice with a little fat. It was then carefully coloured like a bullet, and at a distance could hardly be distinguished from one. When put in a gun and well pounded with a ramrod, of course, it would break all to pieces, and when fired at anything like an ordinary distance for ball firing would be perfectly harmless.

But Mr Ross's cleverness had been too much for the rogues, and so he had changed the bogus affair for a genuine bullet of lead. To his servant, who was to fire, he explained exactly how matters were, and had said to him:

"Do not kill the rascal, but give him a wound that will forever stop his boastings, and break his power over the poor deluded hundreds, who firmly believe he can do what he has so boastfully declared."

The low, shrill whistle call had made a great change upon the conjurer in the tent. He was now all boastfulness, and his cries were like the shouts of triumph:

"Waters cannot drown me; bullets cannot pierce me; fires cannot burn me."

"Are you sure you are ready?" said Mr Ross.

Shouting his defiance, the conjurer came out from the tent, and walking to a place where he knew the fine sand in the bullet of bear's grease would not hurt him, he boldly stood up, and stretching out his hands defied the shooter to do his best.

"You are sure, are you, that bullets will not hurt you?" said Mr Ross.

Very haughty was the conjurer's reply. Then said Mr Ross again; "If you are hurt, no one will be to blame."

"No, indeed," was the conjurer's reply, "for I have given the challenge, and my familiar spirit has told me that the bullets cannot pierce me."

"If you are struck, then you will give up your conjuring, and go and hunt for your own living, like other people?"

He hesitated for a moment, but the low, shrill whistle was once more heard, and so he fairly shouted out:

"If bullets can pierce me I will forever give up my conjuring, and destroy my magic drum and medicine bag."

"All right," said Mr Ross; then, turning to his servant, he said, "Now, Baptiste, fire!"

Taking deliberate aim, the man fired, and, as the report rang out, from one of the uplifted hands of the conjurer who was standing about fifty yards away—there fell a finger, as neatly cut off by the bullet as though a surgeon's knife had done the work.

With a howl of rage and pain most decidedly un-Indian-like, the conjurer began dancing about, much to the amusement of the boys, who a moment before were pale with pent-up excitement; for it is rather trying to look on and see in the hands of a skillful marksman a gun loaded with ball and pointed at this boastful man, who was willing to put his magic against the skill of the finest shot of the country.

Much to the surprise of all but Mr Ross and one or two others who saw through the trick, the old fellow, with his wounded hand still profusely bleeding, rushed over to his confederate and began abusing him most thoroughly for having deceived him. This attack the man resented, and a first-class quarrel was the result. Around them gathered numbers of Indians, and in the mutual recriminations of these two the truth came out, and the people saw that they had long been deluded by a pair of impostors. From that, day they were discredited men, and never after regained any power or influence.

That evening Mr Ross explained to the boys the whole affair. He showed them the bogus bullet, and explained to them how it was made. The boys admitted that it was a clever trick, and were not satisfied until they had made several of them in the manner described.

Thus ended their first and last experience with Indian conjurers, and it thoroughly convinced them that they are only cunning impostors.

# Chapter Fifteen.

**Outing—Alec and Mustagan's Shooting Contest, or Gun versus Bow and Arrow-Shooting the Swans—Was Sam Cross-eyed?—The Return Trip—The Escape of the Doe and Fawn from the Wolf.**

As Mr Ross had quite recovered, it was resolved to go again on an extended trip to the country in the region of Montreal Point, and have some hunting in that section of country. Some Indian hunters had come in from that place, and reported the entire absence of wolves. This was not to be wondered at, on account of the number that had been shot in the fierce conflict which there took place. It is also a fact well-known to wolf hunters that when a pack has been severely defeated the survivors at once retreat to some distant regions.

As the weather was very fine, Mrs Ross and the younger members of the family accompanied them as far as to the Old Fort. They travelled in a large and roomy canoe especially made for them. It was manned by four Indians, who were very proud of their charge. Frank and Sam, with an Indian hunter, occupied another canoe, while Mr Ross had with him Alec and Mustagan.

As the ducks and other gamy birds were numerous, they had some good shooting from their canoes as they paddled along. At times they were able to fire into large flocks, then again they tried their skill on a single bird as it rapidly flew by.

Said Mustagan to Alec: "You take gun, I take bow and arrow, and we see who shoot best."

"All right," said Alec, "I'll try."

So it was decided that when the next duck flew over them Alec was to try first. If he missed, Mustagan was to shoot, and thus they would alternately fire—first Alec, and then Mustagan; then Mustagan first, and then Alec. The one who killed five ducks or other game first was to be considered victor. Mr Ross, who entered heartily into the spirit of the contest, took the steering paddle while the white lad and the old Indian tried their skill. It was a contest between gun and powder *versus* bow and arrow.

Soon a fine mallard duck came flying along. Alec let drive at it, and missed. Quick as a flash Mustagan's bow was up and his arrow sighted and sent after it with such accuracy that it caught it fairly under one of the wings, killing it instantly.

"The best shot I ever saw!" shouted Alec, in genuine admiration.

The head of Mustagan's arrow was the thigh bone of the wild swan, which is about solid, and makes a capital arrow head for duck shooting, as it is heavy, and can be made so sharp as to easily pierce the body of the game.

The next object was a solitary beaver sitting on a bank quite unconcerned. Mr Ross said afterward that in all probability it was an old, sullen fellow that had been driven away by the others from some distant beaver house, and had come and dug a burrow somewhere in that bank and was there living alone.

As it was Mustagan's turn to shoot first, he carefully selected his heaviest arrow, the head of which was a piece of barbed steel. Having examined the shaft to see that it was perfectly straight, he shot it with all his strength. No need for Alec to fire, for deep down into the skull of the animal had the steel head gone, instantly killing him. When it was lifted into the canoe Alec was surprised at the size of its tail, and more than amazed when told that it was one of the luxuries of the country. It was one of the favourite dishes of the supper that evening. The other luxuries, Mr Ross added, were the bear's paws and the moose's nose.

As they paddled on Mustagan suddenly shaded his eyes for a moment, then quickly said:

"Wap-i-sew! wap-i-sew!" ("Swans! swans!")

Word was quickly shouted to the other boats of their coming, and to try and shoot some of them if possible. Swans' feathers are much prized in that land for beds. Their meat, however, is not considered equal to that of the wild goose. As they fly with great rapidity they were not long in coming within range. There was a large flock of them, and they were flying, as they usually do, in a straight line. This flock must have risen up very recently, as they were not more than fifty feet above the water.

"I killed beaver. Your turn first now," said Mustagan to Alec. "But I fire just after you."

Alec had at Mr Ross's suggestion dropped a half dozen big buckshot in the barrel of his gun on the top of the charge of duckshot. The instant the first swan of the long straight line was in range he fired. To his amazement, while the first and second passed on unhurt, the third swan dropped suddenly into the water; and a second or two after another, about the twentieth in the line, also fell. Soon reports from other guns were heard, as the friends in the other canoes in the rear fired, and Mrs Ross was delighted to have the feathers of six beautiful white swans to take home with her when she returned.

The most perplexed one in the party for the time being was Alec. Mr Ross had observed it, and half suspecting the cause asked what it was that was bothering him. His answer was:

"I cannot understand how it should have happened that when I aimed and fired at the first swan it and the second should pass on unhurt and the third fall dead."

He was very much surprised when Mr Ross explained that he had not calculated for the speed with which the wild swan flies. Although such a large and heavy bird, the swan flies with a rapidity excelled by very few. The wild ducks and geese are easily left behind by the beautiful and graceful swans.

When the swans were picked up the journey was resumed, and the friendly contest between Alec and Mustagan continued. Soon a large flock of ducks flew over them. It being Mustagan's turn he fired, and as his arrow returned it was in the heart of a splendid duck. Alec, watching his opportunity, fired where a number were flying close together, and had the good fortune to bring down four at the one shot. This, of course, gave him the victory. And no congratulations could have been more kindly or sincere than were those of the big-hearted Mustagan.

In the meantime those in the other canoes had their own adventures and excitements. Sam had the good fortune to kill one of the swans, although he said afterward that he thought he must have been cross-eyed when he fired, as the one which fell was the third or fourth behind the one at which he aimed.

In his amusing way Sam's irrepressible spirit was up, and, in a half-moralising way at such erratic shooting, he said: "indeed, when I saw that swan fall I began to think I must have been like the old schoolmaster that my father used to tell about, in the old times when he was a boy, that when he was angry would shout out, 'Will that boy I am looking at stand up?' And do you believe it, ten or a dozen would rise trembling to their feet in different parts of the schoolhouse."

The Old Fort was reached early in the afternoon, and at one of the favourite camping places on the western side of the rushing waters of the great river that comes pouring out of Lake Winnipeg they went ashore. The active Indians soon had an abundance of dry wood cut and gathered. The fires were soon brightly burning, and the meal was prepared. Around it clustered the happy hungry ones, and very much did they enjoy their dinner out in the sunshine amid the beauties of this romantic spot.

Mrs Ross and the children, escorted by Mr Ross and our three lads, went for a long ramble through the woods, looking for some rare and beautiful ferns which here abound. They succeeded in getting quite a number of fine specimens, which they carefully dug up to be planted in the grounds around Sagasta-weekee. Some beautiful wild flowers were also found, and several small young mountain ash trees were carefully dug up and carried home.

After this delightful ramble, which was without any exciting adventure, they all returned to the camp, where they found that tea had already been prepared for them by the thoughtful Indian canoemen. When this was partaken of, Mrs Ross and the young people embarked in their capacious canoe for the return trip, and under the vigorous paddling of their four canoemen reached Sagasta-weekee before midnight.

The only excitement they had on the way was the seeing a beautiful deer and her young fawn swimming in the water a long way out from the shore. They gave chase and caught up to the beautiful frightened creatures. Mrs Ross would not allow the men to kill either of them, as she did not want the children to be shocked by the death of such beautiful, timid animals, especially as the solicitude manifested by the mother deer was very interesting to observe.

At first even the experienced Indians were perplexed at the sight of the deer with her young fawn in this broad water so far from land. Generally while the fawns are so small the mother deer keeps them hid in the deep, dark forests, only going to them when it is necessary for them to suckle.

It was not very long before these Indians had an idea of the cause for the unusual conduct of this deer. So they began watching very carefully the distant shore, from which the deer had come, and after a while one who had been shading his eyes gave a start and whispered earnestly:

"Wolf! wolf!"

And sure enough there was, for trotting up and down on the shore was a great, fierce, northern grey wolf, he must have got on the trail of the deer and alarmed her, but not before she had time to rush from her retreat with the fawn and spring into the water. They must have got quite a distance out from shore before the wolf reached the water, as the Indians said, judging by the way the wolf ran up and down on the beach, trying to find the trail; he had not seen them in the water.

Wolves do not take to water like bears. It is true they can swim when necessary, but they cannot make much of a fight in the water. A full-grown deer can easily drown a wolf that is rash enough to dare to attack him in the deep water. The Indians would have liked to have gone ashore and made an effort to get in the rear of the wolf and had a shot at him, but this was at present out of the question. So they only paddled in between the swimming deer and fawn and the shore from whence they had come. This enabled them to escape to the shore opposite from the wolf. Shortly after, as the wolf, so angry at being baffled of his prey while the scent was so hot on the shore, came running along in plain sight. The Indians carefully fired a couple of bullets at him. These, while not killing him, went near enough to cause him to give a great jump of surprise and alarm, and to suddenly disappear in the forest.

"Sometime soon we get that wolf," said one of the Indians.

How he did get it we will have him tell us some time later on.

# Chapter Sixteen.

### The Old Fort again—Aurora Borealis—Unexpected Arrivals—Fur Traders—Head Winds—Camp Annoyances—Camp Fire Yarns.

We must now return to our other friends, whom we left at the Old Fort. Some days were spent at this favourite old hunting ground.

With Mr Ross the boys visited the site of their former camp, where the cyclone wrought such havoc, and where they had had such a narrow escape. They were all amazed as they examined the trunks of the trees twisted off, and saw how, like a swath of grass cut through a meadow, the irresistible hurricane had swept through the dense forest.

Never had any of them seen anything to equal this, and they were very grateful for providential deliverance. They investigated the rocks and boulders, and Mr Ross gave them his ideas as to the formation of the great prairies of the West, over which he had so often wandered, and where Sam, Alec, and Frank expected, in a year or so, to spend some happy months.

To the boys the evening camp fire on the rocks, with the rippling waters of lake or river at their feet and the dark back ground of unexplored forest, was always intensely interesting, with its review of the day's adventures, the picturesque Indians, and preparation for the evening meal, enjoyed with such glorious appetites. Then, after the sun had gone down in splendour, and the long twilight began to fade away, the stars came out of their hiding places, one by one, until the whole heavens seemed aglow with them, for they shone with a radiance and beauty that was simply indescribable. Then, if not too tired to wait for their arrival, how fascinating often were the auroral displays, the mysterious "northern lights." If they were sleepy and tired, when some of these field night displays began, they soon forgot their weariness as they gazed, at times fairly fascinated by the wondrous visions that were theirs to witness. Never did they see a glorious display exactly repeated. There was always a kaleidoscopic change; yet each was very suggestive and beautiful. Sometimes they mounted up and up from below the horizon like vast arrays of soldiers, rank following rank in quick succession, arranged in all the gorgeous hues of the rainbow. They advanced, they receded, they fought, they conquered, they retreated, and they faded away into oblivion. Then great arches of purest white spanned the heavens, from which streamers red as blood hung quivering in the sky. Then, after other transformations, a corona filled the zenith and became a perfect crown of dancing, flashing splendour that long hung suspended there above them, a fit diadem, they thought, for the head of Him who was the creator of all these indescribable glories.

Thus in the beauties of the night visions, and in other sights peculiar to the North, there were compensations for some of the privations incident to being so remote from the blessings of civilisation. These new scenes, both by night and by day, were sources of great pleasure to the boys, as their tastes were fortunately such that these visions had a peculiar charm for them. Then, with their full program of delightful sports, they were indeed having a most joyous holiday.

But our readers are not to understand that during all these months there was nothing but continued enjoyment without some genuine hardships. There were at times some very serious drawbacks, and the boys had to muster up all their courage and face some annoyances that were exasperating in the extreme. And these hardships and trials were as likely to meet them when they would have rejoiced in refreshing slumber as during the weariness of a heavy day's marching on the trail of some game.

One of the great drawbacks to quiet slumber during the sultry hours of the hot summer nights were those intolerable pests, the mosquitoes. At times they were simply unendurable. They came in such multitudes that they were irresistible. They presented their bills so importunately that payment had to be made promptly in blood. Some nights the boys could hardly sleep at all. Every expedient was tried to drive them off. Smoke fires were kindled, and all other known remedies were tried, but all in vain. Blistered hands, swollen faces, eyes that would only half open, some mornings told of the long-continued, unsuccessful battles that during the nights past had been fought; and, to judge from appearances, the lads had been most thoroughly defeated. Said Sam one morning, after a night of misery with the insatiable pests:

"I see now why the rascals are called pious animals—because they have been singing over us and preying on us all the night; but in spite of all their efforts I am sure I am none the better, but much the worse, both in body and spirits."

"I say, Big Tom," said Alec, "what is the good of mosquitoes anyway?"

"To teach young white gentlemen patience, to see what stuff they are made of," said the old man, while all were amused at his apt reply.

"We hardly notice them," continued Big Tom, in his slow, deliberate manner; "and so it will be with you all after a time. Mosquitoes are peculiar, and have their likes and dislikes. One of their likes is to be fond of fresh blood, and so they go for the latest arrivals, and one of their dislikes is not to care much for tough old Injun. When you have been here some time, and have been bitten by a great many, you will not mind them so much."

"How many?" said Frank.

"About a million," replied Big Tom, "though I don't know how many that is."

This answer was too much for Sam, so he sprang up in a hurry and, in a semi-tragic manner, exclaimed:

"When does the next train start for home? I want to see my mother."

This inquiry from the irrepressible Sam provoked roars of laughter, and caused them to forget the mosquitoes and their bills.

When the boys arose one morning they were surprised to find a whole brigade of boats drawn up on the shore, and the men at various camp fires busily preparing their breakfast. They had slept so soundly that they had not heard the slightest sound.

Mr Ross and the men were up quite a time, and had gone over to chat with the two officers of the Hudson Bay Company who had charge of the brigade, which was from the Cumberland House and Swan River district, and was now on its way up from York Factory with its cargo of goods for the next winter's trade.

As breakfast was now ready, Mr Ross invited the two officers of the company, Mr Hamilton and Mr Bolanger, to eat with them. This invitation was gladly accepted, and to them were introduced Frank, Alec, and Sam, who became very much interested in them, and in the recital of various adventures and reminiscences of trading with the Indians in various parts of the great country.

The officers, on their part, were very anxious to hear all about the gunpowder explosion that had occurred at Robinson's Portage, as all sorts of rumours had gone abroad throughout the country about it, and especially a story that many persons were killed, among them some young English gentlemen, who for a bit of a lark had laid the train of gun powder which caused the general flare-up. The boys were amazed and indignant at first, then vastly amused as they saw by the twinkle in Mr Ross's eye that he was well acquainted with fondness for banter, which was a strong characteristic of some of those Hudson Bay gentlemen.

At first the boys hardly knew how to reply to this absurd reflection. Sam was the first to thoroughly understand them, and so in the richest brogue of his own green isle, which we will not try to produce in all its perfection, he said:

"Och, thin, it's roight ye are, av course. An' wasn't it too bad intoirely, the spalpeen to the loikes of you, an' he too an Englishman! Shure, thin, an' didn't he fire the powther through downright invy. Do ye believe me now, didn't he, an' Alec, the Scotchman, sitting there foreninst ye, wish to blow John Company, body and breeches, all at wanst into the Nelson River for your rascally chating the poor Injuns, that they might be after starting a company thimselves."

This sally of Sam's created roars of laughter, and even the slap he gave them about their close dealings with the Indians was much enjoyed. Soon all were on the best of terms, and it was a mutual pleasure, in that lonely place, to meet and interchange the news of the country, as well as to have the flashings of wit and fun and pleasant raillery.

Of course the men of the brigade were anxious to get on, as they still had a journey before them. They had only come from Norway house, a distance of twenty miles, the previous day. They had started, as was customary, quite late in the afternoon. The wind was anything but favourable, and so they were obliged to remain where they had drawn up their boats. Their old guide, after scanning the heavens and watching the movements of the different strata of clouds, declared that a fierce south wind was brewing, and that if they dared to start they would soon be driven back to that place. This was bad news to all, especially to the young officers, who were very anxious to get on. They very much dislike long delays in their journeys. Then it is always in favour of an officer seeking promotion in the service if it is known that he has a good record for making speedy trips with his brigades.

Here, however, were reports from one whose word was law; so there was no help for it, and thus they were here to remain until the wind changed. As the indication was for high winds, with perhaps heavy rains, orders were issued for the complete safety of the boats and cargoes. In making their preparations for a severe storm the crews of two or three of the boats seized hold of the strong rope which was attached to the stem of each boat, and by their united strength dragged them, one after another, well up on the sand, out of the reach of the waves. As there are no tides in these great American lakes the boats have not to be shifted. Heavy tarpaulins were carefully lashed down over the cargo, thus preventing the rain from doing any damage. These precautions turned out to be quite unnecessary, as the threatened storm either did not appear or passed round them. Still the wind blew constantly from the south for a number of days, and thus the brigade was obliged to remain. So long, indeed, was it detained that the officers had to order the removal of the cargo from one of the boats and send it back to Norway House for an additional supply of food.

This delay of the brigade was a glorious time for the boys, for among the men were some remarkable characters from the great prairies and the distant mountains. Some of them were full of incidents of thrilling adventures and wonderful stories; and so, while waiting during the long days for the wind to either change or go down, many a capital story was told at the pleasant camp fires. Some of them were narrated with wondrous dramatic power. These Indians are true sons of nature, and, while not taught in the schools of oratory, have in many instances a kind of eloquence that is most effective, and a dramatic way of speaking that is most telling.

There were stories of war parties and of scalping scenes, as well as of thrilling horse-stealing escapades. In addition there was the narration of various kinds of hunting adventure from these bronzed old hunters, who had frequently met in deadly conflict various kinds of fierce animals, from the mountain lion to the grizzly bear.

Sinking in the Quicksands.

# Chapter Seventeen.

### The Story of Pukumakunun—Loosing his Tongue—His Early Days—Excursion for Buffalo—Treacherous Quicksands—Sinking Mother—Sagacious Horse—Sneaking Wolves—Rattlesnake and Prairie Dog.

One old Indian with a splendid physique much excited their curiosity. They were specially anxious to know the story of that fearful scar across his face. He was evidently getting up in years, and was treated with much respect by his comrades. However, he was so quiet, and at times so reticent, that hardly a word could be got out of him. That there was some thrilling adventure associated with that scar the boys were very confident. The question among them was how to get him to tell it. They made friends with some of his Indian associates, and tried to get from them his history. But all the information they would impart was:

"Yes, he has a great story. It very much please you. You get him tell it."

This, of course, only increased their curiosity to hear his narrative. For a time all their efforts met with poor success. At length Alec, the shrewd Scottish lad, said:

"I have an idea that I can break through his reserve and get him to talk."

"Let us hear what your scheme is," said Frank.

"It is this," replied Alec. "I have been watching him, and I have noticed that the only two things he seems to have any love for are his red-beaded leggings and his brilliant red neckerchief. So I have been thinking that if I offer him that red tartan shirt of mine it will so please him that it will break through his reserve, and will get his story."

"A capital plan!" shouted Sam; "and if you succeed in getting the adventure from him we will gladly pay for the shirt."

The question now was how to find out if this plan would be successful. Some of the Indians are very sensitive, and require careful handling. However, Mustagan, the famous Indian guide, who had become so very friendly with this Indian, undertook at the desire of the boys to present their request and, as it were, incidentally to hint at the present of the brilliant shirt.

The scheme worked admirably, and here is his interesting story:

His name was Pukumakun, which means a club or a hammer. He was a Kinistenaux Indian, and when he was a boy his family and people lived a part of each year on the banks of the Assiniboine River. Here he grew up as other Indian lads, and was early taught the use of the bow and arrows, and how to skillfully throw the lasso. He had his share of excitements and dangers, living in those days when warlike tribes were not far away. The war-whoop was no unusual sound, and so they lived in a state of constant expectation of defence or attack.

Living on the prairies, he was, as soon as he was large enough, taught how to ride the fiery native horses until he could manage the wildest of them. Living such a life, he naturally had many adventures. The one that is most vividly impressed on his mind, and the constant reminder of which he carries in the great scar on his face, is the one that he here gives the boys.

It was many years ago when, as a boy of about twelve years of age, he was living with his father and mother in an Indian village not far from the Assiniboine. As game was not very plentiful that season in that part of the country, it was decided that they should break camp and go on a great buffalo hunt, which would last for several weeks. While the men went to kill the buffalo the women had to go also to dry and pack the meat and to make pemmican. The buffalo herds were far away, and so it was many days' journey before they were found.

One day while they were travelling along over the prairies Pukumakun had the misfortune to be bitten on his leg by a poisonous snake. His mother, having first killed the snake, then sucked the wound until she had drawn out nearly all the poison. By this brave act she undoubtedly saved his life. However, there was still enough of the poison left in his system to make him very sick and cause his leg to swell greatly. The result was he could not travel as fast as the buffalo hunters, who were anxious to reach the herds. So it was decided that he should be left with his mother to follow as rapidly as they could. So painful became his leg from the exercise of the riding that at length he was unable to mount his horse. His brave mother stuck to him, and continued to help him along for some days. To make matters worse, one of their two horses disappeared one night. Still, on they pushed as well as they could with the remaining one, and at length reached a river with many sandbars. Here the noble woman, in trying to carry him across, got into the quicksands and began to sink. In vain she tried to pull her feet out of the treacherous sands. When she would try to lift up one foot the other only sank deeper and deeper. Failing to succeed in this way, she lifted him off her shoulders, and, placing him gently beside her, tried again to struggle loose from the sands. But it was all in vain. She was held with too tight a grip. Seeing this, and fearing that Pukumakun might also begin to sink in the sands, she again put him upon her shoulders, and then both of them shouted and called loudly for help. But no help came. No human beings were within many miles' distance. Some prairie wolves heard their voices, and came to the river's bank to see what it meant. They found the bundle of meat there and quickly devoured it, but they did not dare to attack the horse, that was eating the grass not two hundred yards away. When they had fought over and devoured the food they came to the bank again, and their howls and yelps seemed to mock the cries for help of the perishing ones, as deeper and deeper they sank in the treacherous quicksands. But that woman never wept, for she was the daughter of a chief. But we must let Pukumakun tell the rest of the story, which fairly thrilled and fascinated the boys:

"By and by my feet began to touch the water, which ran a few inches deep over the bad sands, that had so caught hold of my mother, and into which she was sunk now nearly up to her waist. Still she cried not, but spake brave words to me. Hoping some Indians might be near, we called and called, but the wolves only answered with their mocking howls. Deeper and deeper we sank, until the waters were up to my mother's neck, and my feet were beginning to feel the grip of the treacherous sand.

"All at once I saw the horse coming down to the water to drink. Around his neck was tied the long Indian lariat made of braided deerskin, and therefore very strong. As I saw the horse, hope sprang up in my heart, and I began to feel that we were going to be saved. The water was now close up to my mother's lips, but we both called to the horse, which had been in our camp for years. He raised up his head and seemed startled at first, and then he plunged into the river. It did not take him long to get through the deep water, and then as his feet began to touch the quicksands he seemed at once to know that it was not right, so he kept lifting up his feet one after the other very rapidly. Still on he came, until he was so close that I was able to seize hold of the lariat.

"Then spake my mother: 'My son, you will escape. Tie the lariat quickly around your waist, and the horse will be able to drag you out. Here I must die. The spirits of my ancestors call me away to the happy hunting grounds, and I must obey. Remember your mother tried hard to save you, and only failed with her life. Tell my people how I perished, and give my message to the avengers of blood, and tell them not to be angry toward you. Farewell. Remember you are the grandson of a chief.'

"At first I wanted to die with my mother. It seemed dreadful to leave her alone, but she would not hear of it. As the waters were coming into her mouth she cried, 'Obey me, my son; obey me, and do it quickly, for the horse is impatient and knows the place is dangerous.'

"So I called sharply to the horse, and he sprang forward, and with a great wrench jerked me from my mother's shoulders out of the quicksands, and dashed through the water with me to the shore.

"As soon as I could loose myself from the lariat I turned round to look, and there I saw my mother's head just sinking out of sight. I was wild with terror and sorrow, and bitterly chided myself for not having died with her. But I had the consolation that she herself had insisted on my escaping when the strange chance offered itself.

"What was I to do now? My father and other friends were far away; my mother had perished; and here I was an almost helpless cripple on the great prairies, and night was rapidly approaching.

"Fortunately my horse stuck to me, and I saw that I must keep him close to me all night, or the wolves that were prowling around would, in the darkness, make short work of me. So, miserable and wet though I was, I tied the loose end of the lariat around my waist, and selecting a spot where the grass was good, I sat down in the middle of it, there to pass the night.

"It was, indeed, of all nights the saddest and most miserable. I could not sleep. I was full of sorrow. If I tried to shut my eyes, there was before me the sight of my mother, sinking, sinking down, down in that treacherous quicksand.

"The wolves were very troublesome. They would sit out in the gloom and howl in their melancholy way. Then they would arouse themselves and try to get hold of me. But my horse, well accustomed to fighting these animals, would rush at them as far as the lariat would allow, and would either strike at them with his fore feet, or, swinging around quickly, would so vigorously lash out with his hind legs that the cowardly brutes would quickly skulk back into the gloom.

"The long night ended at length, and the welcome morning came. I found that my poor leg, which had caused all the trouble, was much better. Perhaps this was from having been so long in the water. I was able to ride, and so I hurried away from the sight of the river that had so cruelly swallowed up my mother. My faithful horse, that had already been my deliverer, was very patient while, in my crippled state, I managed to get up on his back. I had eaten nothing since yesterday, but I thought nothing of that; I only wanted to get my sinking mother out of my eyes, and get away from that dreadful river which we had to cross. Horses are very wise about these quicksands, and so I just held on to the lariat, which I had made into a kind of a halter, and let him choose his own course. Very quickly and safely did he convey me across, and soon did we find the trail along which my father and the other hunters had travelled. We hurried on very rapidly, until my horse was tired, and then we stopped for a few hours in a ravine where we were well sheltered from hostile Indians, if any should be lurking about. The grass was luxuriant and abundant, and my horse enjoyed it very much.

"When the hottest part of the day was over we again found the trail and pushed on until sundown. Where the grass was good I tethered my horse with the lariat, and for the first time began to feel hungry. But I had nothing to eat, neither had I bow nor arrow. However, I noticed that the burrows of the prairie dogs were quite numerous where we had left the trail. So I took the strings of my moccasins, and making in the ends of each a running noose I fastened them over the burrows that seemed very fresh. Returning to my horse, I there waited for a time, and then went back to see if anything had been caught. I was much startled to find that in the first noose a great rattlesnake had been caught. He was lashing the ground at a great rate, while his rattles kept up a constant buzz. With a pole from some dried willows I soon killed him, for I wanted the moccasin string with which he was caught.

"I was more fortunate with the other noose, for in it was caught by the neck a fine young plump prairie dog. Quickly killing him, I carried him and the two strings back to the protection of my horse. As I had my knife, it did not take me long to skin the prairie dog, and as I had no fire I had to eat him raw. It tasted very good, for I was now feeling very hungry. As I had done the night before, I slept with my horse close to me as a protection from the wolves."

The Avenger of Blood.

- 115 -

# Chapter Eighteen.

**Pukumakun's Story Continued—Searching for Friends—Pathless Prairie—Angry Relations—Avengers of Blood Unappeased—Race for Life—Overtaken—First Conflict—Arrow against Tomahawk— Opportune Arrival.**

"Thus I travelled on for some days. At times it was I difficult for me to keep the trail, but my horse was very wise, and somehow he seemed to know that he was following-up his comrades.

"I was often very hungry, as I had nothing else to depend upon with which to hunt except my two strings, and then I could only use them when my horse was resting. However, I caught a few more prairie dogs, and one night I caught a prairie chicken, which was very good.

"One day, as I rode over a big swell like a hill in the prairie, I saw not very far away a herd of buffaloes. So I knew I must be near my friends. While I was pleased at the sight I began to feel very much alarmed. They would say at once, 'Where is your mother?' Then, if they did not believe my story, what then? So I was much troubled in my mind, and, while looking for my people, I dreaded to meet them. I felt that my father would believe my story, but I was afraid of my mother's brothers, the sons of the chief. They had never had any love for me, or I much for them. Why this was so I found out one day when they were upbraiding my mother in the wigwam for marrying my father, instead of a chief of another village, to whom they had promised her. They thought I was asleep, or they would not have spoken as they did. I remember that my mother spoke up, and said that she was the daughter of a chief, who had given her the right to choose her own husband; and that she was contented and happy in her choice. Just then their sharp eyes seemed to know that I was not very sound asleep, and so their strong words ceased; for Indian men and women do not let their children hear their quarrels.

"So I now remember their words, and was afraid. Not long after I saw some of the hunters, and when I met one whom I knew, I inquired for my father. He told me where I would find him, and so I rode on. My father was resting with some others after a great run, in which they had killed many buffaloes. When I drew near to him, although I was the grandson of a chief, I lifted up my voice and wept. At this he was very much surprised and hurt, for as yet he knew not of our great loss. Others jeered and laughed at seeing a young Indian weeping. Then my father arose and led me away and began to upbraid me, for he knew not the cause of my sorrow, but supposed my mother had joined the other women, who were very busy cutting up and preserving the meat of the buffalo. But I could only continue my weeping, and at length was able to cry out: 'My mother! my mother!'

"At this my father quickly ceased his reproofs, and becoming alarmed cried out: 'tell me what is the matter.'

"So I told him all. And as I saw his great sorrow as he listened to my story I knew how great had been his love for my mother, who, in her love for him, had preferred him to the chief whom her brothers wished her to marry. He was crushed to the ground and speechless with sorrow, and as I saw him so overwhelmed with his grief I wished I had died with my mother.

"For a time he thus remained, while I, the most miserable, could only sit by and look at him. No words or tears came from him, but the great sorrow had taken such a hold upon him that he seemed as one who would there have died.

"Suddenly, as voices were heard and we both knew that some persons were coming near, he turned to me and with a great effort said:—

"'My son, you must flee at once. Your mother's brothers, who love us not, will not believe your story; and as they are the nearest of kin, the avengers of blood, they will seek your life. You have no witness to your story, not even the body or a grave to show. When they find your mother has not arrived their suspicions will be aroused. I believe your story, strange as it is. When they demand of me the cause of your mother's non-arrival I will tell them as you have told me; but they will not believe it, and so you must not meet them, as in all probability they will kill you, in spite of all that I can do. So you must flee away from the avengers. You, my only son of your mother, must not fall by the hands of her brothers. Meet me here to-night when the moon is at her brightest, and I will then have decided what you must do. Flee quickly.'

"It was indeed time for me to go, for hardly had I slipped away, and hidden in the deep grass, ere I heard angry voices in reply to my father's quiet words. But I could make out nothing at the time of what was said. For hours I there remained. The day passed on, and the night followed, and yet I waited until the old moon came up to its brightest point. Then, returning to the appointed spot, there I found my father waiting for me. His great sorrow was still on him, his love for the son of her whom he had loved so well had shown itself in his acts. He had with him a good horse and a warrior's bow and quiver of arrows. In addition he had a supply of food and some other necessary things. He embraced me more tenderly than I ever remember his having done before, and then for an instant his strong Indian nature broke, and with one convulsive sob he said, 'Kah-seke-at' ('My beloved'), which was his pet name for my mother. But quickly he regained his composure, and, pointing to the north star, he said I was to direct my course so much west of that and try to reach the friendly band of Maskepetoon, the great chief of the land of the Saskatchewan. He commanded me to ride fast, as he feared trouble, as my uncles, to whom he had told my story in the presence of all the relatives, would not be pacified, but had demanded that I be delivered up. So I was armed and mounted, but ere my father would let me go he drew me down to him and kissed me, and then said:—

"'Be brave, my son; never begin a quarrel; but if the story of your mother's death is true—and I believe you, for you have never deceived me—then in your innocency, if you are followed and attacked, use your weapons, and if you must die, fall bravely fighting, as does the true warrior.'

"In the moonlight there I left him, and dashed away in the direction pointed out.

"My horse was a good one, and carried me along without any stumbling, although the prairie was rough and uneven. It was well for me that he was so steady and true, for I was only a boy, and so crushed by my great sorrow that I was hardly able to care for myself. With this good horse I was able to get on rapidly. However, in spite of all the progress I had made, I discovered about the time the day-dawn was coming that I was being followed. My pursuers were my fierce uncles, who had never forgiven my mother for marrying my father; and now that they had heard that she was dead resolved to take vengeance on me, whom they had always hated. They knew that, as was the custom of our people, they as the nearest relatives were the avengers of blood. In vain had my father pleaded for me, and that I was not guilty of her death. They would not be appeased, even though he had offered, as gifts, about all of his possessions. When, in anger and sorrow at their unrelenting spirit, he left them, they cunningly watched him, that they might find where I was hidden away.

"But my father was too quick for them, and so was able to get me off, as I have mentioned, before they found my hiding place. However, they were soon on my trail, but they had to ride many a mile before they overtook me, as I had sped on as rapidly as I could. Although I was only a boy I was able to see, when I detected them following after me, that they were not coming as friends. Then also my father's words had put me on my guard. They seemed so sure of being able to easily kill me that they resorted to no trick or disguise to throw me off my guard. So I remembered my father, and being conscious that I was innocent of my mother's death I was resolved to die as a warrior. Carefully stringing my bow, I fixed my quiver of arrows so that I could draw them easily as I needed them. Fortunately for me, my father had taught me the trick of riding on the side of my horse and shooting back from under his neck. Soon with the yells and warwhoops of my pursuers the arrows began to fly around me. One of their sharp arrows wounded my horse, but instead of disabling him it put such life into him that for the next few miles we were far ahead beyond their arrows. But their horses were more enduring than mine, and so they gradually gained on me once more. I did not shoot an arrow until I could hear the heavy breathings of their horses, which, like mine, were feeling the effects of this fearful race. Then, swinging quickly to my horse's side, I caused him by the pressure of my knee to swerve a little to the left, and then, drawing my bow with all my might, I fired back from under his neck at the horse nearer to me. Fortunately for me, my arrow struck him in the neck, and so cut some of the great swollen veins that he was soon out of the race. The uncle on the other horse stopped for a moment to see if he could be of any service, but, when he found that the wounded horse would soon bleed to death, he sprang again upon his own and came on, if possible, more furiously than ever. His brief halt had given me time to get another arrow fixed in my bow as on I hurried, but my horse was about exhausted, and soon again the arrows began to sing about me. One unfortunately struck my horse in a mortal place and brought him down. I could only spring to the ground as he fell, and with my bow and arrow quickly turn and face my pursuer. Very sudden was the end. He drew his tomahawk and threw it with all the fury of his passionate nature. I did not try to dodge it, but facing him I drew my bow with all my strength and shot straight into his face. Our weapons must have crossed each other, for while he fell dead with the arrow in his brain, I fell senseless with the blade of the tomahawk, which, cutting clean through my bow, had buried itself in my face.

"When I returned to consciousness my father was beside me. He had sewed up the wounds with sinew, and had succeeded in stopping the flowing of the blood. How he came there seemed strange to me. He told me all about it when I was better. He had found out that the two uncles, well-armed and on good horses, had discovered my trail and had started after me. He was not long in following, and as he had their trail in addition to mine he was able to push on without any delay, and so caught up to the one whose horse I had shot in the neck.

"They had no words with each other. They knew that as they joined in battle it was to be a fight unto the death. My father killed my uncle and came out of the battle unwounded. Then he hurried on as quickly as he could, and from a distance saw the fight between my uncle and me. When he dashed up, at first he thought I was dead, but soon he discovered that the life was still in me. He at once set to work to help me, but months passed away ere the great wound made by the tomahawk healed up.

"This great scar remains with me to this day, and reminds me of that fierce fight, and tells of how terrible in those days were some of the doings of our people."

Shooting Deer by Torchlight.

# Chapter Nineteen.

### "Fair Wind!"—Fish Spearing by Torchlight—The Shining Eyes—Death of the Deer—Abundance of Game—Additional Excursions—Tradition of Nanahboozoo and the Flood—Was Nanahboozoo Noah?

The boys listened with absorbing interest to this thrilling story. The camp fire had partly burned down and the stars had come out in their splendour, but none seemed to observe these things.

The dramatic power with which Pukumakun accompanied his narrative, his genuine sorrow at the tragic death of his mother, and then his fierce excitement as he described the last long race and its end, simply fascinated our young friends, and they declared that it was the most wonderful story they had ever heard.

Of course the bright tartan shirt, with some other gifts, was handed over, and then all wrapped themselves in their blankets and lay down on the rocks to sleep.

During the night the strong south wind veered around to the north-east, and the alert Indians in charge were quick to observe the change. Soon the cry of "Meyoo nootin!" ("Fair wind!") was heard, and, in a time so brief that it would have seemed almost incredible to persons who have not witnessed it, the boats were afloat, the masts stepped, the sails hoisted, and the journey, so long delayed, was gladly resumed. In the earliest dawn the last of the sails were seen by Mr Ross and our friends to be sinking below the horizon as they sped along toward the mouth of the great Saskatchewan. For the rest of the day they were quite lonesome after the departure of the brigade, and, as the wind was in a bad quarter for them, they decided to rest during the day and then go out spearing fish during the coming night. The Indians were set to work preparing the inflammable torches which would be necessary for their success. These were made of various things. The best were of the fine resinous strips of spruce or balsam, taken from those parts that are saturated with the resinous gum. They were secured in handles which prevented the hot melted pitch from running down and burning the hands of those who held them. Other torches were made of strips or rolls of birch-bark saturated in the balsam gum, which is gathered by the Indians and used so generally in keeping watertight their canoes.

The three-pronged barbed spears were fastened in long light handles, and every other preparation was made for having a successful expedition.

On account of the long evening twilight they had to wait for some hours after supper ere it was dark enough for them to hope for any measure of success. However, the experienced Indians knew when it was best to start, and so, after the inevitable cup of tea and the additional pipe for the smokers, the three canoes were carried down and carefully placed in the water. In each canoe was one of our boys, and they were of course excited at the prospect of this nightly adventure. It seemed so weird to thus embark in this ghostly way and to leave the bright camp fire on the rocks, with the few watchers who remained, Mr Ross being one of them, and to embark in their canoes and go paddling out in the gloom.

Their destination was in the western part of Playgreen lake, where they expected to find abundance of fish of the varieties that afford excellent sport when caught in this way. After several miles of careful paddling in the darkness, where rocks abounded and rapids were many, they reached a place that seemed familiar to the Indians. They easily found a sheltered cove, where they went ashore, and, groping around in the darkness, they soon gathered some dry wood and kindled a fire. Fortunately the wind had nearly died away, and so they anticipated a successful night's sport.

The inflammable torches were carefully arranged, and a couple of them for each boat were ignited. Then all again took their assigned positions in their canoes, and noiselessly paddled to the places where the fish were supposed to be abundant.

At first all the boys could see were dark, shadowlike objects in the water that, after remaining under the glare of the lights, suddenly dashed away in the gloom.

For fear of accident it was decided that the experienced Indians should do the spearing, while the boys looked on and aided with the paddles or helped to hold the torches. The Indian spearmen stood up in the canoe, and, gazing intently into the water where it was brilliantly lit up by the blazing torches, were able to see the fish at a depth of several feet beneath the surface. Some varieties of fish are not attracted by the light, and so are not to be caught in this way. Other kinds, however, seem quite fascinated by the bright light, and will remain perfectly still in its glare, as though under some power they cannot withstand.

The experienced spearmen, with a vigorous thrust, are generally very successful in securing large numbers of them. Still, in spite of all their skill, many escape. Apart from the excitement about this method of fishing, it is not to be compared with the ordinary way of capturing them with gill nets as regards the quantities obtained. The spear cruelly wounds many that escape, and so even the Indians only adopt this plan for the sake of its exciting sport, and for the capture of some varieties of fish that are not easily obtained in any other way.

After the boys had watched the successful operations of the Indians for some time they made their first attempt. For a time they could not understand how it was that when they made a vigorous thrust with their spear at a great big, quiet fish it seemed to strike some place a couple of feet or so away from the fish. So they found that the law of refraction had to be considered, and after a few experiments they did better. Each was successful in securing some fine fish. Some, indeed, were so large that, after the boys had plunged their spears into them, they required the help of the Indians to get them into the canoe.

When the torches burned down others were lighted, and thus the sport continued until the boats began to feel the additional weight of the fish thus secured. The boys were loath to think of stopping, and no wonder, for everything was so strange and weird.

The three canoes with their picturesque occupants, lit up by the blazing torches, the waters so transparent under the light, and phosphorescent-like on every wave, made a picture never to be forgotten. Then so close around was the dense deep darkness of the solitudes that stretched away and away for miles in all directions.

No wonder the hearts of the lads were beating loudly, and in the suppressed excitement of such surroundings no thoughts of sleep there troubled them.

"O, if our friends could only see us here," said Frank, "wouldn't they be pleased with the sight?"

"Ay," said Alec, "and what would not the boys of the old school give to be here for a few hours with us?"

"Hush! What is that?" said Sam, as he pointed his finger to a spot in the dense dark forest of trees that hung down low to the water's edge, not many yards from where they were slowly floating along on the stream.

That there was something was very evident, for there were to be seen two great shining eyes that, owing to the dense darkness around them, seemed to be strangely large and brilliant.

"Will-o'-the-wisp," said Frank.

"Jack-o'-lantern," said Alec.

"A banshee," said Sam.

"A big deer," said Mustagan. "Keep still, and we will soon shoot him."

Quietly and quickly was a gun lifted up, and with a word to the men to steady with their paddles the canoe in which Mustagan was seated he fired, and the report was followed by the plunge of the body of a great deer, as he fell headlong in the water not thirty yards away. The sound of the gun broke the deathlike solitudes and aroused a chorus; and for a long time the cry of the bittern and the loon mingled with the quacking of ducks and the wakeful calls of the sentinel wild goose.

More torches were lit, and the body of the deer was secured with a rope; and, as the night was far spent, it was decided to go ashore, if they could find a safe place, and there rest until morning, as it was utterly impossible with the heavy load of fish to think of returning through the darkness with the additional weight of this splendid deer.

As closely as possible the three canoes had kept together. This made it more sociable in the gloom, and was much enjoyed by the boys, as they could thus freely chat with each other and watch each other's success or failure.

As the locality was known to some of the Indians, a sheltered little sandy beach was soon discovered, and here the now tired party drew up and landed. A fire was speedily built, and a kettle of tea and a lunch were prepared and enjoyed by the hungry ones. Then they quickly rolled themselves up in their blankets, and were soon away in the land of dreams. Nothing softer had they under them than the rocks, and no roof over them but the starry heavens, yet they slept in a way that thousands of excited, weary, restless ones, tossing about in comfortable beds, might well envy, but could not command.

Very early were the boys aroused for the home trip, but, early as they were up, the Indians had already skinned and cut up the deer, and divided it among the boats. Part of the fish were given to some Indian women and children who were encamped on some of the islands, near which they passed on the route back to the camp.

Mr Ross was much pleased with the glowing accounts which the boys gave of the night's adventures. Much praise was given to Sam for having seen the great luminous eyes of the deer, even before any of the Indians had observed them.

Mr Ross, in answer to the boys' inquiries, explained how some deer, like fish, seemed to be fascinated by a bright light, and will allow the hunters to get very near, especially if they are on the water, ere they will try to get away.

The weather proving favourable, the camp was struck, the canoes loaded, and they all proceeded on the way to Montreal Point once more. They only stopped for an hour or so at Spider Islands to melt some pitch, and mend a crack which had opened in the bottom of one of the canoes.

The boys, who in their own land had seen the great iron ships being prepared in the dry docks, were quite amused and interested at the primitive way in which these Indians made watertight their light canoes. When this was done they were all soon under way again, and, not long after, the shores of the mainland began to loom up plainly before them.

They all remembered the last visit, and the battle with the wolves. So they were naturally on the lookout for a herd of deer or the sound of ravening wolves. But not even a "whisky jack" was seen or heard. The desolate land seemed to be much more so by the apparent entire absence of life.

Selecting a favourable spot, they all landed, and then, while some of the Indians made a fire and prepared the supper, Mr Ross, with Frank, Alec, Sam, and Mustagan, visited the scene of the great fight. They took the precaution to carry their guns with them, for who could tell where the rest of those wolves might be, or what other game might not suddenly appear in sight, even if the Indians had reported that the wolves had all disappeared.

Sam and Frank took special pride in pointing out to Alec and Mr Ross where they had stood when, under Mustagan's directions, they brought down the two leading wolves in that memorable and exciting battle, and then where they fought in the terrible hand-to-hand encounter, where it was hunting-axe against teeth. But little was left to tell of the fray. A few whitened, well-picked bones were to be seen here and there, but nothing more, so they returned to the camp fire, where the supper was now prepared, and ready indeed were they for it.

As they had made such a long trip that day, Mr Ross, who was ever mindful of the welfare of his canoemen, decided that there should be no hunting that evening or night. So they gathered round the camp fire, and, with bright and pleasant chat, the happy hours passed away, one of them being specially interesting as Mr Ross, who had made the gathering up of Indian legends a favourite study or amusement when not absorbed in heavier work, was requested by the boys to tell them an Indian legend or story.

Yielding to this request, he cheerfully consented, and not only had he the boys as interested listeners, but the Indians of the party gathered round, curious to hear how well a white man was able to tell one of their favourite stories.

"Before the general deluge," Mr Ross began, "there lived two enormous creatures, each possessed of vast power. One was an animal with a great horn on his head, the other was a huge toad. The latter had the whole management of the waters, keeping them secure in his own body; and emitting only a certain quantity when needed for the watering of the earth. Between these two creatures there arose a quarrel which terminated in a great fight. The toad in vain tried to swallow its antagonist, but the latter rushed upon it, and with his horn pierced a hole in its side, out of which the waters rushed in floods, and soon overflowed the face of the earth.

"Nanahboozoo was living at this time on the earth. Observing the water rising higher and higher he fled to the loftiest mountain for refuge. Perceiving that even this retreat would soon be inundated, he selected a large cedar tree, which he purposed to ascend should the waters come up to him. Before the floods reached him he caught a number of animals and fowls and put them into his bosom. At length the waters covered the mountain. Nanahboozoo then ascended the cedar tree, and as he went up he plucked its branches and stuck them in his belt, which girdled his waist.

"When he reached the top of the tree he sang, and beat the tune with his arrow upon his bow, and as he sang the tree grew, and kept pace with the water for a long time. At length he abandoned the idea of remaining any longer on the tree. So he took the branches he had plucked, and with them constructed a raft, on which he placed himself with the animals and fowls. On this raft he floated about for a long time, till all the mountains were covered and all the beasts of the earth and fowls of the air, except those he had with him, had perished.

"At length Nanahboozoo thought of forming a new world, but how to accomplish it without any materials he knew not. At length the idea occurred to him that if he could only obtain a little of the earth, which was then under the water, he might succeed in making a new world out of the old one. He accordingly employed the different animals he had with him that were accustomed to diving. First, he sent the loon down into the water in order to bring up some of the old earth; but it was not able to reach the bottom, and, after remaining in the water some time, came up dead. Nanahboozoo then took it, blew upon it, and it came to life again. He next sent the otter, which, also failing to reach the bottom, came up dead, and was restored to life in the same manner as the loon. He then tried the skill of the beaver, but without success. Having failed with all these diving animals, he last of all took the muskrat. On account of the distance it had to go to reach the bottom it was gone a long time, and came up dead; on taking it up Nanahboozoo found, to his great joy, that it had reached the earth and had retained some of the soil in each of its paws and mouth. He then blew upon it, and brought it to life again, at the same time pronouncing many blessings on it. He declared that as long as the world he was about to make should endure, the muskrat should never become extinct.

"This prediction of Nanahboozoo is still spoken of by some Indians when referring to the rapid increase of the muskrat. Nanahboozoo then took the earth which he found in the muskrat's paws and mouth, and having rubbed it with his hands to fine dust he placed it on the waters and blew upon it. Very soon it began to grow larger and larger, until it was beyond the reach of his eye. Thus was spread out the new world after the great flood. In order to ascertain the size of this newly created world, and the progress of its growth and expansion, he sent a wolf to run to the end of it, measuring its extent by the time consumed in the journey. The first journey he performed in one day; the second trip took him five days; the third consumed ten days; the fourth a month; then a year; then five years. Thus it went on until the world became so large that Nanahboozoo sent a young wolf that could just run. This animal died of old age before he could accomplish his journey. Nanahboozoo then decided that the world was large enough, and commanded it to cease from growing.

"Some time after this Nanahboozoo took a journey to view the new world he had made, and as he travelled he created various animals suitable for the different parts of the new world. He then experimented in making man. The first one he burnt too black, and was not satisfied. Then he tried again, and was no better pleased, as this one was too white. His third attempt satisfied him, and he left him in this country, while the first two he had made he placed far away. He then gave to the men he had created their various customs and habits and beliefs.

"Thus Nanahboozoo, having finished his work, now sits at the North Pole, which the Indians used to consider the top of the earth. There he sits overlooking all the transactions and affairs of the people he has placed on the earth.

"The northern tribes say that Nanahboozoo always sleeps during the winter, but previous to his falling asleep he fills his great pipe and smokes for several days, and that it is the smoke rising from the mouth and pipe of Nanahboozoo which at that season of the year produces what is called the Indian summer."

The boys listened to this Indian tradition of the flood with a great deal of interest, and the next Sabbath they got out their Bibles and tried to see the points of resemblance between the account given of Noah and that given of Nanahboozoo.

They decided that Nanahboozoo was the Indian name for Noah, and the raft was the substitute for the ark. The sending out of the various animals to discover and bring some earth stood for the sending forth of the raven and the dove. In some other conversations with Indians on the different traditions about the flood, Mustagan told them that, in some of the tribes he had visited, they had, in addition to what has here been narrated, a story of a bird coming with a little twig, and sticking it in the newly formed world of Nanahboozoo. This little twig took root and rapidly grew into a large tree, and from it all the other trees and shrubs had come.

A Royal Battle.

# Chapter Twenty.

**The Call of the Moose—Preparations For Capture—Midnight March—Rival Bulls—A Royal Battle—Frank's Shot—Big Tom, the Successful Moose Hunter—Young Moose Calves—Their Capture—Sam's Awkward Predicament.**

In the morning the boys were informed that during the night the call of a great moose bull was heard, and that an effort would be made the next night to kill him if possible.

The moose is the largest animal that roams in these northern forests, and is exceedingly difficult to kill. His eyes are small and not very good, but he has the most marvellous powers of hearing and smelling given to almost any animal. Then he is so cunning and watchful that very few Indians are able, by fair stalking him in his tracks, to get a shot at him. He does not eat grass, but browses on the limbs and branches of several kinds of trees. His horns are often of enormous proportions, but yet the speed and ease with which he can dash safely through the dense forests is simply marvellous.

There are various ways of killing them in addition to the sportsmanlike way of following on the trail, and thus by skill and endurance getting within range of them.

In the winter, when the snow is deep, they have a poor chance against the hunters, who, on their light snowshoes, can glide on the top of the deep snow, while the great, heavy moose goes floundering in the drift.

They have a great weakness for the large, long roots of the water lily, and so are often killed while they are out from the shore and wallowing in the marshy places for these succulent dainties. But the most exciting sport is that which the Indians were here going to adopt in trying to bring this big fellow, whose bellowings the night before had so arrested the attention of those who had been awakened by him.

Mr Ross explained that the bellowings of the previous night were his calls to his mates in the forest. Perhaps they had been alarmed by some hunters or chased by wolves, and had become widely separated. So nature has not only given to the moose of both sexes this wonderful power of hearing, but to the males this great voice, which in the stillness of the night in those northern solitudes can be heard for a number of miles. The reply call of the female moose is much softer, and the Indians have a plan by which they can so successfully imitate it that they can often call the old male moose close enough to them to be shot; and cases are known where the infuriated beast, maddened by the deception played upon him, has rushed upon his deceiver and made it lively work for him to get beyond the reach of his great antlers.

For fear of driving the moose out of the neighbourhood, it was decided that there was to be no firing of guns that day, as the Indians were certain there had been no answer to the call of the male on the part of the other sex, and judging from their knowledge of the habits of the animal they decided that, if not alarmed, he would be within hearing distance about ten o'clock that evening.

The question then was, "How are we to spend the day?" This was speedily answered when the Indians reported that there were any number of sturgeon seen jumping in the shallows among the rocks not far out from the shore. The method of securing them was by spearing them from the canoes. A good deal of calculation was required in managing the canoes so that they would not be upset in the excitement of the sport, and then a great deal of strength had to be exerted to hold on to the spears when once the great big sturgeon, from four to six feet long, was transfixed.

There were some amusing upsets, and the boys in turn came back to the camp drenched, but happy with the varied adventures of the day. Nearly a score of fine sturgeon rewarded them for their efforts. These the Indians cut into flakes and dried, while the valuable oil was distilled and put away in most ingeniously constructed vessels made out of the skin of the sturgeon themselves.

But in spite of the fun and success of the sturgeon fishing the boys were simply wild in anticipation of the events of the coming night. The very uncertainty and weirdness of it had a fascination for them that made it impossible for them to shut their eyes and have a short sleep in the early hours of the evening, as Mr Ross suggested. The very idea of sleeping seemed an utter impossibility. So they kept awake, and were alert and watchful on the movements of the Indians, who made their final preparations to take advantage of the natural instincts of these great animals to meet each other.

These preparations were not very many. From the birch trees that grew near they stripped off long rolls of new bark. These they carefully made into a horn-shaped instrument the end of which was much wider than the other. Then they put on their darkest garments, as the appearance of any thing white would alarm the wary game and frighten them away.

The evening was exceedingly favourable. But little wind was blowing, and that was from the land toward the lake; thus the scent would not be carried toward the moose, if they appeared.

The next question was, who were to go and where had they better be stationed? So it was decided that as Mr Ross had caught the contagion of the hour, he and Alec should take a position at a designated rock, both well-armed, while out near the lake one of the clever Indians, armed with one of these oddly constructed birch-bark horns, should be placed. The reason of this was the expectation that, if the old moose heard the call, while perhaps too wary to come within range of the man sounding it, he might be near enough for a good shot from Mr Ross and Alec. In the same manner Frank was stationed with Mustagan, and Sam with Big Tom, while two other Indians, acting the part of trumpeters to them, were stationed in the rear near the water's edge.

For a couple of hours very eerie and weird seemed everything to these excited boys. No moon was in the heavens, but the stars shone down upon them with a splendour and a beauty unknown in a land of fogs and mists. No conversation was allowed, as the hearing of the moose is most acute. For a time the silence was almost oppressive.

After watching at their different stations for about half an hour or so, there wailed out on the silent air a cry so wild, so startling, so blood-curdling that it filled with terror and dismay the hearts of our three boys, who had never heard anything like it. Strung up as they were to such tension by their surroundings out there in the gloom of that quiet night, and then to be thus startled by such a cry, no wonder each lad clutched his gun and instinctively crowded close to his experienced companion in that trying hour. Yet such was their confidence in them that they remained silent, but were soon relieved when they were told, in a whisper, that it was only the cry of the lynx, and, blood-curdling though it was, it was really a good sign for them. When this harsh, doleful sound had died away in the distance, from a tree near them some great owls began their strange hootings, and the Indians again said, "Good signs."

About midnight the first note of the sound for which they were listening was heard. It was far away in the forest directly east from them, with the wind coming from the same direction. The Indians remained perfectly still until the roaring became somewhat louder, and then the boys were somewhat startled at hearing, but in a much softer key, a sound very similar in their rear. This latter sound was made by the men through these queer birch-bark horns they had been so industriously working at during the day. From long practice some of these Indians can so perfectly imitate the sounds of the female moose that they can deceive the males, and thus bring them toward them. These artificial sounds were not long unanswered. Louder and louder still were the roarings that came at intervals from the deep forest. Soft and varied were the responses as the

Indian in the rear of Mr Ross and Alec blew his inviting notes, but in the rear of the others there sounded out the enticing strains.

"Listen," said Mr Ross, "there is the roar of another old moose, and we are in for a battle."

Fortunately the wondrous auroras came shooting up from below the horizon and flashing and dancing along the northern sky; they almost dispelled the darkness, and lit up the landscape with a strange, weird light. This necessitated a quick change of base on the part of the hunters, and so, as soon as possible, they retired under the shadows of some dense balsam trees. Hardly were they well hidden from view before a great moose showed himself in full sight in a wide opening, where the fire, years before, had burned away the once dense forest. In response to his loud calls the three Indians with their horns replied, and this seemed to greatly confuse him. He would move first a little in one direction and then in another, and then hesitated and sent out his great roar again. Quickly, and in a lower strain, did the Indians closely imitate the female's call. Before there could be the responsive answer on his part to them there dashed into the open space from the forest, not many hundreds of yards from him, another moose bull that roared out a challenge that could not be mistaken.

The Indians with their birch horns again imitated the calls of the female moose. This they did with the purpose of bringing the bulls within range before they engaged in battle.

It is a singular characteristic of many wild animals that when the rival males battle for the possession of the females they like to do it in the presence of those for whom they fight. Their presence seems to be a stimulus to nerve them to greater courage. So it is with the moose and other deer species, and so by the light of the dancing auroras the three boys and those with them watched these two great moose, each standing at the foreshoulders over sixteen hands high, as they thus came on toward the spot where Mr Ross and Alec were well hid from observation, and behind whom the Indian kept now softly lowing like a moose cow.

In their hurried movements they had gradually approached each other, and so when not far from Mr Ross and Alec's hiding place they suddenly appeared in a clear, elevated spot, and supposing they were now close to their companions they turned suddenly and gave each other battle. And a royal battle it was! A moose bull at the best is not handsome, but an angry, infuriated moose bull, when his temper is up, is one of the most hideous of monsters. The long, coarse hair of his head and neck seems to be all turned in the wrong direction, his small eyes have a most wicked gleam in them, and, taking him altogether, we know of no picture more likely to cause a person who sees him to have the next night the nightmare.

With a roar they rushed at each other, and as their great antlered heads met in the shock of battle it was a sight not often seen. They each seemed as though they were resolved to conquer in the first round, and appeared surprised at not having been able to succeed.

It undoubtedly would have been interesting to some people to have witnessed the battle between these two well-matched moose bulls to a finish, but the practical Indians know a thing or two about their meat, and one is that the meat of a moose that has been in battle for a couple of hours or so is apt to be so soft and spongy and full of air bubbles that a hungry dog will hardly eat it. They also know, on the other hand, that moose meat when in prime condition is the finest venison in the world. The Indians were also well aware that the bulls now engaged in battle would take but little heed of any other foes. They therefore quickly gathered in with Frank and Sam to the spot where Mr Ross and Alec were hidden, and there in quiet whispers arranged their plans for the killing of the two great moose ere the fierce battle had much longer continued.

The Indians were anxious that the boys should have the honour of killing them, but Mr Ross hesitated to expose any one of them to the fierce rush of an infuriated wounded moose bull in case the bullet had not done its work. The Indians, cautious though they are, however, saw here an opportunity such as might not for a long time be theirs, and so pleaded for them, and promised to so place themselves as to be ready with a reserve fire if it should be necessary.

To Frank and Alec the honour of the first fire was given. If this did not immediately bring both of the moose down Mr Ross and Sam were to fire next, while the Indians would be as a reserve in case of emergency. Mustagan was given charge over all in case of any need arising. After a short survey of the fierce conflict it was decided that they must quietly work round the combatants and fire at them from the forest side. Under the guidance of Mustagan the single party quietly drew back a little, and then, making a detour, were nearly in the rear of the fighting animals when a quick, sharp word from Mustagan caused them all to drop flat upon the ground, for there, clearly visible in the light of the dancing auroras, not two hundred yards away, was a large moose cow with two young calves at her side. So intently was she watching the battle that she had not the slightest suspicion of the presence of these hunters.

This was a new complication. What was to be done? If possible she must be killed. The meat of a cow moose is very much superior to that of the bull. Gliding past the boys like a panther went Big Tom from the front to consult with Mustagan, who was at the rear. Soon it was settled that Big Tom was to get that cow, while the bulls were to be killed as arranged.

But a few seconds for consultation were needed between these two Indian hunters, and then to the eyes of the boys it seemed as though Big Tom, the largest man in the party, literally sank into the ground, so small did he seem to make himself, as with his gun in the fickle light he silently glided away. Mustagan then, with the party close behind him, moved on again to the scene of the battle, which was still fiercely raging. The ground was very uneven, and as every advantage was taken of it the boys were able to secure a most advantageous position not more than fifty yards from the combatants.

The fierce battle was a sight sufficient to try the nerves of much older persons than our boys. The bulls seemed simply wild with rage, and as in their mad rushes their horns struck together Frank and Alec declared that they saw fire flash from them; others, however, said it was only auroral reflection as they turned at certain angles. Mustagan beckoned the two boys who were to have the honour of the first fire, and placing them side by side he quietly said:

"Wait until in their fighting they turn their sides to you, then aim to strike them behind the foreshoulders."

They had not long to wait ere the double report rang out on the midnight air, and as an echo to it another one was heard not far away. That the balls struck was evident, for the thud of the bullets was heard distinctly by all, so close were they to their game. The effect of the firing on one of the bulls was seen to be immediate, for, although his huge horns seemed almost locked in those of his antagonist, he slowly sank to the ground. The other moose, although badly wounded, gave a last vicious plunge at his opponent. Then proudly lifting up his head, and seeing for the first time his new antagonists, and being still mad with the excitement of battle, he, without any hesitancy, rushed to the attack.

"Fire straight at the centre of his head," were Mustagan's words. Hardly were they uttered ere from the guns of Mr Ross and Sam the death-dealing bullets flew on their mission and the great, fierce animal stumbled forward a few more yards and fell dead, pierced to the brain by both of the balls. In a few minutes they were joined by Big Tom, who quickly said:

"Moose cow shot, and little calves run into woods; catch um next day, if wolves not too quick."

It was the report of his unerring shot that rang out so quickly after Frank and Alec had fired.

The reaction after the complete silence and the long-strung-up tension, together with the fierce battle witnessed and the decisive victory, was very great. No need of silence now, but the boys were so excited they hardly knew whether to laugh or cry. Frank said he wanted to howl. Alec said he wanted to dance. Sam said he wanted to swing a shillalah. And they all said, "What would not the boys at home give to be here?"

A fire was quickly kindled, and a couple of Indians remained as watchers while the rest returned to the not very distant camp. The Indian in charge had supper ready for them, which was much enjoyed, and then as speedily as possible they were wrapped up in their blankets and doubly wrapped in sweet, refreshing sleep. Very few were their hours of slumber. Daylight comes early in the summer time in high latitudes, and so when the boys heard the Indians moving about and preparing breakfast they sprang up also, and after a hasty bath in the lake were ready for their breakfast and eager to be off, not only to see where their bullets had struck the moose bulls, but to find out how it was that while one dropped so quickly the other was able to make that fierce charge upon them.

When they reached the scene of last night's exciting adventures they hardly recognised that locality, so different does a place look in daylight from what it does when illumined by the ever-changing auroras.

However, here was the place sure enough, for some Indians had already nearly skinned the great animals, and had traced the bullets that had been fired. Frank's bullet had pierced the heart of the one that had so quickly dropped in the fight; Alec's had gone through the lungs, and, though the wound was a mortal one, it did not so suddenly result in death; hence his ability to make that fearful charge, which was so promptly stopped by the balls of Mr Ross and Sam, both of which were taken out of his brain. This was very satisfactory to the boys, and so they were bracketed with equal honours all round by Mr Ross, much to their delight, for three nobler, more unselfish lads never chummed together. The success of one was the success of all, and when one seemed to fail, or make a miss, the others were uneasy until he was at the head in the next adventure.

But the question now was, "Where are those young moose calves?" The Indian watchers could give the boys but little information. All they knew was that after the auroras faded away in the dark hour just before dawn they heard them moving about; but they did not frighten them, as Mr Ross had left orders that they were not to be disturbed, unless some prowling wolves should appear as though on their trail. None, however, were heard, and so the Indians had remained very quiet.

So the search for the young moose immediately began, and although it was prosecuted with a good deal of vigour, still not a sign of the young animals was discovered. At length Mustagan, who had watched the younger members of the party at work, said:

"You want to see those calves quick, just wait."

Quietly taking up one of the birch-bark horns, he began softly blowing into it. The sounds he made were like those of the mother cow when she calls her young from its secluded retreat, where she has cunningly hid it away from its many enemies while she is off feeding.

Now high, now low, now prolonged and in different tones, came out from that great birch-bark horn those peculiar notes, some of which were not unlike the sounds made by the domestic cow when separated from her calf. For once in his life Mustagan was a complete failure. For blow as much as he would—and great were his exertions—no calf appeared in answer to his calls.

Said Big Tom, who was a famous moose hunter, and who had listened to Mustagan with a good deal of interest and some amusement: "Let me have that horn, and I will show you how it ought to be done. You boys watch the woods and be ready to run."

Then putting the birch horn to his mouth he cooed out such a tender moo-oo-o-o that the boys were fairly startled by the similarity of its sound to the familiar notes in the barnyards at home; but soon other things excited them, for hardly had the echoes of Big Tom's mooings died away before there came rushing out from the forest the two moose calves. On they came directly toward the spot where Big Tom had uttered his call. So sudden had been their appearance that all remained perfectly still to watch their movements. Certain that they had heard their mother, they were now anxiously looking for her. They were a pair of fine-looking moose calves, about three months old, and so it was resolved, if possible, to capture them alive and tame them. It turned out not so easy a matter as had been anticipated. With as little display as possible the boys and Indians tried to surround them before they become alarmed. So confident did the young creatures seem that they had heard their mother that it was some time before they became suspicious of danger, and then only when they were about encircled by the hunters. Then the fun began. Turning toward the point in the forest from which they had emerged, they made a dash for liberty. Frank and Alec threw themselves on one, and getting their arms around its neck made a desperate effort to hold it. They were amazed at its strength, as it easily carried them along, and not until they succeeded in tripping it up and throwing it on the ground were they able to hold it.

Sam and a young Indian tackled the other one, and found him much more pugnacious. With a vicious kick he struck the Indian in the stomach, who at once decided that he had had enough of that sport and quickly retired, leaving Sam now to struggle with him alone. Sam at first seized him by his long ears, but was unable to bring force enough to arrest his progress in that way. Then he tried to seize him by the neck, but a few strong blows with his fore feet made that a difficult and dangerous task, and so Sam had to let go. This seemed to interest the calf, and so from being the one attacked he became the aggressor. The pugnacity of the calf, and the lively way in which he butted his opponent, caused great amusement to the onlookers. Sam could not stand this, and so he threw himself desperately on the animal, and hugging him around his neck, held him so closely that he could neither use his hard little head nor his fore feet, with which he had been fighting so vigorously. Sam was in an awkward predicament. Gladly would a number of Indians have rushed to his help, but Mr Ross wanted him to have the honour of capturing the young moose alone, and so held them back; but all watched the odd struggle, which was intensely amusing.

Sam still pluckily held on, but the calf evidently considered himself the aggressor, for he tried hard to shake Sam loose from him, his object evidently being to strike him with his head or feet. This Sam endeavoured to prevent, until at length he was afraid to let go his grip for fear of the now vicious young animal, and so, in his desperation, he called out most comically:

"Will somebody come and help me to let go of this calf?" Help was soon there, and strong arms quickly captured the spirited young creature. It, as well as its companion, was securely tied and taken back with the party when they returned to Sagasta-weekee.

So great was the quantity of meat and other things secured that a canoe was hastily sent back to the home, and the next day a large boat, similar to those used by the Hudson Bay Company in the fur trade, arrived with a good crew. Everything was placed on board, including the two young moose, that already would eat the young branches gathered for them by the boys. A strong yard, inclosed with planks and logs, was made for them, and they soon became quite tame and gentle.

Harnessed to a cariole, or dog-sled, they travelled with great speed, and seemed to enjoy the fun. But they drew the line at the saddle, and no Texas bronco could more easily rid himself of a tenderfoot than these lively animals with their enormous forequarters could send their would-be riders into the snow or grass.

Our illustration gives us a good idea of how they looked when ready the next spring to be shipped by the Hudson Bay ship to one of the big zoological gardens in Great Britain.

# Chapter Twenty One.

**Excursion to Sea River Falls—The Cranberry Picking—The Contest—"Where are the Children?"—Wenonah and Roderick lost in the Forest—First Night's Unsuccessful Search—The Tracks in the Sand—Mustagan's Startling Discovery.**

Thus pleasantly passed the bright weeks away at Sagasta-weekee. Every day had its duties and amusements. Mr Ross, although the best of masters, was almost a martinet in his affairs, both in the home circle and among those in his employ. This strict disciplinary method is absolutely essential for comfort and success in such a land. If there is a lax method of living and conducting business, soon everything is in confusion and wretchedness.

Yet while everything went on with almost military precision in the home life, there was nothing about it to make it otherwise than pleasant and enjoyable. So the boys ever returned to this happy home with delight from the excitements of their various hunting and fishing excursions.

One of the great deprivations of living in a land where the summer is so short and the winter so long and cold is the lack of native fruit. No apples, pears, cherries, or peaches grow in that northern land. These fruits must be brought to it in a preserved or dried condition.

In some sections wild plums are to be found; in others, abundance of cranberries grow most luxuriously. A few wild strawberries spring up in the clearings where great fires have destroyed the forests. A sweet bilberry also abounds in some parts of the country. This fruit is much prized by the Indians, and frequently used, mixed with dried meat, in the manufacture of their finest pemmican.

The Indian women in the neighbourhood of white settlements or trading posts bring in large quantities of the cranberries, which they gather in the marshes and forests, and sell to those who are able and willing to purchase.

Sometimes cranberry parties were organised, and nearly all the members of the post and families interested would join together and go off on an excursion of several days to places where the berries were abundant, and thus secure large quantities, which were an acceptable addition to their rather meagre bill of fare.

This year, as the berries were reported by the Indian women to be very abundant, Mr and Mrs Ross, at the urgent request of their own children, as well as to give the boys the unique experience, decided to have a cranberry outing on quite an extended scale, and one that would last for several days. It turned out to be unique and memorable in various ways.

It was decided that they should go into camp below Sea River Falls, on the Nelson, and pick berries at their leisure in the great section of country lying north-west from that point, as there they were to be found in large quantities.

For the comfort and convenience of the family a couple of large tents were sent on and pitched by some Indians. The various utensils and supplies necessary for a good time were also forwarded, so that when Mr and Mrs Ross, with Minnehaha, Wenonah, Roderick, and our three lads, arrived they found everything arranged for their comfort.

It was an ideal place for an outing. Before them was the great river with the music of its rushing, roaring rapids, down which it was so exciting to run in the canoes under the skillful guidance of the cautious, experienced Indians. The great granite rocks in picturesque beauty were everywhere to be seen. Back of the sandy beach and grassy sward, where stood the tents and camp fires, was the deep, dark, unbroken forest, that stretched away and away for hundreds of miles.

So delightful were the surroundings, and so good the fishing, as well as novel and interesting this running the rapids, that two or three days were thus spent ere any definite arrangements about the cranberry picking was thought of.

To aid in gathering a large quantity of berries Mrs Ross had engaged a number of Indian women, who were famous as noted berry pickers. These women brought with them a large Indian vessel called a "rogan." It is made out of birch-bark, and is capable of holding about twenty quarts of berries.

There are two kinds of cranberries in this land. One is called the high-bush variety, while the other is known as the moss cranberry, as it is generally found where moss is abundant, and grows on a small vine on the ground. It was this latter kind that here abounded and that they had come to gather.

As the outing was not merely for the purpose of gathering berries, they did not pick very steadily. Mrs Ross well knew that her faithful Indian women would see that she had her full supply. So the members of the family picked berries, went fishing or hunting or canoeing, more or less frequently, as their inclinations prompted them. Several days thus passed in varied sport and work.

One evening as the Indian women came in with their heavy loads they reported finding, not very far distant, a splendid place, where the berries were very plentiful, and the ground dry and mossy and free from muskegs and rocks. So it was decided that, with the exception of some of the servants, who would remain and take care of the camp, all should go and have a big day of it at berry picking, and then they would make their arrangements for returning home.

The preparations necessary were soon made. A number of large and small rogans were made ready, and, in addition, the men took the precaution to carry with them their guns and ammunition.

Minnehaha and Wenonah were very happy and proud of the honour of taking charge of their little brother Roddy, as they loved to call him. As the children were anxious to do their share of picking berries they were each supplied with a little birch-bark vessel, and with great delight did they gather quite a number of the bright red berries that were so abundant.

As they had left the camp early in the morning they were able to do a capital forenoon's work. At midday they all assembled at a designated place, and much enjoyed the dinner that the servants had prepared for them. Then again they separated, and men, women, and children were once more very busily employed in gathering in the fruit, while pleasant chat and merry laugh would be heard from various parts.

To add a little zest and excitement to the pleasant work the whole company had been divided into two parties, and between them there was a lively contest as to which should succeed in gathering the greater quantity of berries.

Little Roderick and Wenonah were placed on one side as being equal in their picking abilities to their older sister, Minnehaha. Very proud were the little folks as they filled their dishes and came and emptied them into the large vessels. Thus the contest raged, and, as the two parties were about equal in picking abilities, the excitement rose very high, and all exerted themselves to the utmost that their side might be victorious.

It had been previously arranged that the contest was to cease at sundown, so as to give them plenty of time to return to the camp in the beautiful gloaming.

Some able-bodied Indian men were employed to carry the large birch rogans to the selected spots, where the berries were to be measured and the victors announced. Some time was spent in this work amid the excitement of all, as the contest was very close.

"Where is Roderick?" said Mrs Ross.

"O, he is with Wenonah," said Minnehaha.

"And where is Wenonah?" was the question now.

No one seemed to know. And so the cry of the sweet musical name rang out on the air:

"Wenonah! Wenonah!"

But to that call, and also to that for the little brother Roderick, there was no response.

At once there was excitement and alarm.

"Who saw them last, and where were they?"

Many more such questions were uttered, while some persons ran one way and some another. Several young men seized their guns and fired several shots in quick succession, but Mr Ross stopped them as quickly as possible.

Mr Ross, although alarmed, was the first to get some order among them, and on the closest questioning it came out that none were certain that they had seen the children since about three o'clock, and that was when they were emptying their little dishes of berries into the larger receptacles. Then, excited by the contest, they had rushed off for more.

A rumbling of thunder in the west startled them, and so, prompt must be their movements. To the point where the little ones were last seen a dozen or more had hurried, and ere they scattered in the forest to begin the search they were told that the firing of the guns would be the signal of success or failure. One report meant they were not found; two reports, close together, was the signal that they had been found, and for the searchers to return. Immediately all those who were able to act as searchers, without themselves becoming lost, scattered to their work. On account of the vastness of the forest Mr Ross positively refused to allow Frank, Alec, or Sam to go any distance away on the search. This was a keen disappointment to the boys, but Mr Ross was wise in his decision. The searchers had very little to assist them in their work. There were any number of signs where had walked the busy feet, but the trouble was there had been so many pickers at work, and they had travelled so far, that it was impossible to pick out the tracks of the two lost children.

Only an hour or so were the searchers able to do anything that night; for the thunderstorm was on them, and in spite of all they could do they were all drenched through and through. Mrs Ross, although stricken with grief, kept firm control over herself, and, surrounded and comforted by Minnehaha and the three boys, huddled under the slight protection which some Indian women had hastily prepared against the fierce storm. Mr Ross had done all that was possible in directing the watchers as they brought all their Indian experience to their aid. Thus the hours passed. The storm spent its fury in the heavy downpour of rain, and then was gone. The stars came out from behind the flying clouds, and the night again became one of beauty. Still there were no signs of the children. Somewhere out in the forest, alone, were those little ones whom none as yet had been able to find. The heavy rain had completely obliterated every vestige of a trail. So the searchers, sad and quiet, came in one after another, grieved and vexed at their failure.

Mr Ross tried to induce Mrs Ross, with Minnehaha, to return to the camp and obtain refreshment and rest, but she most positively refused.

"My children are out in the wild forest, exposed to many dangers. I cannot go to bed until they are found," she passionately exclaimed.

So a great fire was built out of dry logs, blankets were sent for from the tents, and the saddest and longest night to those terrified ones slowly passed away. Mr Ross had not only sent for food and blankets for all, but he had also dispatched swift runners to go by land and water and cease not until they had found Mustagan and Big Tom and told them of his loss and sorrow.

Soon after sunrise these grand old men walked into the camp. A hasty council was summoned, and these old men closely questioned the Indians who had been present the previous day, and who had searched until the storm and darkness stopped them.

When they were told that a number of guns had been fired off in quick succession they were much annoyed, and said:

"Great mistake. Lost children in the woods always hide when they hear guns."

But no time must be lost. The country was to be marked out and a code of signals explained by which they could communicate with each other as soon as any trail was found. Not in straight lines were they to go, but in enlarging circles until they should cross the trail of the children. When it was found, they were to report as speedily as possible, that there might be a concentration from that point and thus no waste in fruitless search.

Not until about noon was the first sign struck; then it was a number of miles away from the camp. It is simply marvellous the distances that lost persons, even little children, will travel. The clue discovered by Big Tom was where the children had left the dry, rocky lands, which left no trail of the little feet, and had crossed a small, shallow stream. Here the sands were clearly marked by the little footsteps, and Tom's big heart gave a great thump of joy as he saw the signs so clearly indicated before him. At first he feared to fire the signal, lest he should add to the terror of the lost children; but as soon as he examined the footprints he saw that they had been made the evening before, and by little ones who were hurrying on as rapidly as possible.

As quickly as he could he followed them up until they were lost again on the dry rocks on the other side; then he fired his gun, and while waiting the coming of others he kept diligently searching for some other signs of the wanderers.

Not long had he to wait ere he was joined by Mr Ross, Mustagan, and others. They were all excited, and glad to see these footprints, but judged by the hardness of the sand in the steps that the children had passed over the creek some hours before dark the previous evening. This being the case, they might have travelled some miles farther before they were stopped by the storm and darkness. But no needless time was spent in surmises and conjecturing. A new starting point had been found, and from it the search was again renewed with all the vigour possible.

If Wenonah and Roderick had been pure white children, brought up in a civilised land with all the ignorance incident to such regions, they would have been found long ere this; but their part Indian blood and thorough training in that wild north land was now really to them a misfortune— first, because they had the strength and training to push on with such wonderful speed and endurance; again, it also made them wary and cunning, and so fearful of being tracked by wild beasts or hostile Indians that they carefully, but rapidly, moved along in a way that children not brought up in such a land would never have dreamed of.

So, while the Indians were looking for traces of the children, the wandering lost ones were doing all they could not to leave behind them the vestige of a trail. Thus hours passed on, the sun went down in beauty, the shadows of night began to fall; still not another sign of the wanderers had been found.

Discouraged and annoyed at failure, one after another of the searchers returned to the spot where the footsteps had been discovered. Here the camp had been made, and here had come Mrs Ross, with the boys and others.

The sight of the tiny footsteps of the hurrying feet of her little darlings nearly broke her heart. But she crushed down her great sorrow, that nothing in her should divert anyone, even her husband, in the search for those who were still exposed to so many dangers—lost in the great forest of so many thousands of square miles.

The last to come in was Mustagan, and his face was that of a man who has bad news but, by intense effort, shows it not in his countenance, but keeps it locked up in his heart. Few and yet searching were the words uttered at the camp fire as each one had declared to Mustagan that there had been no fresh signs. He himself had not given any answer, and, by asking questions of the others, had thus thrown off suspicion as regarded himself. But nevertheless he had seen signs, and what he had seen had nearly driven him wild. But darkness had come on him almost suddenly from the arising up of a black cloud in the west, and so, in spite of all his experience and anxiety, he had been compelled to return shortly after making this startling discovery. What he had seen had so alarmed him that he dare not tell, even to Mr Ross.

Very sad, indeed, was that second night around the camp fire. Mr and Mrs Ross were nearly broken-hearted. Frank, Alec, and Sam spent the night in sleepless sorrow. The Indians, who all dearly loved the lost little ones, sat back in the gloom and were still and quiet. A kind of stupor seemed to be over them all, with one exception, and, strange to say, that one was Mustagan. Sharp eyes were on him, and some wondered why he was so strangely agitated and was so restless and excited.

A little after midnight he abruptly sprang up, and speaking to Big Tom and a couple of other Indians they all withdrew some distance back into the darkness of the forest. To them in quiet tones, so as not to be heard by the sorrowing ones at the camp fire, Mustagan told what he had seen just as the darkness had set in. When they heard his story they were as much excited as was he.

His story was this: he had pushed on in the direction he had selected in the hunt for the children, and toward evening he had reached a part of the country where the berries were very plentiful. Here he had found traces that bears were numerous, and as they are fond of these berries they had been feasting on them. This, of course, alarmed him, and so he cautiously began making a circle around this place, and at length, in a depression in the forest, he found the dried-up channel of a creek. He cautiously hurried along on the dry sands, and, after going on only a few hundred yards, he found a number of fresh tracks, not only of bears that had recently crossed but also among them the footsteps of the lost children!

Children in the Custody of Bears

# Chapter Twenty Two.

### Children's Footsteps and Bears' Tracks—Children in the Custody of the Bears—The Plan of Rescue—The Boys' Part—The Bird Call—Success.

This was terrible news; and only Indians that have such perfect control over themselves could have heard it without making an outcry. As it was, Mustagan had to utter some warning words to maintain the perfect silence that was desired. In a few sentences he quietly stated that the children were not then running, and, judging by their footsteps and the broken branches of berry-bushes from which they had been picking the fruit, they were not frightened. He judged, also, from the tracks that there were four bears, two large ones and two that were quite small. What astonished him most of all was that the tracks were so numerous, and seemed to say to him that both the bears and the children had crossed and recrossed the place several times. When he made this discovery he hid himself at once, for fear his presence might anger the bears and cause them to destroy the children; he listened, but could hear no sound.

After waiting quietly for a time he returned to the trail and followed it until it entered among the dense bushes and great rocks. If the light had not so quickly faded he could have easily followed them; as it was, he was perplexed to know what to do. If he should come up to them in such company he was not sure how he would be received. So he thought the best thing he could do was not to anger the bears, who were evidently not disposed to hurt the children, and so he quietly withdrew and came back to the camp.

Old hunters as they were, here was a new experience to almost every one of them. Big Tom was the first to speak.

"My words are," said he, "that we go and tell the master and mistress at once. It will comfort them to know the little ones are alive, even if they are in such company. We shall yet get the children. As the bears did not kill them at first, and there are plenty of berries, they will not kill them soon."

To this suggestion of Big Tom's they all agreed, and immediately after returned to the camp fire, where Mustagan, in his simple yet picturesque way, told the story of his discovery.

The poor mother could only say:

"Thank God! He will yet restore to me my children."

Mr Ross's lips quivered, but crushing down his own fears he said, as he comforted his sorrow-stricken wife:

"Yes, thank God! Perhaps he has made even the wild animals of the forest to be their guardian angels."

Frank, Alec, and Sam had listened to Mustagan with bated breath. As Alec said afterward:

"My heart seemed to stop beating while I listened."

When it came out that the bears were friendly, and not disposed to injure the children, the lads could hardly restrain the hearty cheers that somehow, in spite of themselves, would try to burst out.

There was no more sleep that night. As it was at least five miles to the spot where the tracks had been discovered, the strict orders of silence were cancelled, and soon there were noise and activity. Food was prepared and eaten with an appetite unknown since Wenonah and Roderick were of the happy party.

The absorbing question with Mr and Mrs Ross, in consultation with Mustagan and Big Tom, was how they were to proceed when the morning came.

To follow them up and rush in upon them might anger the bears, and the children might suffer. To stalk them so quietly as to be able to get within range and shoot the bears might terrify the children, or they might be wounded by the bullets. There was much talking and many suggestions. A remark from Mustagan gave Mrs Ross a hint, and so a woman's quick intuition solved the perplexing question.

Mustagan had said that, as he carefully examined the tracks, he found where the children had evidently filled their birch dishes with berries and fed them to the little bears, whose many tracks had shown that, like young dogs, they had gambolled and played around them.

Said Mrs Ross as she heard this:

"Those bears seem well disposed toward children, so the brave boys will go on ahead with similar dishes of berries, and they will find that the animals will rather eat the fruit than do the lads any harm."

This suggestion so delighted the boys that, without a moment's thought of the risks they would run, they gladly consented, and were eager to carry out the suggestion.

Mr Ross and the Indians were old bear hunters, and they could not at first think that any such plan would be at all possible. However, think or plan as much as they would, they found it utterly impossible to settle on any other scheme that appeared to them either safe or suitable. The result was that daylight found them still in perplexity, and altogether undecided as to the correct method to adopt in this novel expedition, so unique in all of their experiences.

Mrs Ross, however, and the boys, stuck to her suggestion, and pleaded that it be attempted. As nothing else was suggested the Indians and Mr Ross at length consented. However, they took many precautions to save the lads and prevent disaster, either to them or to the children.

The preparations were soon made, even to the rogans of berries, and heavily armed with their guns the party set out under the guidance of Mustagan. Mrs Ross went with them, as her anxieties were so great for the rescue of her darlings.

When within a half mile or so of the spot where the tracks had been seen they halted, and, after some final consultation, Mustagan and Big Tom decided to go on and see if there were any further developments. Very cautiously and yet rapidly did they advance from covert to covert, until they were so close to the sand of the dried-up stream that it was quite visible to them, although they themselves were well hid from observation.

Here for a time they waited, for they shrewdly conjectured from Mustagan's description of the numerous tracks, crossing and recrossing, that for the present, at least, the bears were abiding in that vicinity.

Not long had they to wait ere they were convinced of the correctness of these conjectures, for coming out of the forest on the other side of the dried-up stream were to be seen four bears and the two lost children.

Crouching down low on the ground, and peering through the dense bushes behind which they were hidden, did our two Indians watch them for a time, that they might decide on the best method of rescuing the little ones. The wind was blowing from the bears toward the Indians, and so there was little fear of the animals scenting danger at that distance, which was still a good quarter of a mile away.

Why the children had remained so long with the bears was perplexing to these hunters until the mystery was solved by the fact that was now evident to their eyes, that the children were really prisoners and the bears would not let them escape. As the men watched they saw Wenonah seize Roderick's hand in hers, and, starting on a run, she tried to go up the channel on the sands. This movement was stopped by one of the large bears as speedily as possible by putting himself in the children's way. Then children, still hand in hand, turned to the opposite direction, and when trying there to escape were stopped by the other large bear. In the meantime the little ones played around them like lively young dogs.

Foiled in their efforts to go either up or down in the dried-up channel of the stream, after some time spent on the sands the children and bears came up, and, entering among the berry-bushes, began to eat of the abundant fruit.

They were now much nearer to the Indians, and it was evident that the young bears were looking to the children to help them in picking their breakfast of berries.

When convinced of this the Indians' eyes brightened, and they said:

"The mistress is right; the boys will feed the young bears, and we will shoot the old ones."

Noiselessly they withdrew from their hiding place and rejoined the rest of the party, who had with almost feverish impatience awaited their return. Quietly and rapidly they reported what they had seen, and then the final preparations were made.

Quickly they all moved on, and soon were at the brow of the last hill, from the top of which the whole of the great plain, densely covered with the berry-bushes, could be seen, with the thread of shining sand in the distance, already referred to.

Here on the hilltop Mr and Mrs Ross were seated behind some dense bushes, through which they could look without creating suspicion. Then the Indians, taking the boys along with them, started on their dangerous course. Like panthers they moved quietly along, keeping as close to the ground as possible, until they reached a ledge of rocks. Here the Indians, with their guns loaded with ball, were placed, while the boys, with nothing but their baskets of berries, in company with Mustagan went on a little farther. Then Mustagan, giving the boys their final instructions and charging them to keep cool and be brave, no matter what might occur, withdrew with his gun, and hid himself behind a rock, a little way in the rear of them.

It was an exciting time for the boys, but they had learned to have such confidence in these grand old red men that such a thing as fear was now about unknown in any of them, even at the most trying moments.

While there sitting they were startled by a shrill bird call from not far behind them. They could hardly believe their ears when they found it came from the lips of Mustagan. In a minute or two it was repeated, and then again and again, with short intervals between.

To their surprise another bird call some hundreds of yards ahead of them was heard, and after a time it was repeated. Then the blackbird's notes rang out from behind, and then another note came from the front. Ere the voice behind could again reply a solemn "Hoot-a-hoot-a-hoo" came from the front.

For a time all was still, and then the song of the robin was heard in front, and only a chirp was heard in the rear.

Sharp and quick was the ending.

Soon after this chirp the boys heard the bushes rustling in front of them not fifty yards away. Then they saw in the opening the two children, closely followed by two young bears. As the children slowly moved along they kept plucking the berries and feeding them to the greedy young animals. The children were ragged and sadly changed as, from their still hidden position, the boys watched them; they could see that Wenonah, at least, seemed to know that they must act cautiously, and they observed that frequently she spoke to the little fellow at her side.

It was her bird notes that had answered Mustagan. Little did they realise, a year or so before, as he taught Wenonah these calls of the birds and what they meant, that her very life would so soon depend upon her knowledge of them.

Still cautiously advancing with little Roderick at her side, and both of them feeding the little bears, she at length reached a spot where she caught a glimpse of the boys. Without at all raising her voice she said:

"Crouch down as well as you can and bring the berries."

This they quickly did.

"Feed these greedy young ones while I give a basket to the old ones, so that while they are eating them we can get away."

Poor girl! She knew not of the number of guns that were now within range of anything that would dare to harm her, and the boys were warned not to speak.

Taking one of the baskets of berries, she quickly disappeared among the dense bushes, while the boys, with the other full baskets, had made friends with the young bears. When Wenonah returned, she found the young bears were filling themselves with the fruit. So thoroughly terrified had the children become, through fear of the bears, that although the boys by expressive signs urged them at once to hurry in the direction of safety and deliverance, they hesitated, and even when they started kept fearfully looking back.

The instant they reached Mustagan he shouted to the boys to return, and not a moment too soon, for crashing through the bushes came the two old bears, fierce and savage, and showing that in some way they had become suspicious of danger.

Coolly picking up the two baskets which the two young bears had upset, the boys, keeping their faces to the fierce, savage brutes, slowly retreated. The bears, at first only seeing the boys, came rushing toward them, but when they reached their young ones they stopped for a time, and then came on to attack the boys.

To the ledge of rocks Mustagan had carried the now happy children. They had nearly smothered "dear old Mustagan," as they loved to call him, with their kisses. Wild, indeed, were they with joy as father and mother rushed forward and received them as from the dead. They could only lie clinging to them while they wept out their bliss.

From it they were startled, as out rang a volley from the guns, and two great, fierce bears rolled over each other, each shot through more than one vital spot.

"Capture the little fellows alive!" was the cry.

And soon, after a lively chase and some sharp struggling, two four months' old cubs were so tied up as to be unable to do any injury either with teeth or claws.

Very anxious had the boys been during the search for the lost children. Their only regret was that they were so powerless as to be unable to join in the search. Very proud, however, were they to have had some share in the exciting events of the last hours of their strange deliverance. Tears were in their eyes and dimmed their vision as they first saw them in the company of the wild beasts, showing by their appearance what they must have suffered during the long days and nights of such hardships.

The story of the children's account of their adventures and hardships will be given in another chapter. Suffice here to say that very quickly was the march taken up, after the half-famished little ones had been fed, for they had had nothing but berries to eat, and, as Roderick put it:

"Naughty bears, they kept me all the time picking berries for them."

The return to the camp on the banks at Sea River Falls, and then to Sagasta-weekee, was soon made.

Great were the rejoicings there as well as at the mission, and at the Hudson's Bay Company's fort, when the news of the finding of the lost ones reached them. A special thanksgiving service was held the next

Sabbath at the mission church, at which whites and Indians from near and far gathered, and entered heartily into the spirit of the service.

Roderick and Wenonah in the Bears' Cave.

# Chapter Twenty Three.

## Wenonah's Story of their Marvellous Adventures with and Deliverance from the Bears—Roderick's Comments.

It was wisely decided that, as the children were so exhausted, at least a couple of days should be allowed to pass before they were asked to give anything like a full account of their marvellous adventures.

Wenonah, of course, was the principal speaker, but Roderick often put in some quaint remark, which gave additional interest to the story. Seated in her father's arms, while Roderick monopolised those of his mother, while Minnehaha and the boys, with some friends from the Fort and mission, gathered round, Wenonah told in her own way the story of their strange adventures:

"Roderick and I were to try and gather as many berries as Minnehaha; so we took our rogans, and we went to where the berries were thickest, and once we came back and emptied our dishes, and then we hurried away where we had seen a good many. But we did not find as many there as we hoped, and so we went on and on, and it took us a long time to fill our rogans, and when we did we started to come back, but we did not find the way, and so we hurried on and on. Then after a while we called, and called, and nobody answered us. So Roddy and I said we would not cry. So we hurried on and on, to try and get back. Then we came to some high rocks, and we climbed up as high as we could, and when we called again we thought we heard voices answering us from some other rocks, and so we hurried over there, but there was nobody, and no voice. Then we pushed on, and on, and soon we heard the thunder, but we never stopped, but just tried to get back before the rain.

"Soon we left the rocky land, and went down a long hill where we saw a little stream. This we crossed where the water was not deep.

"We wanted to get home, so we tried not to feel tired or to cry; but, although we tried ever so hard, we could not find the way. We had held on to our dishes, but now they were not half full, and so we stopped and ate some of the berries. Soon after it began to thunder very hard, and there was lightning, and so we hurried up to some big trees, and while we were standing under the branches to be out of the rain we saw one old tree that was all hollow on one side, and as the rain was coming down through the branches we went and got into this hollow tree. I had Roderick go in first so that I could keep him dry, and I stood at the outside."

Here Roderick spoke up and said:

"I wanted to stand on the outside because I was the boy, but Wenonah said she had better because she was the biggest."

"Then," continued Wenonah, "as it soon got very dark, and none of you came for us, we began to cry, and we could not help it, for there we were all alone in that hollow tree in the dark."

"After a while a big owl in one of the trees began to call. I knew what it was for Mustagan had taught me. At first Roddy said it was somebody calling him."

Again Roddy, who was now nestling in his mother's arms, spoke up and said:

"I thought it was somebody saying to me, 'Who, who, who!' and I said, 'We are Roddy and Wenonah Ross, and we are lost.'

"Then, when it called again, it only said:—

"'Oo! oo! oo!' So then we knew what it was, as we had often heard it at night here at home."

"We were glad to hear it," said Wenonah, "for all was now so dark and lonely. We could not lie down; we just had to stand up there all night. I held Roddy up as well as I could. Once we heard the cry of the wild cat, and that made us keep very still. I must have nodded some, as I leaned against the inside of that old tree, but it was an awful long night, and we were glad when it was light enough to see. Then we left that old hollow tree, and took up our dishes, and as we were very hungry we went out among the berry-bushes and ate some of the berries. We were careful to leave no tracks, because of that wild cat. We ate a lot of berries, but we did miss our good breakfast at home. We filled our dishes, and then started for home; but we could not find it. While we were going on among the bushes we came out into a little opening, and there were the two little bears. We thought at first they were two little black dogs. They came right up to us, and when they sat up so funnily on their little hind legs we saw they were bears, and of course we were afraid.

"Then they came and smelled our baskets of berries, and as we held them out to them they seemed very hungry, and at once began eating."

"But they were so greedy; they were worse than little piggies," said little Roderick; "they made such funny little noises all the time they were eating."

"But," continued Wenonah, "that sound of theirs seemed to call the old bears, that we had not yet seen. They came rushing through the bushes, and we were so frightened we could not even cry out or let go of our baskets.

"When they rushed at us the little bears, that were between them and us, seemed to think that all the old bears wanted to do was to get at the berries too, and so they kept so funnily twisting their little bodies between the old bears and us, while all the time they were eating the berries. When the old bears saw this they stopped looking so fierce and savage, and just sat down on their hind legs and looked at us feeding their young ones.

"Then we began to wonder what would happen when the little bears had eaten all the berries that were in our baskets.

"Little Roddy seemed to know just what to do; for as there were some berries growing close to him, while he held his basket in one hand he picked some more berries and fed them to the little bear. Then I did the same to the one that had been eating out of my dish. Soon we began moving slowly among the bushes for more berries, to find plenty for the greedy little fellows, but we kept them as well as we could between the old bears and us.

"As the old bears kept moving around we could not keep their little ones between them and us very long, and so by and by they came close up to us, but they did not now seem to be very angry. One of them got close up to Roddy, and there he stood up and looked so big beside my little brother that I almost screamed out, I was so frightened. But I did not do it for fear he might hurt him. He only moved a little, and then he came down again on all his four legs, and as he put his big mouth close to him Roddy just put in it a handful of berries. After that there was no more trouble with him except to get berries enough."

"Yes," said Roderick, "I just thought that if big bears like berries as well as little bears perhaps they would rather have them than eat us little children; so I just chucked that handful in his mouth, and he just did like them."

"I was slower in making such good friends with the other bear," continued Wenonah, "because the little one I was feeding was such a greedy little pig. He would not, for a long time, let me gather a handful and give to the big bear that, once or twice, got so close to me as to put its cold nose against my face. My! it made me shiver. But I said in my heart, 'I will be brave, for I want to save Roddy,'" and the child's voice broke. "I did want to see my father, and my mother, and Minnehaha again."

"But we did not cry here, did we?" said Roderick.

But the memory of that event was too great for them now, and throwing themselves in each other's arms they burst out in a passionate fit of weeping, that was so contagious no eyes remained dry in that group of loved ones there gathered to hear their pathetic story.

When calm again Wenonah went on with the story:

"After a while the little ones had enough, and then they began wrestling and playing with each other. They acted as if they wanted Roddy to play with them, and I told him to do so, but not to hurt them, and perhaps the old father and mother bears would not hurt us before we could run away."

"Yes," said Roddy, "I had great times with them, but they always wanted to wrestle with me more than any other kind of sport."

"I kept gathering berries," said Wenonah, "while Roddy played with the young bears. The old ones kept me busy now and were just about as greedy as the young ones had been.

"After a while I said to Roddy, 'We must try and get away from here,' for we did want to come home and see you all.

"We did not talk very much to each other, for our voices seemed to make the bears angry. But we found that when we tried to get away they got right in front of us and stopped us with their big bodies. This made me feel very bad, but I did not tell Roddy. Some time early in the day I heard some one calling, and I tried to answer, but one of the bears struck me such a blow with one of his paws, and showed his dreadful teeth in such a way, that I was so frightened that I dare not call again."

Said little Roddy, once again: "When I saw that naughty bear hit my sister with his paw I wanted to hit him with a stick."

"This voice of whatever it was seemed to frighten the bears, and so off they started," said Wenonah, "and they made us go along with them. We had to go; for if we stopped, or tried to go some other way, they growled at us, and pushed us with their noses, and so we had to go with them. Soon they came out of the bushes and crossed over the sand, and went up on the other side into the dark woods. We were very much afraid, but we whispered that we would not cry, but just be brave, for we knew you would soon come and fight those great big bears.

"The way the bears made us go was this. One big bear went on before, then the little ones followed next, then they made Roddy and me follow next. We had to do it, for just behind us was the other big bear, and he would growl at us if we did not just walk right along.

"Then, after we had travelled some time, we came out of the dark forest among some, O, such big rocks, bigger than houses. Among them we had to go, until we came to a dark opening like a big door, and into this we had to go. It must have been the home of the bears.

"Roddy cried out, with fear, but the bears growled again and showed their great teeth, and so we had to go in."

"I didn't want to go in," said the poor boy, as he put his arms around the neck of his mother; "it was worse than a cellar, it looked so dark. But the old bear behind just kept pushing me along with his nose, so I had to go."

"It was not such a bad place after all," said Wenonah, "when we once got into it. It seemed dark at first as we went in out of the sunshine; but when we were in it, and looked back, there was a good deal of light. In it were big piles of leaves and dry grass, and on them the bears soon lay down. One of the big bears lay down between us and the door, so we could not get out. We sat down by the little bears, and I whispered to Roddy to be brave, for God would take care of us and our friends would surely find us. Then we lay down on the dry grass and, being very weary, soon went to sleep, with our arms around each other.

"How long we slept we knew not, but were suddenly roused up by the little bears playing and tumbling over and around us. So we got up, and the bears made us go back again across the sands into the berry-bushes, and there we all ate berries, as there was nothing else to eat. The little ones kept poking their noses into our hands, and thus begged us to pick berries for them."

"The lazy little fellows," said Roderick, now smiling as he thought of them; "little greedy piggies that never had enough."

"There we stayed in the bushes," said Wenonah, "until nearly night, and then they made us go back again with them in the same way to the same place. It seemed so dreadful to have to spend the night in that place with those wild bears; but we whispered, 'We will be brave,' and so we lay down between the little bears, for in some way or other we felt the little ones were our best friends, and it was because of them the old ones did not kill us.

"I thought we could never spend the night in such a place, but we did. We just whispered our prayers as there we lay, and ended with, 'Now I lay me down to sleep.' And sleep we did until the little bears woke us up again the next morning.

"The old bears were now so friendly that they let us pat them, and so I thought that perhaps they would let us go; and so, when we came to the sand, I whispered to Roddy, 'Let us try and get away.' But those wicked bears would not let us go; for when we tried to go along the sand in one direction one of the big bears got in our way and made us go back; then we tried to go the other way, and they stopped us there. I now felt that we were like prisoners, and that we had to go with them. They led us again into the berry-bushes, and Roddy and I ate a good many, for we were very hungry, and the little bears teased us so much we had to pick a lot for them. It was when I was feeling the worst, and fearing that perhaps they would never let us leave them, that I heard the bird note. O, how sweet it sounded! For I knew it was from Mustagan, and that it meant we would soon be free. But I saw that the bears had heard it, and were very uneasy, as they had been at all sounds. For a time they stopped eating berries and stood up and listened. However, when it came again and again, so bird-like, they lost their fear and again began eating the berries."

Said Wenonah: "I was afraid to answer, for the bears had always been so angry at us when we made any noise; but I knew that sweet call meant rescue and home, and must be answered, and so, while putting a big handful of berries in the mouth of the fiercest old bear, I gave the answering call. Then came the reply.

"I must have been trembling, for in my reply I shook in my voice, and the bears were angry and growled at me. How ever, I knew I could correctly give the owl call which Mustagan knew was our signal of danger. So when I passed behind a tree I gave it as loud as I could, as though from an owl in the tree above me. When all was right again I gave the robin song, and you all know the rest."

# Chapter Twenty Four.

**Congratulations—Other Incidents of Lost Children—Long Excursion by the Boys—Indian Legend—"Why is the Bear Tailless?"—Oxford Lake—Black Bears as Fishermen—The Lookout from the Trees—Fish-Stealing Bears—The Conflict—Bears versus Boys and Indians—Sam's Successful Thrust—Plenty of Bear Meat.**

The thrilling adventures and escape of Wenonah and Roderick were, of course, the great sensations that were most talked about for many a day. Children have wonderful recuperative powers, and so the two little ones recovered from the effects of their strange mishaps long before Mr and Mrs Ross or even Minnehaha did. But time is a great healer, and soon all were well and in good spirits again.

The event produced a deep impression upon Frank, Sam, and Alec, and drew out from the older servants at the home and some of the Indians some very interesting stories. It is simply amazing what a difference there is in people in respect to their ability to find their way out of a forest when once the trail is lost. Some people invariably get lost in as small an area as a hundred-acre forest, and are almost sure to come out on the opposite side to the one desired. Indians, perhaps on account of their living so much in the woods, are not so liable to get bewildered and lost as white people. Still some of them are as easily perplexed as other people.

One of this class went out hunting and lost himself so completely that his friends became alarmed and went searching for him. When they fortunately found him, one, chaffing him, said:

"Hello, are you lost?"

To this he indignantly replied:

"No, Indian not lost, Indian here; but Indian's wigwam lost!"

It would never do for him to admit that such a thing could possibly happen as his being lost.

So popular and beloved were Mr Ross and his family that not only did the congratulations on the recovery of the children come from the Hudson Bay Company officials and other white people from far and wide, but Indians of other tribes, who had known Mr Ross in the years gone by, when he was in the company's service, came from great distances, and in their quiet but expressive way indicated their great pleasure at the restoration of the little ones to their parents. Mustagan was, of course, the hero of the hour, and as usual he received the congratulations with his usual modesty and gave great credit to Big Tom. He also had nothing but kind words for the brave white lads, who had so coolly and unflinchingly played their part in the closing scene of the rescue. His only regret was that he had not had them take their guns with them when they went to the front with the berries, so that they might have had a share in the grand fusillade that stopped so suddenly the rush of the furious bears. The actions of the bears in thus sparing the children's lives brought out from the Indians several remarkable stories of similar conduct known to have occurred elsewhere.

One Indian told of an old mother bear that boldly attacked an Indian woman who, with her young babe, had gone out into the forest to gather wood. The mother fought for her child until unconscious. When she came to herself both the bear and the papoose were gone. She returned to her wigwam and gave the alarm, but as the men were away hunting several days passed ere they could begin the search.

When at length they discovered the bear's den they found the child was there alive. In killing the bear they had to take the greatest care lest they hurt the child, as the bear seemed in its ferocity to think more of defending the child from them than of saving its own life. The child when rescued was perfectly naked, yet was fat and healthy, and cried bitterly when taken away from the warm den and the body of the dead bear that it had suckled with evident satisfaction.

To this and other wonderful stories the boys listened with the greatest delight. The fact is, while the children were lost they were as miserable a trio as could be found, and now the reaction had come, and they were just bubbling over with delight and ready for any story that had, even in the remotest degree, anything similar to what had so excited them.

Indians love good companions, and they found them in the boys; so it was not long before some of those who had come from Oxford Lake invited them to return with them, and they promised them some rare sport. At first Mr Ross was a bit fearful about letting them go so far, but as Big Tom and Martin Papanekis offered to go in charge of the two canoes he at length yielded. So, in company with the Indians from that place, they started off in great spirits, well supplied with guns and ammunition, and all the necessary camping outfit for a ten days' or two weeks' excursion.

It was with very great delight that the boys set off with their fresh, dusky, red companions on this trip. It was principally down the rapid lakes and rivers up which the boatmen gallantly rowed on their journey from York Factory. The running of the rapids, especially a wild, dangerous one through Hell's Gate, very much excited the boys.

On one of the beautiful islands in Oxford Lake they pitched their tents, and had some capital sport in fishing for the gamy trout which there abound. The only drawback to the fishing in such a land as this, where the fish are so abundant, is that the sportsmen soon get weary with drawing up the fish so rapidly. The finest whitefish in the world are to be found in Oxford Lake. They, however, will not take the hook, and so are caught only in gill nets.

Black bears are quite numerous in this part of the country. They are very fond of fishing, and so it was proposed to try and get a shot at one or two, as the Indians well knew their favourite resorts. Indeed, the Indian tradition of why the bear has such a short tail is the result of his preference for fish diet. They say that originally the bear had a beautiful tail, so long that with it he could easily whisk the flies off his ears. One winter a greedy bear, not content to stay in his den and sleep as bears ought to do, wandered out on a great frozen lake. There he met a fox hurrying along with a fine fish in his mouth. The bear being the larger and stronger animal, he rushed at him to capture the fish. The fox, seeing him coming, quietly dropped it on the ice, and, putting his forepaw upon it, said to the bear:

"Why bother yourself with such an insignificant fish as this, when, if you hurry, you can get any number of fine large ones."

"Where are they to be found?" asked the bear.

"Why," said the fox, "did you not hear the thunder of the cracking ice on the lake?"

"Yes, I heard it, and trembled," said the bear.

"Well, you need not fear," said the fox, "for it was only the Frost King splitting the ice, and there is a great crack, and the fish are there in great numbers. All you have to do is to go and sit across the crack and drop your long, splendid tail in the water, and you will be delighted to see with what pleasure the fish will seize hold of it. Then all you will have to do will be to just whisk them out on the ice, and then you will have them."

The silly bear swallowed this story, and away he rushed to a crack in the ice. These cracks are very frequently found in these northern lakes in bitter cold weather. They are caused by the ice contracting and thus bursting.

Down squatted the bear on his haunches, and, dropping his beautiful tail in the water, he patiently waited for the bite. But the water in these cracks soon freezes again, especially when it is fifty or sixty degrees below zero, and so it was not long before in this crack it was solid again. And so when the bear got tired waiting for a bite, or even a nibble, he tried to leave the place, but found it was impossible without leaving his tail behind him. This he had to do, or freeze or starve to death, and so he broke loose, and ever after has been tailless.

This is one of the many traditions that abound among the Indians. They have traditions to account for almost everything in nature. Some of them are interesting, ingenious; others are ridiculous and senseless. It is well-known, however, no matter how the bear lost his beautiful tail, if he ever had one, he is still very fond of fish, and often displays a great deal of ingenuity in capturing them.

So it was decided that, if possible, the boys should have a chance to see him at his work, and, if possible, get a shot or two, as this was the favourable time of the year, as certain kinds of fish were spawning in the shallows of the streams, and for them he would be on the lookout. As these regions were the hunting grounds of the Oxford Indians, whom they had accompanied from Mr Ross's, they knew every place likely to be frequented by the bears; and so three canoes were fitted out, with one of our boys in each, and away they started, full of pleasurable anticipation, not so much just now to shoot or kill, as to find the place where they could see bruin at what was at this season his favourite occupation, namely, that of catching fish.

Oxford Lake, when no storms are howling over it, is one of the most beautiful in the world. As the weather was now simply perfect, the boys enjoyed very much the canoe excursions, and, in addition, a fair amount of shooting. Ducks, partridges and other birds were shot on the wing, or at the points where they stopped to rest and eat.

They were rewarded in their search by finding several places where the bears had undoubtedly been at work at their favourite pastime. The shrewd Indians were also able to tell as to the success or ill luck of the bears in their fishing efforts.

At places where only a few bones or fins were to be seen scattered about, the Indians said:

"Poor fishing here; only catch a few, eat them all up."

However, they found other places where only part of the fish had been eaten, and here the Indians said:

"This looks better. When fish plenty, bear eat only the best part."

At length, however, they reached a place that made even the eyes of the generally imperturbable Indians flash with excitement. It was on the north-eastern part of the lake, where the river that flows from Rat Lake enters into Oxford Lake. Here, not far from the mouth of the stream, were some gravelly shallows which were evidently favourite resorts for the fish during the spawning season. Just a little way out from the shore were several broad, flat granite rocks that rose but a little above the surface of the water. Between these rocks and the shore was quite a current of water that ran over a gravelly bed.

On the mainland opposite this flat ridge of granite rocks were to be seen a large number of fish, each ranging in weight from eight to ten pounds. What most excited and pleased the Indians was that while the numerous tracks indicated that several bears had been there fishing only the night before, yet each fish had only had one piece bitten out of it, and that was on the back just a little behind the head. Bears are very dainty when they have abundance to choose from, and so, when fish are very plentiful, especially the whitefish, they are content with only biting out that portion containing some dainty fat, which is, as we have said, on the swell of the back just behind the head.

When this discovery was made the men in the other canoes were notified, and quietly and quickly, plans were made to not only see the bears at work that night, when they would return, but to have some shots at them; for the Indians said:

"Bears not such fools as to leave such a place while food so plenty."

The impression among those who knew their habits was that even now the bears were sleeping not very far away in the dense forests. So the place was carefully looked over, and the best spots for observation were selected. An important consideration was to form some idea as to the direction from which the bears would come, if they returned that night to this spot. Indian cleverness, sharpened by experience in such matters, enabled them to solve this very important question by studying the trail along which they had been cautiously coming and going very recently. This they found to be almost a straight line running directly back into the depths of the dense forest.

To climb trees as points of observation from which to view bears is, as a general thing, a dangerous experiment, as bears themselves are such capital climbers. But there are times when it is the only possible course available for those who would observe their action, on account of the flatness of the country thereabout. So, speedily as possible, the trees were selected that were considered most suitable. These were situated a little north and south of the spot where the bears had thrown their fish on the shore. They were a little distant from the trail along which it was likely the bears would come. Three trees were thus selected, and it was decided that Sam, Alec, and Frank should each have one Indian in his tree with him in case of attack. The other Indians were to remain out from the shore in their canoes, sheltered from view by some rocks that were not far distant. They were not so far away as to be beyond call, if they should be needed.

All these matters having been decided upon, they entered their canoes again and quietly paddled out to one of the rocky isles, not far distant, and on the side opposite to the mainland they gathered some dry wood and had a good dinner, for which they had capital appetites. Then the Indians lit their pipes and curled down on the rocks for a smoke and rest, and urged the boys also to try and get some sleep. They at first thought they were too excited, in view of the coming night's adventures, to sleep, but as the Indians so desired they lay down near the shore, and the rippling waves were such a soothing lullaby that, strange to say, they were soon in dreamless slumber.

A couple of hours was all that could be allowed them, for, as the Indians said:

"Sometimes bears move around early, and we must be all there in the trees before they come."

All the preparations were soon made. The guns were freshly loaded with ball, and some extra ammunition was taken in the pockets of each one. Their hunting knives were given a few rubs on the stones to see that they were keen and sharp. In addition, much to the boys' surprise, there was given to each one of them a good solid birch club, about eighteen inches in length and an inch and a half thick. As an extra precaution against their being dropped, the Indians, who had prepared them while the boys slept, had bored a hole through one end, and inserted a deerskin thong to slip over the wrist. How they were to be used, and the wisdom of preparing them, we shall see later on. The Indians were similarly armed, but, in addition, they stuck their hunting hatchets in their belts.

A few final instructions were given and the signals decided upon, and then the boys and their Indian comrades were noiselessly paddled to the shore. They were landed as closely as possible to the trees into which they were to be ensconced, so as to leave but little scent of their footsteps on the ground.

In the two trees selected on the north side were Frank and Alec, each with an Indian hunter, while Sam and his comrade took up their assigned station in a fine large tree on the south side. It was about an hour before sundown ere they were all quietly stowed away in these peculiar resting places. The other Indians quietly paddled back to the places designated beyond the rocks.

For a couple of hours they had to sit there in silence, broken only by the singing of some birds around them, or the call or cry of some wild animal in the forest. They were first aroused by hearing the crunching of bones where they had noticed the fish lying. On peering out from their hiding places they saw an old black fox, with a litter of half-grown ones, making a hasty meal out of the fish. The Indians would have loved to have captured them, as the skin of the black fox is very valuable. However, it was not foxes they were now after, but bears; and, besides this, the skin of the fox is only prime in the cold, wintry months. So they had to be content with watching them as there they greedily devoured the fish. Suddenly they were disturbed in their repast, and dashed away, each with a piece of fish in its mouth, and the watchers observed that what had caused their sudden retreat was a large wolverine that had quite unexpectedly appeared upon the scene. He, too, seemed to be fond of fish, and at once began to feast upon them.

Not long, however, was he permitted to thus enjoy himself, for out in the beautiful gloaming a great black bear was seen emerging from the now dark forest upon the shore. At his coming the thievish wolverine at once slunk away. The bear did not attempt to eat any of the fish that were still remaining; but, after a short survey of the coast up and down to see that all was clear, he boldly plunged into the water and crossed over to one of the shallow rocks only a few yards away. Hardly had he reached it ere another, and then another, bear came out from the forest along the central trail which the men had earlier in the day discovered.

They were not long in joining their comrade on the smooth, wide rocks which we have described. After they had spent a little time in inspection they lay down on the rocks facing the shore, as close to the water as they could without really touching it. These movements could be distinctly seen by the boys, as they were looking out toward the west, where the sky was still bright and the few clouds golden.

For a few minutes the bears were very still, then there was a quick movement on the part of one of them as he shot out one of his handlike paws into the water under a passing fish, and threw it from him across the stream, high and dry, up on the shore. Soon the other bears were similarly employed, and the fish were rapidly being captured. The boys excitedly watched these sturdy fishermen, and were astonished at the cleverness and quickness with which they were able to throw out the fish upon the shore. Although they had to throw them quite a number of yards, they very seldom miscalculated and allowed any to fall short and thus drop back into the water.

But before the pile of fish had become very large there happened something else to divert the attention of the spectators from the three four-footed fishermen out on the flat rocks. Suddenly they heard the sounds of tearing flesh and breaking bones. On looking down to see who were these new intruders, they were able to see not many yards below them a couple of other bears that, in their prowling around and looking for their supper, had found their way to this capital supply of fish. As the watchers peered down at them it was evident by the greedy way in which they attacked the fish that they were so hungry as not to be at all particular.

Their sudden appearance and attack on the fish were not at all appreciated by the industrious trio that had been so skillfully catching these fish for their own supper. They had no disposition to be fishermen for others, and so with growls of rage they suddenly dashed into and across the water, and sprang upon the intruders. It was a fierce battle, and but little of it could be distinctly seen, especially when under the shadows of the trees. When, however, in their struggles they came out on the bright, sandy shore, there was still enough of the western twilight in which to witness a good deal of terrific fighting. Bears have thick fur and tough hides, and so their battles are generally carried on until one side is shaken into exhaustion or knocked into submission. But so stubborn was the fight here that it continued with but few intermissions until the moon, which was nearly full, had so risen up that everything was made about as bright as in the daytime.

It was evident that the two intruding bears were so hungry that, although they had been well shaken, they were loath to consider themselves beaten or to leave so sumptuous a supper, and so they again returned to the conflict. The battle was renewed in all its fury, and when the three were again victorious the vanquished ones, instead of again retreating into the forest, each shaking off his opponent rushed to the nearest tree and began its ascent, one followed by two bears and the other by one.

These two trees, up which the five bears were now climbing, happened to be the ones in which Frank and Alec and their two Indian companions were hid.

Bears are capital climbers, and these two fellows, stimulated by the cuffs and bites of their antagonists behind them, made good time in the ascent. Now, for the first time, the boys saw for what purpose they had been armed with those handy birch clubs. A bear's tenderest spot is his nose. This the Indians well know, and so, when they are chased by a bear, always defend themselves by there striking him. A bear that will stand heavy blows with a club on his skull, or shoulders, or even paws, gives up the fight at once when rapped over the nose.

Secrecy was now no longer possible, and so the quiet command of the Indians to the boys was:

"Hit them on the nose whenever you can."

The two angry bears were so taken up with the attack of their own species behind them that they little imagined that there were enemies above, and so about the first suspicions they had of the presence of the boys and Indians were the smart raps they received on their noses.

Whack! whack! whack! fell the blows upon their snouts, and down they dropped suddenly to the ground, each of them carrying with him an assailant that happened to be just below him. The sudden discomfiture of the bears brought a cheer from the boys. This, of course, startled and excited the other bears, that were in a very pugnacious mood.

The two were additionally angry at the ugly blows that had met them, and the other three fishermen seemed to imagine that fresh assailants were there in the trees ready to come down and rob them of their supper of fish. This they resolved to resist, and so the fight was on in good earnest.

The Indians declare the bears know how to talk with each other; anyway, these five seemed for the present to proclaim a truce among themselves, that together they might attack their common foes, who were ensconced up there above them in the trees.

Fortunate was it for our friends that the moon was now so high in the heavens that they could see every movement of the bears as distinctly as though it had been daylight. For a time the bears moved about excitedly below them, and occasionally made a feint, as though they were about to climb the trees and again attack them. They hesitated, however, and kept moving angrily about from tree to tree. Sam and his comrade in the third tree were soon discovered, and two or three of the bears made a pretence of climbing it, but soon desisted and dropped back to the ground.

In the meantime the rest of the Indians out in the canoes had heard the growlings and fightings among the bears, and had paddled in much nearer to the shore. By their expressive calls the Indians in the trees had given to those in the canoes some idea of how the conflict stood, and that they were still able to defend themselves.

The bears at length seemed to have come to some arrangement among themselves, for they so divided that they began attacking the three trees at once. The two that had come last attacked the tree in which Sam and his comrade were ensconced; two of the other three began climbing the tree in which were Alec and his comrade; while Frank and his companion had only to face the remaining one.

"Strike them on the nose," was still the cry of the Indians. And although the bears made the most desperate efforts to defend their tender nostrils while they still advanced, they eventually had to give up the attempt, one after another, and drop back to the ground fairly howling with rage and pain. Angry bears have a great deal of perseverance, and so this phase of the fight was not over until each bear had tried every one of the three trees in succession ere he seemed discouraged. After moving round and round, and growling out their indignation, they tried the plan of as many as possible of them climbing up the same tree together. However, as the trees were not very large this scheme did not succeed any better, and they were again repelled.

"What trick will they try next, I wonder?" said Frank.

"Get your guns handy," was the answer, "for you may soon need them."

And sure enough the bears, after talking in their whining, growling way to each other again, rushed to the attack; and while three of them began each to climb one of the trees in which were our friends; the other two began climbing a couple of other trees, whose great branches interlaced with those of the trees in which were two of the boys.

The Indians were quick to notice this ruse, and said:

"The bears must never be allowed to get up those trees above us, for if they do it may go hard with us."

Very cunning were the bears, for they tried as much as possible to climb up the trees on the sides opposite the places where were hidden Frank and Alec and their Indians. However, they could not keep entirely hid, and so, at the command of one of the Indians, there rang out the simultaneous discharge of the four guns. One of the bears suddenly dropped to the ground, but the other one continued his climbing until he reached a position quite close to Frank on the branch of the tree in which he had ascended. The boys and men had not time to load their guns, as they were single-barrelled muzzle-loaders. In addition to watching this attack on the two bears, they had to vigorously use their clubs on the noses of those attacking three. As before, these three were speedily defeated, and now the excitement was to see how Frank and his comrade would deal with the big fellow that had succeeded in reaching a position on a branch that was in a line with them. They could observe him cautiously working his way on a great branch of the tree which he had ascended, and was endeavouring to get into the branches of the tree in which they were located.

After some clever balancing he managed to get hold of a long branch that reached out horizontally toward him, and steadying himself on it, and holding on to a much smaller one above, he gradually began making his way toward them. The Indian at once saw his opportunity, and told Frank, who was on this upper branch to which the bear with his forepaws was clinging, to bravely crawl out on it as far as he safely could, and keep up a vigorous attack with his club on the bear's nose. This Frank gallantly did, and while thus employed the Indian drew his axe and began vigorously chopping the large limb of the tree on which the bear was standing. Assailed by Frank's blows he made but little headway, and so, before he knew what was up, the branch suddenly gave way under him and he fell to the ground, a badly stunned and discouraged bear. This gave time for the guns to be carefully reloaded, and then the besieged, thinking they had had excitement enough for one night, became the assailants, and so began firing down upon the bears below them.

Sam, in his excitement, had put too much powder in his gun, and when he fired the kick of the weapon caused him to lose his balance and he tumbled to the ground. It was fortunate for him that he fell in a soft place, and was not in the least hurt or stunned, for the only unwounded bear soon made a rush for him, but was not quick enough to find him unprepared.

Sam now knew more about bears than he did when he rushed into the camp with one not far behind him. So here there was no desire to even try and regain his position in the tree, from the branches of which he had so suddenly descended. Springing up from the spot where he had fallen, he drew his keen-bladed knife, and placing his back against the tree he awaited the attack. He had not long to wait. The bear, maddened by the battle that had been going on, and doubly excited by the smell of blood from his wounded comrades, rushed at him with the intention of making short work of him by hugging him to death. But he little knew what was before him. With all the nerve and coolness of an old Indian hunter, Sam waited until the big fore paws, like great, sinewy arms, were almost around him. Then with a sudden lunge he drove the knife firm and true into the very heart of the fierce brute. There was one great convulsive shiver, and then the bear fell over dead.

The next instant there was a great shout from those who had landed from the canoes in time to witness this brave act. The shout was caught up by the others, who, when they saw Sam's unceremonious descent from the tree, began to descend more slowly, and were in good time to see him give the deadly thrust.

Sam had indeed redeemed himself, and was the hero for many a day. Alec and Frank were very proud of him, and hearty indeed were their congratulations. Sam cheerfully accepted their congratulations, but had his own opinion of himself, first, for putting too much powder into his gun, and secondly, for so ignominiously tumbling out of the tree.

On looking over the ground they found four dead bears. One, badly wounded, had managed to crawl away into the forest.

They had had enough excitement for that night, so they gathered up some dry wood, made a fire, and cooked some fine whitefish in thorough Indian style. They had good appetites for a good supper, and after it were soon sound asleep. As usual the boys were the last to wake up the next morning, and found that the Indians had already tracked and killed the wounded bear that had escaped in the night.

Some time was spent in skinning them, and then, loaded with the robes and meat, they returned in high spirits where they had left Big Tom and Martin Papanekis and the other Indians.

There were great rejoicings at their success, and even quiet Big Tom had some cheery congratulatory words to say to Sam, which Sam prized very much indeed.

# Chapter Twenty Five.

A Successful Mission—Peculiar Address—The Visit to the Beavers—
Commodious Houses—Well-constructed Dams—The Moonlight
Sight—Strange Interruption—Stealthy Wolverine—Crouching
Wolves—More Cunning Men—A Mixed-up Battle—Delighted
Boys—Return to Sagasta-weekee.

They rested that day, and then, the next being Saturday, they decided to go to the upper end of the lake and there camp, so as to be near the newly formed mission, established by a Reverend Mr Brooking, and thus be able to attend the service on the Sabbath.

They met with a cordial welcome from Mr and Mrs Brooking, who, living in such a lovely place, were delighted to welcome them, especially the boys, who were all to give them a great deal of information about friends in the old land, which they had not visited for many years.

The boys were very much interested in the mission and the school. As they remained camped in the vicinity a few days, they saw and heard a good deal of the genuineness of the work done, and always, in after years, were they strong advocates for foreign missions. And yet there were some amusing things, which showed how wise and patient a missionary has to be in leading a people up from the darkness and ignorance of paganism.

The missionary told them many amusing stories. Here is a simple one: One of his converts was anxious to preach to his fellow-countrymen, and in this laudable desire he was encouraged by the missionary. As long as he stuck to his subject, and talked about the Gospel, he did very well indeed. But soon his ambitions led him to tackle subjects about which he was not very well informed.

One day, in addressing a company of his countrymen, he exclaimed:

"My friends, the missionary says the world is round, but he is mistaken; it is flat, yes, as flat as the top of that stove," he said, pointing to the great iron stove in the centre of the room.

When the missionary heard this of course he had to give Metassis a lecture in geography. He showed him a map of the hemispheres, and, as he thought, so fully explained the matter that there could be no further mistake.

The next time Metassis stood up to speak he said:

"Friends, I made a mistake. The world is round, but it is flat one way for sure."

This he said from having seen the flat maps on the wall. It was thus evident that another lesson in geography was necessary, and a school globe had to be brought into requisition before he could be convinced that it was round. His apology did not much mend matters. Here it is:

"My friends, I made another mistake. The world is round, but then it stands on three legs."

This he said owing to the fact he had had his last lesson in geography from a globe that worked in a frame that was supported by a tripod stand.

To see the industrious beavers at work was one of the sights that long had been desired by the boys. At many a camp fire they had heard the Indians talk about these most industrious of all animals, and tell such wonderful stories of their cleverness; and so now, as the moon was still bright, it was decided to accept of the very kind invitations of some friendly Indians, and go and visit a large beaver dam that they had discovered was being constructed by a large colony of these animals. Nothing could have given greater pleasure to the boys than this invitation, and so it was gladly accepted.

In view of the fact that the moon was already waning, it was decided to set off that very afternoon in order to reach that place by sundown, so as to be in good positions to see, ere the beavers began the night's varied occupations.

Of the many wonderful things which have been written and told about the beavers we need not here repeat; suffice to say that those Indians who most hunt them, and thus have the best opportunity of studying their ways and doings, are the ones who speak most strongly and enthusiastically about them.

Of the size of the trees they can cut down with their teeth, and of the length and strength of the dams they can construct, as well as the reason and instinct they seem to exercise in giving the right curve to these dams at the dangerous places, so that they will be most able to resist the force of the current, even when swollen by heavy floods, we need not here describe in detail. It is enough to say that stumps of trees over two feet in diameter are still to be found with the marks of the teeth of the beaver, that had so cleverly and accurately felled the great trees that had stood there defying every storm, proud monarchs of the forests, until these industrious animals laid them low.

Dams hundreds of yards long, and wide enough and strong enough for great wagons to easily travel over and pass each other, can still be traced out in regions where the beavers have long been destroyed.

Vast beaver meadows are still prized by the farmers for the hundreds of acres of richest hay land that have been formed by the gradual filling up of the rich lands, brought down in times of freshets from the high regions beyond, and year after year deposited in these beaver ponds, until at length they were so filled up that what was once like a great inland lake has become a prairie or meadow of rich waving grass.

Their houses were in some instances not only larger, but in every case much more cleverly and thoroughly built than were the habitations of the pagan Indians.

Their forethought in cutting and depositing upon the bottoms of the waters and ingeniously fastening there vast quantities of the birch or willow, the bark of which was to serve as food during the long winter months, was far ahead of the habits of the improvident people, who literally took "no thought for the morrow," and so were often at starvation point, while the industrious beavers in their warm, cozy homes had enough and to spare.

As soon as it was decided to go the preparations were soon made, and, bidding farewell to the noble missionary and his heroic wife, from whom they parted with regret, the canoes were pointed to the east again, and after some hours of hard paddling they reached a fairly large river, up which they were to go to a large creek which entered into it, and upon which the beaver dam now being constructed was to be found.

At the mouth of the river they went ashore for a rest and supper. Here the whole program of the night was talked over and all arrangements made. It was necessary that everything should be thoroughly understood and carried out, as beavers are very watchful and timid animals; the least alarm sends them to their retreat, and it is a long time ere they resume their work. As a precaution against surprise from bears or wolves, or even wolverines, who are very fond of beaver flesh, it was decided to take their guns along.

The creek, which was more like a small river, ran through a beautiful valley, and on either side were hills, some of which rose up so precipitously from the water that they formed admirable positions from which the cautious sightseers could watch the operations of the busy toilers when they were at work in the waters below.

The wind was everything that could be desired, and so our three boys were able to be together; but they had to wait quite a time in the most complete silence for the appearance of the industrious but timid workers.

It is amazing how all animals seem to be acquainted with the natural sounds that come from the woods or prairies, and are but little disturbed by them, while a sound that is unnatural is at once detected. For example,

Big Tom was more than once heard to say in his quiet way that, when hunting moose, he noticed that a storm might be raging, and the great branches of the trees snapping and breaking in the gale, yet the moose seemed to pay no attention to any of these sounds; but just let the hunter be careless enough to let a dry stick snap under his moccasined foot, and the moose was alarmed and off like a shot. So it is with the beaver. The ordinary night sounds disturb them not, but the report of a gun, it may be a mile away, sends them instantly to their retreats, while the slightest evidence of hunters so disturbs them that perhaps for twenty-four hours they will keep under cover without making the slightest movement.

The moon was quite high up in the heavens ere the first rippling sounds were heard upon the waters. The first arrivals seemed to be the watchers, who had come to report. They appeared to swim almost from end to end of the great pond that had already been made by the strong dam, which seemed about finished.

As soon as they had in some way reported that the coast was clear, others appeared upon the scene, until between twenty and thirty were at the same time visible. Some were industriously employed in carrying additional stones and mud to the dam, and carefully filling up every crack and crevice. Others were guiding great logs down the current, and fastening them in position where they would strengthen the dam against possible floods and freshets. The majority, and they were principally the smaller ones, were employed in cutting down small birch and willows, which they dragged by their teeth to the edge of the pond, and there they suddenly dived with them to the bottom. The pieces that they could not firmly stick in the mud they fastened down in the bottom by piling stones upon them to keep them from floating.

The boys were too far away to see by the moon's light the beavers actually at work among a clump of large trees that stood on the shore some way up the stream, but the crashing down of a couple of trees into the water told very clearly that some were there industriously at work. Thus for a couple of hours the boys and Indians watched with great interest these clever animals, and then there was an abrupt ending. It was not caused by any of our party, as the Indians, having abundance of food, had no desire to now kill the beaver. Then, in addition, the skins, so valuable in winter, were now of but little worth.

As we have stated, the beavers have many enemies. Their flesh is very much prized as food by all the carnivorous animals of that country. And so, while our party was watching with such pleasure the varied movements of the beaver, there were other eyes upon them, full of evil purposes, and, strange to say, they were not very far away from where our boys and Indians were hid.

As before mentioned, our party was on the top of a hill that abruptly rose up from the pond, caused by the backing up of the waters by the beaver dam. From this point of observation they looked out toward the west. On the left side were some hills much smaller and less abrupt. Just about the time they were thinking of retiring, the sharp eyes of one of the Indians noticed a dark object on the small hill nearest to them. Giving a whispered word of caution, they all lay as low as possible and watched. On and on, and at length out from the shadows of some bushes into the clear moonlight, came the creature, and now the sharp eyes of the Indians saw that it was a wolverine. The fact of our party being so high above it was the only reason they had not been detected.

It was evident from its actions that it was on a beaver hunt. At every extra noise the busy animals made in the water, as logs were rolled in or the beavers plunged in with birch or willow saplings in their mouths, the wolverine stopped and listened. There was but little wind, and so it was evident that even when the cruel beast had nearly reached the shore, and there crouched behind a small rock, the beavers were still unconscious of his presence. There was only a little strip of land about a yard between this rock and the water; but along this narrow strip of land the beavers had been coming and going while at their varied duties. This, in some way or other, the cunning wolverine seemed to have discovered.

But while the boys and some of the Indians were intently watching his movements, others of them, as the result of long experience, had occasionally cast a searching glance in every direction around them.

"Hist!" in a quiet whisper arrested the attention of all. Without a word, but by a gesture scarcely perceptible, they were directed to look along the very trail the wolverine had made, and there stealthily moving along, now in the light and now in the shadow, were two large grey wolves.

This was complicating matters, and making things interesting indeed. The Indians, leaving the boys their guns loaded with ball, and enjoining perfect silence upon them, took up their own weapons and noiselessly withdrew. So gloriously bright was the night in that land where fogs and mists are almost unknown, and where the rays of the moon cast a clear and distinct shadow, that everything passing was distinctly seen.

There out in the waters, and around the shore and on the dam, were perhaps thirty beavers hard at work. Here to the left below them lay crouching, like a ball of black wool, the savage, alert wolverine, patiently waiting until an unsuspecting beaver, loaded with wood, stones, or gravel, should pass along that trail within reach of his deadly spring.

A couple of hundred yards behind the wolverine, and yet high enough up on the hillside to observe his every movements, and yet not be observed by him, were the two wolves, now crouching down flat upon the ground. As they remained so quiet, the boys were surprised and wondered, if they were after the wolverine, why they did not attack him. But, while they watched the wolverine, it was not wolverine meat they were after, but beaver. But their wish and hope was that the wolverine might obtain it for them. How far their expectations were realised we shall soon see.

"Hush!" said Alec, "look!" And sure enough there were the Indians, some hundreds of yards behind the wolves, and spread out like a third of a circle, cautiously moving on toward the two wolves, which were intently watching the wolverine, which was watching the beavers. It was to the hunters an interesting sight, and so fascinated the boys that they could hardly keep still. Soon the tension was broken and there was a sudden change.

A couple of fine large beavers came in sight along the trail on the shore with a large stone, which they were evidently wishing to take to the dam. So intent were they upon their work that they knew not of danger until with a great spring the wolverine had fastened his sharp teeth and claws in the back of one of them, which uttered a cry of pain as he was dashed to the ground. The other beaver instantly sprang into the water, as did all the other beavers within sound of that death-cry.

In a few seconds the wolves, with great bounding leaps, had cleared the space between them and the wolverine. They fiercely attacked him and endeavoured to at once secure the beaver. But the wolverine is a plucky animal when thus assailed, and he made a good fight for his hard-earned supper. In the meantime, the instant the wolves started, the Indians, who from their higher ground had seen the movements, also began to advance; and so, ere the wolves and wolverine had settled the matter as to the ownership of the dead beaver, a volley of bullets killed the wolves, while the wolverine turned and began climbing up the steep place of the hill where the boys were hid.

"Shoot him!" shouted the Indians. A volley rang out from the guns of the boys, and a dead wolverine with three bullets in him went tumbling back to the bottom of the hill.

No need of silence now, and so the long-continued hush was broken with a will, and there were many shouts and congratulations. The boys speedily and safely descended the side of the hill, that sloped downward in the direction of the men, and joined them at the spot where they were examining the dead wolves and beaver. The wolverine had not had much time to kill the latter ere the wolves were upon him, and so he was not very much torn. The splendid broad tail was uninjured, and was eagerly examined by the boys. The dead wolverine was dragged in by the men, and it was decided, as dry wood was abundant, for some of them to make a fire, while others went for kettles, food, and blankets, and there spent the rest of the night.

They had two objects in view. One was to be on hand to skin the animals early in the morning, and the other was to have the opportunity of inspecting the beaver dam, and seeing the size of some of the stumps where those wonderful animals, with their teeth alone, had cut down some great trees.

A tired, sleepy trio of boys were they even ere their midnight meal was eaten, and so very quickly after they were rolled up in their blankets and stretched out on the smooth rock fast asleep.

As there are many wild animals in this part of the country, the Indians, ere they lay down to sleep, took the precaution of rolling some of the logs cut down by the beavers on the fire. These would keep up a blaze until at least sunrise, after which there would be no danger.

Refreshing and invigorating is the sleep which comes to those who have the courage and enterprise to visit these lands, and in this way live out a great deal in the open air. The night was never close and sultry. The air seems full of ozone, and scented with the balm of the great forest. So it was here as in many similar experiences with these hearty, healthy lads. So soundly did they sleep that it was after eight o'clock ere they opened their eyes. As they sprang up, half ashamed of themselves, the Indians chided them not, but one, in broken English, comforted them when he said:

"Plenty sleep, strong men, clear eye, firm grip; good medicine."

So they were comforted by this, and ever after when they overslept themselves they called it "good medicine."

The wolves and wolverine were already skinned, and so as soon as the boys had had their breakfasts, which had long been waiting them, they set off to visit the beaver dam. When they reached it the boys could hardly realise how it was possible that animals not heavier than an ordinary retriever dog could build such a structure. It was in shape like a crescent, with the outer curve up stream. It was thus able to meet and best resist the force of the great currents in times of freshets and floods.

Many of the logs used in its construction would have been prized as valuable for timber in saw mills. Then, in addition to the large logs, there were great numbers that were smaller. The stones, gravel, and mud used would require many men, with horses and carts, for many days to transport. Yet here visible to the eye were gathered all of this material by these animals, that have no tools but their teeth and paws, and all piled up and arranged in a manner so scientific and accurate that the finest engineer in the land would not have lost anything in his reputation to have claimed the work as his most careful planning.

The beaver house was also visited. It was apparently all built on the land, but it so overhung the lake at one side that the water ever found access, and there was abundance of room for the beavers to swim out or in whenever they desired. No attempt was made to break it, nor in any way to disturb it, neither would there be in the winter months, when the Indians would make the attack upon them. A more clever and successful way for their capture is well known, and this would be put in practice. But we must not anticipate an interesting adventure at this very spot.

The return to Sagasta-weekee was made in a few days. With the exception of an upset of a canoe in one of the rapids, where they were trying to work up stream instead of making a portage, nothing of a very startling nature occurred. Alec was the boy who was in this canoe, and he was quite carried under by the rapid current, and only reappeared above the surface a couple of hundred feet lower down. Fortunately there were some canoes near at hand, and he was quickly rescued. But the accident gave them all a great fright. They lost everything in the canoe that would not float. They most regretted the loss of three reliable guns. After this they were much more cautious, and the boys were taught the admonitory lesson that these sports and adventures were not to be enjoyed without many risks, and that there was at all times as great (a) demand for caution and watchfulness as there was on certain occasions for daring and courage.

A Painter's Vision, a Poet's Dream.

# Chapter Twenty Six.

### The Excursion in the Reindeer Country—Numerous Herds—The Battle between Reindeer and Wolves in the Lake—Reaching the Herds—The Long Stalk for the Leader—Alec's Successful Shot—Consternation of the Herd—Abundance of Venison.

To see and, if possible, to hunt a herd of reindeer, both on land and in the water, was one of the ambitions of the boys. They had frequently heard some remarkable stories of these animals from northern hunters whose homes were in regions where they occasionally visited in their migrations, and so they were much pleased when Mr Ross, returning one day from the Hudson Bay Company's Fort, informed them that a number of the Indians from that land were there trading, and that he had obtained the permission of the Hudson Bay Company's officials for them to return with these Indians for some sport in that land. He also added that the Indians themselves had stated that the herds of reindeer this year were numerous, and that it would be a very great pleasure to take charge of the young "palefaces," who were so highly spoken of by the red men, and do all they could to assist them in their sports in their country.

This was glorious news, and, as the weeks were now rapidly going by, no time was to be lost.

Alec deeply regretted the loss of his favourite gun, but Mr Ross speedily replaced it with another; and so, well supplied, and with a couple of Mr Ross's Indians as servants to look after the camp and be on hand in any emergency, the journey was commenced under the happiest auspices.

We need not repeat the description of the trip down or up the river and across the portages. There were several nights when they slept as usual at the camp fires on the rocks. There was a good deal of sunshine and a few storms.

They passed through some lakes of rarest beauty, that simply fascinated the boys and drew from them the warmest expressions of admiration of which they were capable. Even Sam at some glimpses on these lovely sheets, where the water was so transparent that at times it seemed as though they were paddling through the air, lost his powers of speech for a time, and then when the spell was broken he exclaimed, in almost sorrowful tones, "That beats Killarney!" How glorious must have been the sight when even a loyal Irish boy would make such an admission!

The Dominion of Canada has in it more fresh-water lakes than any other country in the world. Some of them are equal, if not superior, in the clearness and purity of their waters, in the distinctness of the reflections cast upon their limpid surface by surrounding hill or forest, and in the wild, weird beauty of their environments, to any of the world's old favourite ones that have been long praised in song and story. They are slowly being discovered and prized, for some of them are as a poet's dream and a painter's vision.

They saw various wild animals, but as they were in charge of the trading outfit for the Hudson Bay Company's post in that region of country they were under obligations to push on as rapidly as possible. The only time they did make a stop of any length was in Split Lake, where, as they were rowing their boats along, they saw a great commotion in the water a long way ahead of them. When they drew near to it they saw it was a battle between a couple of splendidly antlered reindeer and four wolves.

It was evident that the wolves were being badly worsted in the fight, as the reindeer were now the aggressors. From the Indians' idea of it, it looked as if the wolves had either chased the deer into the lake or, seeing them in there swimming, had plunged in after them. The deer, at first much alarmed, had boldly struck out into the lake, and were followed by the wolves. Of course, it was impossible to say whether the wolves had been able to reach them and make the attack, or whether the reindeer, when they had drawn them a long way out, had not then turned upon them.

The reindeer has large lungs, and so swims high on the water. He is not only able to use his antlers, but can turn while swimming and kick most viciously. A wolf can only swim like a dog, and as his head is so low he cannot make much of a fight. And so here the boys had the rare sight of seeing a couple of deer chasing with great delight four of their most dreaded foes on land.

They passed across the bows of the boat near enough for them to see quite distinctly the deer suddenly give a spurt and then strike the wolves with their great horns. Every effort of the wolves to attack seemed to meet with complete failure, until at length their only ambition seemed to be to reach the shore, and in this way two were successful. The deer succeeded in drowning the other two.

The victory of the deer over their cruel and relentless foes gave very much delight to the Indians as well as to Frank, Alec, and Sam, and it was decided not to fire at the beautiful creatures, but to leave them to enjoy their victory.

After several days more of travel and varied adventure they reached the trading post and Burntwood River, and shortly after started off to Lake Wollaston, as the hunters had reported the reindeer were there in great herds. To that place they now travelled in birch canoes, and in them the boys were much happier than in the big boats in which, with the company's goods, they had travelled from Norway House.

They saw traces of bears, beavers, wild cats, and other animals; but they were after reindeer, and just now cared but little for any other kinds of game. At a camp fire, where they were having supper, the old Indian who had been appointed captain on account of his experience in this kind of hunting gave the boys some instructions how to act should they discover a large herd. He told them it would not be very difficult to get within range of one or more of them, but they were to crawl up as close to the herd as possible on the leeward side, and there, from their hidden places, watch them until they saw the great one that was the leader of the herd. They would not have any trouble to pick him out. They would soon see how he bossed the rest, and was always at the head when the herd moved.

What they were to do was to keep moving along with the herd, skulking from one rock to the shelter of another, and, taking advantage of every inequality in the ground, to get within range of the leader, "but never let him once get sight of you." It was not so very particular about the others, as they would not run until the leader started, unless very much frightened. They were told to take, in addition to the gun and ammunition, some food, a small axe in their belt, as well as their trusty knife. They were not to be discouraged if hours passed before they got a shot at the leader. They were to be patient and they would succeed. The boys were amazed when the old Indian told them that sometimes he had followed a great herd for three days before he got at the leader. "But," he added, "it well paid me, as I shot twelve deer ere they had a new leader."

How this could happen was a mystery to the boys until he explained to them that when these herds come down fresh from the great barren lands under the guidance of the leader they have such confidence in him, or are in such fear of him, that when he is shot down the whole herd is thrown into confusion, and they run here and there and jump about in such a foolish manner, waiting for their leader to show them the way, that a quick, clever Indian, hid behind a rock or standing in some dense bushes, can keep loading and firing until he shoots from six to a dozen of them. Then another great deer gives a snort and dashes off, and they all follow him as the new leader. They are now so frightened that, under his leadership, they will generally run a great many miles ere they stop.

Early one morning, shortly after this information had been imparted by the experienced old Indian to the boys, some scouts who had been on the lookout came in with the information that two herds of deer were visible. They were in different parts, and could be hunted at the same time without any difficulty.

At once all preparations were made. As but one boy and one Indian could go together, it was decided that Frank and Alec should make the first attempt to show their skill in this kind of hunting. The old captain took Alec with him, while another almost equally experienced hunter accompanied Frank.

Sam was left boss of the camp, but he determined to do a little hunting on his own account while the rest were off after the reindeer.

The clothing of the boys was inspected by the Indians, and everything of a bright nature was discarded. They were all dressed in smoked leather suits, with caps to match. This made them almost the colour of the rocks and dried ferns, or bracken, among which they would have to do a good deal of crawling. The deer hunters left the camp about six o'clock in the morning, Alec and the captain going in a north-easterly direction, and Frank and his companion about due west. The understanding was to be back, if possible, not later than midnight. Each Indian, however, took the precaution of strapping on his back a grey blanket in case of delay.

The adventures of Alec and the captain we will have.

They started off in a north-easterly direction, and had to travel several miles ere, from an eminence far away, the herd was sighted. They were feeding as they leisurely moved along, and seemed to have no suspicion of danger. It was in our hunters' favour that the country was very much broken with a succession of hills and dales, rocky ridges and ravines, clumps of spruce forests, and long stretches of marshy lands, in which the dried ferns and bracken were very abundant. The first thing after the discovery of the herd in the distance was to find out from them the direction in which they seemed to be moving, and then to notice the direction of the wind, as it is always best to be on the lee side on account of the scent.

All arrangements being made, the two started off quite rapidly, as it was possible to push on for quite a time without much precaution, owing to the character of the country. Alec's trips to the Highlands of his beloved Scotland, and his excursions with the experienced gillie there, stood him in good service here. After about an hour's swift travelling the Indian said:

"We are not far from them; stay here a few minutes while I go to that large rock and see how they are moving, and, if I can, make out the leader. Keep where you can see me when I come down a little from the side of the rock, and if I stretch out my arms for a sign come on and join me there."

Alec was not kept long in waiting, for soon after his companion had crawled to the summit of the rock that rose up before them he speedily drew back a little, so as to be out of sight of the deer, and, gave the signal to advance. It did not take Alec long to join him. The Indian informed him that the herd was a large one, and that some of the deer were so close that they could easily be shot from the top of the rock.

Very cautiously did Alec with his companion climb to the point of observation, and there, carelessly moving before them, was a magnificent herd of several hundred splendid deer. As their food was abundant they were in splendid condition and were a beautiful sight. Numbers of them were very heavily antlered, and as Alec tried to count the numerous points he saw many pass muster as "royals" in his beloved Highlands. It was evident the leader was not to be distinguished from that position, and so the keen-eyed Indian watched for a few minutes the gradually receding herd until he was perfectly satisfied of the direction they intended to keep, and then he indicated to Alec their probable route, and stated that in all probability several hours would pass ere they would get a shot.

So, carefully retreating, they began their careful march in a line parallel with the herd, but generally from two to four hundred yards distant, according to the cover the country afforded to screen them from observation. Several times did the Indian leave Alec carefully hid from observation while he, as we have once described, took advantage of some high rock, or steep declivity, to crawl forward and observe the position of the herd. On one of these tours of inspection the Indian observed that before them was now a long valley, and the appearance of the country was as though two hills were quite close together with only a narrow passage between them. Almost as by intuition—perhaps it was the result of long experience—the Indian reasoned, "If we can reach that spot ahead of the herd we are almost sure to be successful. But can we do it? is the question."

Rapidly returning to Alec, he told him what he had seen, and what he thought might be accomplished.

"Let us try," excitedly said Alec, and off they started.

The Indian was amazed at the endurance of this Scotch lad, who so generally kept close to him in his rapid march. When well sheltered behind great rocky ridges or in ravines they ran without fear of being discovered, but when it was on a barren plain, with scores of deer in plain sight, it was a different matter. There they had to crawl snakelike along the ground. Thus on it went, the Indian repeatedly uttering a cheery word of encouragement to Alec, who had so won his admiration by his pluck and endurance.

"What is that?" they both said, as they crowded as low as possible.

"Wait till I see," said the Indian, as he crawled forward to discover.

Soon he came back with the word that it was all right; only a big buck crowded up too near the front, and the leader turned on him and they had a battle, in which the intruder was soon conquered and driven back.

This delay stopped the herd for a time, and so Alec and his companion were now about in a line with the front of the herd.

Only about a mile more had they to make ere they reached the desired position, and so about half an hour before the deer arrived they were well hidden and ready for action. They had taken the precaution to get out, ready for use, their ammunition, so that, if they threw the herd into confusion, they might have several shots ere the herd dashed away.

Soon the deer were so close to them that they could hear them very distinctly. Cautiously the Indian watched them, and then, as arranged, he signalled to Alec, who was stretched out behind a rock that had a narrow cleft in it. This break was just large enough for a lookout, and it would also serve as a good rest for the gun. As Alec cautiously peeped through this narrow opening his heart gave a great thump, for there within fifty yards of him were the most magnificent deer he had ever seen. There was no difficulty now in picking out the leader.

So, pulling himself together, he waited until his heart stopped thumping, and then, carefully and coolly aiming, so as to strike the game immediately behind the fore shoulder, he fired. The deer gave one great bound and dropped dead. Instantly there rang out another report, as Alec's comrade fired, and another great deer fell dead. Now there was one of those panics that occur among these reindeer when the leader is suddenly shot down. They made no attempt to escape. They ran up to where lay the fallen leader, and then they retreated a hundred yards or so. Some ran one way and some another, and then veered around and returned again.

In the meantime Alec and the Indian were carefully loading and firing, until perhaps between them a dozen deer had been killed. Then the Indian gave the signal to stop firing; but they continued to watch them for several minutes more while panic-stricken and bewildered they aimlessly ran from point to point.

"Look," said the Indian, "quick, see the new leader!"

And sure enough there was a great, handsome fellow snorting out his notes of authority and defiance. None now disputed his guidance, and so off he started, and in a few seconds not a deer, with the exception of those that were shot, was visible. No hunters could get within range now, nor for many a day to come.

"Why did you give the word to stop firing?" said Alec.

"Because," answered the Indian, "we have killed as many as our people can eat before the meat will spoil, and we must not kill the deer if we do not need the meat. The Great Spirit gives us these things for food. We must not make him angry by killing more than we need of such animals."

Well done, red man! Would that some white hunters, when bent on the wholesale destruction of valuable animals just for the mad ambition to kill, had some of his wisdom and religion!

The deer were bled, and, when the entrails were removed, they were placed where they could be found next day by those who would come for them. The Indian cut out a splendid haunch, which he strapped on his back, then the return trip was begun, and the camp was reached in the small hours of the next morning. Very tired but very proud was Alec as he strode with his Indian companion into the camp. The fire was burning low, for all the rest of the party were sound asleep, and it looked as though they had been so for hours. Alec, who had been so successful, was anxious to hear how it had fared with Frank, who had started off with another Indian after the other herd that had been sighted.

However, he was too tired and sleepy to say much then, and so Alec did not trouble him. Alec enjoyed the hastily prepared supper, for which he had a glorious appetite, after such a long, heavy day's exciting sport. Then he rolled his blanket around him and cuddled between Sam and Frank, and was soon wrapped in dreamless slumber.

The chief and favourite part of the breakfast the next morning was the broiled steaks of that famous haunch of venison which Alec's comrade had brought back to the camp.

Alec Shoots the Leader of the Reindeer.

# Chapter Twenty Seven.

**Frank's Adventures—The Reindeer followed—Unwelcome Interlopers—Cowardly Wolves stalking the Fawns—Repelled by the Gallant Bucks—Close Quarters—Successful Shots—Different Game than Reindeer—Visions of Splendour.**

Frank's experience was a very different one from that of Alec. He and his companion had started out in a westerly direction until they sighted the herd of deer a few miles away. They followed them up until they came so near as to have been able to have shot some, but, like other hunters, they were anxious to kill the leader, so as to throw the herd in confusion. With this object in view they carefully skulked along, hiding behind the clumps of bushes and rocky ridges that were quite numerous.

All at once they heard a snorting and a sound of rushing hither and thither among the deer, and so they carefully climbed up some rocks and cautiously looked over to try and find out what was the cause of the commotion. At first they could not make out what was the matter, but after a while they saw that the herd had other hunters than themselves after them. These were a pack of wolves.

They were at the front of the herd, and so Frank and the Indian quickly drew back from the rock, and hurried on to see the battle. Fortunately for them, the reindeer were so excited by the presence of the wolves that our two hunters were able to get among some large jagged rocks that rose up fifty or sixty feet, not very distant from them. Here they had a capital view of the valley in which were the deer and the wolves. There seemed to be about a dozen wolves in the pack, and perhaps two hundred reindeer in the herd, including about thirty young ones that seemed about five or six months old.

The object of the wolves seemed to be to evade the great antlers of the bucks and to capture those very pretty young fawns. It was very interesting to watch the skill and courage with which the great antlered bucks would close up, like a company of cavalry, and charge the wolves when they ventured too close to the herd. The wolves never waited to receive the charge, but ignominiously turned tail and ran for their lives. They, however, soon returned when no longer pursued. There seemed to be a thorough understanding among the deer as to the position each should take while menaced by the wolves. The large antlered ones formed the outside circle. Next inside were the hornless males and the does, while in a compact body in the centre were the fawns.

Thus on they slowly moved, while the wolves attempted at various parts to break through, but always quickly retreated when a company of the bucks gallantly charged them.

This strange conflict was watched by Frank and his companion for some time with intense interest, until it had an abrupt ending. It came about this way. In one of the determined charges made upon the wolves by, perhaps, thirty reindeer, they drove their cowardly enemies right up among the rocks just beyond where Frank and his companion had hid themselves. The close proximity of the wolves so excited Frank that he whispered to the Indian:

"Let us fire at the wolves and never mind the deer."

The fact was that Frank's sympathies had so gone out for the deer, as he watched the incessant schemings of the wolves to get at the beautiful fawns and the gallant efforts of the older ones to defend them, that he had no heart to fire into the herd. He could well see that their firing into the herd would so terrify and disorganise them that the wolves would easily destroy the little ones.

From where they were hid the two hunters noticed that the wolves, now no longer chased by the reindeer, were again clustering near the rocks, utterly unconscious of the fact that between them and the herd were some more dreaded foes than even the antlered deer.

"All right," said the Indian, in answer to Frank's request, "but be sure and kill two with your bullet."

Simultaneously there rang out the double report, and four wolves fell dead, while the others, terrified by this attack, so unexpected and so close, fled away toward the distant forest.

After seeing that the wolves did not stop in their flight, it did not take Frank and his Indian companion long to reach a position where the herd of deer could again be seen. Frank was delighted to observe that, although they seemed to be somewhat startled by the distant report of the guns, they had not broken their formation, but were more quickly hurrying away. To skin the four wolves and return with their pelts to the camp was all the sport they had, or wanted, for that day.

At first Alec was inclined to boast of a more successful day in reindeer hunting, but when he heard the whole story he was willing to admit that perhaps, after all, Frank's had been the nobler experience.

Sam's characteristic comments were:

"Man, but I would have liked to have had a crack at that great leader! But, after all, I think I would have preferred to have had the satisfaction of knocking over a couple more of those dirty, thievish, murdering wolves."

One more great excursion was arranged ere they returned, and that was to a large lake to which watchers had been sent some days before.

A couple of days after Frank and Alec had had the adventures with reindeer, these watchers returned with word that the deer were numerous on the shores of the lake, and were often seen swimming out in its water. The two days' rest in the camp had been much needed and enjoyed. Now all were fresh and eager to be off again.

Very little time is lost in breaking up a camp when once it is decided to move, and so in a short time the canoes, propelled by the paddles in the hands of the stalwart Indians, were dancing over the sunlit waves to their next destination, some twenty miles away. Here they found the Indians who had been sent as scouts or watchers had already returned and prepared a cozy camp for their reception. A dinner of venison, bear's meat, and ducks was ready for them, and after the score of miles of paddling— for the boys always insisted on each doing his share—they were all, with good appetites, ready to do ample justice to the hunter's fare.

As the anticipated sport would be exciting, and was generally considered to be more successful in the forenoons, it was decided to keep quiet that afternoon and evening. So the guns were all cleaned and oiled and many pipes of tobacco were smoked by the Indians, while the boys wandered along the shores and enjoyed the sights of that picturesque land. Just a little before sunset they had a display of colour such as is seldom given to mortals to see upon this earth of ours. In the west there floated a cloud that seemed to hang in the sky like a great prism. Beyond it the sun in his splendour was slowly settling down toward the horizon. Through this prism-like cloud there were reflected and settled upon the waters all the colours of the rainbow. Every dancing wave seemed at times to be of the deepest crimson, then they all seemed like molten gold, then they were quickly transformed into some other gorgeous hue, until the whole lake seemed literally ablaze with dazzling colours.

The boys were awed and silenced amid these glories, and sat down on a rock entranced and almost overwhelmed. By-and-by the prism-like cloud that had hung for perhaps half an hour in that position slowly drifted away, and the sun again shone out in undimmed splendour and the glorious vision ended.

Then the spell that had so long entranced the boys was broken, and in silence for a time they looked at each other. Frank was the first to speak, and his quiet words were:

"I have seen the 'sea of glass mingled with fire' that John saw in Patmos."

"And I," said Alec, "thought of the city of mansions where the streets are of gold, and the walls jasper, and the gates pearl."

"And I," said Sam, "thought, 'If that is a glimpse of heaven I can understand why one has said, "Eye hath not seen, nor ear heard, neither have entered into the heart of man, the things which God hath prepared for them that love him."'"

With quiet actions, and yet with happy hearts, they returned to the camp from the long stroll.

Reindeer Attacks the Canoe.

# Chapter Twenty Eight.

**Boys' Adventure with Reindeer in the Lake—Gadflies and other Deer Pests—Peculiar Weapons—Dangerous Antagonists—Hoofs and Horns—Frank's Success—Attack on the Leader—Canoe Smashed— Alec and the Indians in the Water—Sam's Stratagem—Success at last—The Return Trip—Significant Signs—Ducks and Geese heading southward—Indians Uneasy—Journey Hastened—Sagasta-weekee reached—Summer ended—Winter begun.**

Refreshed and invigorated by the much needed rest, the boys with their appointed Indian companions started off early the next morning for the lake, which seemed to have become the reindeer's favourite bathing resort.

So early did they arrive at the lake that they had to wait for some hours ere a deer was to be seen. The principal reason why the deer spend so much time in the water seems to be to get rid of a number of troublesome flies that very much annoy them. Some species of gadfly have the power not only to sting them, but to insert their eggs under the skin, which soon develops into a large grub. Some of the skins of the reindeer are so perforated by these pests that they are absolutely worthless to the Indians.

Another reason why the deer were late in coming out into the lake was the fact that, as the summer was nearly gone, the nights were now long and cool; and the gadflies being only troublesome in the warm hours of bright sunshine, it was nearly noon ere they came out from their forest retreats and plunged into the lake.

A herd of reindeer swimming in the water is a very pretty sight. Having large lungs, and thus being very buoyant, they swim high in the water, and being good swimmers they make, when a number of them are disporting themselves undisturbed, a very beautiful picture.

While our party of hunters were waiting in their shady retreat, secluded from observation, the Indians with as little noise as possible cut down and smoothly trimmed for use some poles. When fully prepared they were between ten and twelve feet long and from one to two inches in diameter. To the larger ends of each were securely lashed with deerskin thongs long, sharp, double-edged knives.

It was about eleven o'clock ere the Indian scouts, sent out to watch the movements of the deer, returned with the report that the greater portion of the herd had taken to the water. In order to be sure of success in the hunt it was decided to carefully carry the canoes through the woods, and embark as near as possible to the spot where the deer had plunged into the lake. This would place the hunters in the rear of their game, and thus give them a very decided advantage.

As the Indians were anxious to get as many reindeer as possible for the sake of the meat, a large portion of which they decided to make into pemmican, they decided to send out six canoes on this day's expedition.

Our three boys were each assigned a canoe with some Indian hunters who were supposed to be well versed in this exciting sport. Each canoe was furnished with one of these newly improvised spears, while each boy and hunter had his gun and axe.

The whole six canoes were very noiselessly placed in the water at a spot where some great overhanging branches reached down to the water's edge. All were thus enabled to embark without attracting attention, or in the slightest degree alarming the deer that were now swimming about in the lake. Pushing aside the bushes, they all shot out as nearly as possible together, and, vigorously plying their paddles, began the attack.

The deer, startled and alarmed by the suddenness of the appearance of the canoes, at first attempted to escape by returning to the shore. Finding, however, that their retreat was cut off, all there was left for them to do was to boldly strike out from the land and get, if possible, beyond the reach of their pursuers. As the lake was, however, a very large one there was no possibility of their being able to swim across. The Indians well knew they would not attempt it; but after endeavouring to shake off pursuit by swimming out from land, if unsuccessful they would return and give battle in the water, if there was no other course open to them.

The three canoes, in each of which was one of the boys, started out side by side, and there was a good deal of excitement and rivalry as to whom should fall the honour of bagging the first reindeer.

Fast as the reindeer can swim, Indian canoemen can paddle their canoes much faster, and so it was not long ere the deer were overtaken.

"Kill none but those in prime condition," were the orders received by all; "and let no canoe kill more than four."

As on some former occasions in similar hunting adventures, the boys were each assigned the post of honour, which was the position in the very front of the canoe, so that they could be the first to attack the deer when they came within striking distance.

As they drew near to the deer, and saw how they swam, the boys were able to see what effective weapons the ones formed by the binding of the knives to the poles really were. Of course the terrified deer made the most desperate efforts to escape; but in spite of all they could do their pursuers steadily gained upon them.

"Do not be in a hurry," said one of the Indians in Frank's canoe to him when he seemed so eager to throw his newly formed spear, as though it were a javelin, at a great antlered fellow they were approaching, but who, as though conscious of their desires to reach his head, very cleverly and rapidly kept them off.

The Indians well know, some by bitter experience, the ability of the reindeer to kick out so viciously and effectively behind, even when swimming, as to smash the canoe that has been paddled up close to them by the over-eager, excited hunters. Hence experienced Indians give that end of a swimming reindeer a wide berth, and endeavour to get within striking distance of his head.

"Ready now!" the man quickly spoke again, as this time by a quick movement they succeeded in getting beyond his heels, and came rapidly alongside of him.

"Strike him just behind the head, and strike hard," were the next words Frank heard, and with all his strength he plunged his spear into the neck of the great animal. He did not, however, as he should have done, strike across the spine so as to sever the spinal cord, and so he only inflicted an ugly flesh wound which irritated the great animal and caused him to turn round and give battle to the canoe and all its occupants. But, rapidly, as he turned, he was not quicker than were the sharp Indians, who, watching every movement and seeing the failure of Frank, suddenly began to paddle back from him. Rendered furious by the wound, and seeing his enemies retreating, he came on as resolutely and rapidly as possible.

"Try the gun," said one of the Indians, and Frank, mortified by his failure with the spear, was not slow to respond. Carefully aiming for the curl on the forehead, between the eyes, he pulled the trigger, and as the report rang out the great deer suddenly turned over dead in the water. A cheer rang out, proclaiming the first one thus obtained. Alec and his men struck out for one of great size that they supposed was the leader of the herd. He not only had a most magnificent set of antlers, but by the way in which he swam in the water he seemed to possess not only magnificent lungs, but to be still trying to have some control over the frightened deer. When he saw that he was himself being attacked he immediately, as became the leader of the herd, turned to meet the advancing canoe and give battle.

It was unfortunate for Alec that his Indian canoemen, while clever hunters, were inexperienced in the tactics of our old, wily reindeer. It would have been wise on their part if, when they saw him swing round and boldly come on to the attack, they had quickly used their guns; but that is considered the last resort in this kind of sport—the great ambition is to kill the deer with their spears.

So here Alec and his comrades wished to carry off honours in this contest; and so, when the great fellow came within reaching distance, they tried, with a couple of spears, to kill him; but a clever, rapid twist of his horns seemed to parry their spear thrusts, and before they knew how it happened the side of the canoe was crushed in as an eggshell, and they were all struggling in the water.

It was well for them that they were good swimmers; and so they struck out for the other canoes, the occupants of which, seeing the disaster, at once began paddling to their rescue. The greatest danger to be feared was that the infuriated deer would take after one or more of them, in which case they would have a poor chance indeed, as a man swimming is no match for a deer in the water. With horns and sharp, chisel-like hoofs, he is able to make a gallant fight, as we have already seen in the case of the deer and wolves.

However, it was soon seen, in this instance, that no danger was to be feared. The deer kept venting his displeasure on the canoe, so that he paid not the slightest notice to those who had so suddenly sprung out of it on the opposite side from him, and were rapidly swimming away. The poor canoe, however, had to be the butt of his ire—as well as of his horns— and soon all there was left of it were a few pieces of splinters floating on the water. The guns, axes, spears, and other heavy articles were at the bottom of the lake.

The swimmers were helped into the other canoes, and the sport was resumed. When several deer had been killed they were fastened by long deerskin thongs, like lariats, to the stern of a couple of canoes and towed through the water to the shore. Alec and his wet comrades went with them, and at a great fire built up on the beach soon dried themselves, and were none the worse for their involuntary swim.

For a time the great deer that had come off so victorious was left swimming around in his glory, none seeming to care to get into close quarters with him. Sam, however, was of a different mind, and was eager for a round with him. Of course it would not have been difficult to shoot him, but, as has been stated, the Indians think there is no honour or skill in shooting a deer in the water, where he cannot swim as fast as they can paddle their canoes. So they were just holding back in each canoe and waiting for some one else to tackle the big fellow.

When Sam told the Indians in his canoe that he wished they would attack him they admired his courage and grit, and one of them, with a bit of a twinkle in his eye, asked:

"You able to swim as well as Alec?"

"Yes, indeed," he replied; "but there will be no need for my trying."

"How you want to kill him?" asked another Indian.

Sam's quick rejoinder was: "I want to spear him, of course."

His enthusiasm was contagious, and the Indians said:

"All right; we will try."

So word was signalled to the other boats that the one in which Sam was would try the gallant old fellow. The Indians in the other canoes heard this with pleasure, and ceased for a time from their pursuits to see the struggle.

The Indians in charge of Sam's canoe wisely explained to him how, if they were possibly able to get him alongside of the deer, to try to spear him across the spinal column as near the head as possible. They also took the precaution to have a couple of guns and axes handy where, in case of emergency, they could be instantly utilised.

When the great reindeer saw them coming down so boldly toward him he at once accepted the situation, and leaving a number of deer that with him had been keeping together for some time he gallantly turned to face them.

When within twenty or thirty yards, as decided upon by the Indian, they suddenly veered to the right, and kept paddling in eccentric circles around him, keeping him as nearly as possible about the same distance in the centre. That he could not reach the canoe and annihilate it as easily as he did the other one seemed to very much irritate him, and for a time he was furious with rage. Yet in spite of his fury they quietly, yet warily, watched him, and kept up their circular movements about him. After a time, seeing it to be an utter impossibility to catch them, he turned and endeavoured to swim to the shore.

Now the attacked became the aggressors, and so, rapidly, the canoe followed in his wake. Several times they tried to draw up alongside to spear him, but a sudden turn of that well-antlered head was enough to cause them to draw back in a hurry. But something must be done, or he would speedily be at the land. So another canoe was signalled to make a feint to attack him from the other side. The one in which Frank was paddling with his Indians soon came up, and when told what was desired of them quickly responded.

The deer, thus worried by the two, had hardly a fair chance, but he gallantly kept up the unequal struggle for quite a time. Sam's canoemen at length saw an unguarded place and so dashed in alongside the big fellow, and at the right minute the Indian steering called out to Sam:

"Now give it to him in the neck, close up to his head."

Sam, however, was not quick enough, and therefore his spear, which he plunged with all the force he was capable of into the deer, while it did not instantly kill, so cut down the side of the neck as to sever some large veins. Unfortunately for Sam, he could not withdraw the spear from the deer, and he was in no humour to lose it, so he hung on to it; but before he knew where he was a great bound of the deer jerked him out of the canoe. However, he fell fairly and squarely on the back of the great deer, and he was not such a fool as not to avail himself of such an opportunity for a ride. So speedily righting himself on this odd steed, amid the laughter of Frank and the Indians, he was evidently in for a good time.

It might have fared badly with him if the deer had been able to have used his horns freely, or have moved with his usual speed in the water; but the additional weight on his back so sank him down that he was powerless to do harm. All he could do, after a few desperate efforts to get rid of his burden, was to start for the shore, and so he speedily continued swimming toward it as though this was his usual employment.

Sam hung on without much trouble, but as they neared the shore he began to wonder what might happen next. But when his antlered steed reached the shallow waters his strength gave way from the excessive loss of blood from the severed veins in his neck, and soon he dropped dead. The great carcass was dragged ashore, while the bodies of the others killed were towed in by the canoes. They killed altogether ten animals, but the reindeer hunt in the water that day, considering the loss of a fine canoe and all its contents, was not voted an unqualified success.

All the Indians present at the camp, which they made near the spot from which they had embarked in the morning, went to work at the venison there landed, and in a few hours they had it all cut into strips and broad flakes and hung up on stagings of poles speedily erected. A smokeless fire under (it), and the bright sun above it, in a few days made the meat so hard and dry that, by using the backs of their axes for hammers and pounding this meat on the smooth wooden logs, they thoroughly pulverised it. Then packing it in bags made of the green hides of the deer, and saturating the whole mass with the melted fat taken from around the kidneys of the reindeer, they had prepared a most palatable kind of pemmican. If well prepared in this way it was considered fully equal to that made from the buffalo on the great plains.

Leaving the majority of the Indians of that country to continue their capturing of the reindeer and the manufacturing of pemmican while they remained in that section of the land, Frank, Alec, and Sam, with their travelling companions, returned to Oxford House. There they made a visit of a few days at the home of the missionary. It was a great joy to meet with this devoted, heroic man and his equally brave and noble wife, who for the sake of Christianisation and civilisation of the Indians of this section of the country had willingly sacrificed the comforts and blessings of civilisation and come to this land. Only twice a year did they hear from the outer world, and only once every year had they any opportunity of receiving any of the so-called "necessaries of life" at this remote station. Yet they said and showed that they were very happy in their work, and rejoiced at the success which, not only to themselves but to any unbiased observer, was so visibly manifested in the greatly improved lives and habits of the natives. Missions to such people are not failures.

They would have been delighted to have lingered longer in this home, and with this delightful missionary and his good wife, who so reminded each of the boys of his own dear mother. But the Indians who were to take them back to Sagasta-weekee were uneasy at the appearances in the heavens and of the birds in the air, and so it was decided that they must return.

Four days of rapid paddling were sufficient to make the return journey. At the close of each day the boys remarked, as they cuddled up close to the splendid camp fire, that they seemed to have an additional liking for its glow and warmth; and for the first time they preferred to sleep as close together as possible, and were thankful that the thoughtful Indians had in reserve for them an additional blanket apiece. The last day of the home journey was quite a cold one, but the vigorous exercise of paddling saved them from any discomfort. They could not but help noticing the large numbers of geese and ducks that were flying over them, and all were going south. The boys would have liked, where they were specially numerous, to have stopped and had a few hours' shooting, but the Indians said:

"Perhaps to-morrow you will see it was best for us to get home."

So "forward" was the word, and on they went and reached home after an exceedingly rapid journey from Oxford Lake.

They met with a right royal welcome at Sagasta-weekee. Mr and Mrs Ross and the children were all delighted to have them back again with them. The faithful canoemen were well paid and given a capital supper in the kitchen, and then dismissed to their several homes.

Frank, Alec, and Sam had each to give some account of their adventures to the household as they were gathered that evening around the roaring fire, which was much enjoyed. Then prayers were offered, and away the boys went to their rooms. They could not but remark to each other how much warmer were their beds than when they last slept in them. However, they found them none too warm as they cuddled down in their downy depths and were soon fast asleep.

When they awoke the next morning the sleet and snow were beating with fury against the window panes, and all nature was white with snow.

Shortly after the wind went down, and then the ice covered over all the open waters, and they saw that that most delightful summer in the Wild North Land was ended, and the winter, with its cold and brightness and possibilities for other kinds of sports and adventures, had begun.